Emma... to Begin Again

DEBBIE BROWN

EMMA... TO BEGIN AGAIN
By
Debbie Brown
Copyright © Debbie Brown 2014
Cover Illustration by Ravenswood Publishing
Published by Mythos Press
(An Imprint of Ravenswood Publishing)

GMTA Publishing Group
6296 Philippi Church Rd.
Raeford, NC 28376
http://www.gmtapublishing.com

Printed in the U.S.A.

ISBN-13: 978-0615787091
ISBN-10: 0615787096

$\mathcal{D}$EDICATION

In memory of my beloved daughter, Emma. You will forever be in my heart.

Clara G. Clark, my editor, thank you for your comments, guidance and insight. Ursula, and Christian, for the endless times you have read and reread this novel from beginning to end.

TABLE OF CONTENTS

CHAPTER 1: COMING HOME

Emma walked into the dark living room and was immediately assaulted by the smell of abandon and neglect. She coughed and raised a hand to her mouth. No matter, she could manage to improve it somewhat, she hoped. Her heart felt heavy as she realized just how lonely this place felt. Unpacking would have to wait until she'd managed to clean up a bit first. In any case, all she had to do was perk it up so she could sell it; then she'd be gone from here for good.

The room looked like something from an old creepy movie, complete with cobwebs and drop cloth covered furniture. This had been her grandparent's farm house, where she had lived with her parents, but the only ghosts here were the ones inside of her. Ghosts that haunted her day and night, no matter what she did. Swallowing her guilt, she held back her tears. It had been five years since her parents had died flying out to her graduation and it was time she took care of business. Life as a nurse and teacher in Vancouver had kept her busy, had allowed her to ignore her responsibilities, but with her roommates moving on, it was time for her to deal with her past. She was done teaching at the university until September, and had taken personal time off from the hospital. She had four months to finally settle her affairs.

Emma surveyed the room again, feeling small before the task at hand, and in all honesty, she didn't know where to start. Dust caught in her nose as she opened the curtains. Room after room, she pulled open the drapes, letting daylight in, and secretly hoping the light would somehow reach her soul. The broom still hung in the mudroom, just off the kitchen as expected. Everything was as she'd remembered, everything that is, except for the loneliness, something that had never been there before. She shivered and pushed the thoughts away.

Back at her starting point, she swept around the covered furniture, pushing the dust right out the door and onto the wooden porch that ran around the two-story house. The vacuum would come later, once the electricity had been restored. No one had come back here since her parents had passed away, since the funeral, she realized, and no one had even bothered to clean out their belongings. As an only child, she couldn't blame anyone but herself. Somehow, she hoped she could go on and rekindle the spark that had fuelled her love of life so long ago. She'd tried to ignore her loss, throwing herself into her work in the city, but with her roommates, Renata and Maggie moving on, the past had come rushing back to slam into her with a force that had shaken her, leaving her right back where she'd been five years ago.

* * *

After spending a few hours getting rid of the dirt and dust from the floors, she lifted the sheets off the furniture, revealing the antiques that had once belonged to her grandparents. Time had stood still in the living room. She removed the heavy drapes from the windows, watching millions of dust particles float on the rays of light that streamed in through dingy windows. "Charming," she said out loud. She'd have to dust again.

"It's about time you showed up," a gravelly voice said from behind her.

Startled, Emma whirled around so fast that she became entangled in the thick fabric of the drapes and tripped, landing soundly on the floor. She clutched her chest. "You scared me." She stared up at Two-Feathers, a close family friend who had been watching over the house these past years.

The old shaman gave a slight smile, but his dark eyes twinkled brightly. "Hmm, apparently." He walked over and pulled her to her feet. Emma recognized the embroidered dream catcher on the left front pocket of his chambray shirt. It had seven feathers representing the seven Kutenai tribes, and he belonged to the Ktunaxa band.

She caught a glimpse of herself in the mirror over the antique settee and grimaced. Her overalls were covered with dust and her blond, wavy locks had come out of her hair clip, sticking out in every direction. Two-Feathers drew her into a hug, in spite of her appearance, and she accepted the gesture, needing the comfort.

"It's good to see you, Emma." He pushed her back after a long moment and took a good look at her, his dark eyes searching her face. "Why did you stay away so long?"

She wrung her hands, the same way she had done as a child. At barely five foot three, and all of one hundred and ten pounds, she still looked like one. Except for the lines around her blue eyes, and the tension around her mouth that betrayed her age, people still occasionally mistook her for a teen. "I've missed you," she said, meeting his gaze but avoiding his question. How was she supposed to answer it, by admitting she'd ignored her past and responsibilities?

He grunted. "Still plan on selling the place?"

Guilt washed over her. She swallowed hard and nodded. "What other choice do I have?" Her mind drifted back to when she was a child, running carefree through the house, laughing. Where had that little girl gone, she wondered. "Why are you here?" she asked him.

He nodded for her to follow and walked out the door to the barn.

She paused a moment before she hurried after him. "You mean to say the animals are still here?" Her heart pounded as she braced for the worst. If the state of the barn and animals looked anything like the house, she wasn't sure she wanted to see.

The familiar smell of hay and horses surrounded her. God, she loved that smell. The barn was well-kept and filled with life. Rooted in place, she looked around slowly, taking it all in.

"I've been tending to the animals since you left, but had I known it would take so long for you to return, I would have moved them elsewhere." Two-Feathers paused. "We use the barn when we come out here for our vision quests, bringing extra horses for the participants. "Here." He handed her Gram's old egg basket, and waved her off in the direction of the nests along the far left wall. "While you're at it, feed them too. You'll probably want to get a few more chickens and another rooster."

There were only five hens left, but each had laid an egg. A cappuccino colored one clucked loudly; announcing her contribution and Emma added it to her basket. Reaching out to stroke one of the colourful brown hens, she half expected it to pull back, but instead, her touch seemed welcome. A smile lit her face

7

as she lightly slid her fingers down the silky-soft feathers, watching as the tiny lids closed over the hen's reddish-brown eyes. It brought her back to a more carefree time in her life.

"Do you think you could give me a hand?" Two-Feathers called out to her. He was holding a saddle blanket. "I come every day to milk the cow and collect the eggs, but I don't take both horses out together, and I can only stay long enough to properly exercise them each once a week." His dark eyes searched her face. "When was the last time you rode?"

She started to answer, but she just shook her head. "I –it's been too long." She gave him half a smile. "I really don't remember."

He nodded and turned away to saddle the dark brown quarter horse. She noticed a few grey hairs mixed throughout Two-Feathers' black braid. She was not surprised when she saw the two owl feathers, tied to a concho with a leather strap, which adorned his hair. He glanced over his shoulder at her. "You gonna saddle yours or not?"

Emma blinked, realizing what he was saying. A spark of anticipation ignited at his suggestion. Why not, she thought. "Let's do it." She could feel a tiny flicker of joy in her heart.

* * *

An hour later, they headed back to the barn. Emma's heart pounded as she worked to keep up with Two-Feathers. The wind cooled her face before it whipped through her hair, and for the first time since her parent's death, she felt as though some invisible weight had been momentarily lifted. Her blood raced through her body, making her feel alive and aware of leg muscles that had been dormant far too long.

"Not bad for a city girl," Two-Feathers teased as he dismounted. He grabbed hold of Emma's blonde quarter horse as she slid to the ground. "I guess I should pull out your mother's old mounting block." He walked the horses back into the barn and handed Emma a brush.

She took the brush and made a face. "The cowboy way," she said. "You want to ride; you care for your horse." She loosened the cinch and flipped the straps over the top to lift the saddle off the horse. God, this thing was awkward. She stumbled slightly.

Two-Feathers took it from her and set it on one of the sawhorses. "The Indian way," he corrected her. "They stole it from us." He winked before turning back to his horse.

They tended to the chores in the barn together, before heading back to the house. The sun had started its descent behind the Rocky Mountains, and without electricity, the house was already dark. Two-Feathers headed to the mudroom and pulled open the electric panel. Pushing the main breaker up, he brought power back to the house and a few lights came on, followed by the hum of the refrigerator.

Emma stared at Two-Feathers. "You've got to be kidding. I thought the power had been cut." She looked around. The house started to feel alive again.

He made a face. "We still needed power in the barn. I'll go prime the water pump," he said, heading for the basement.

She muttered a 'thanks' under her breath. She could do this. Her life was in Vancouver now, so it didn't make much sense to hang on to the house any longer than she had to. If she hadn't been able to come out here while her parents were alive, she couldn't imagine she'd find a reason to do so now.

* * *

It took Emma two days to get the old house back to the pristine state her mother had always strived to keep. "One thing down," she said to herself. Now she would have to get some groceries before she starved. There were jars of fruits and vegetables her mother had canned in the cold room, but she needed more sustenance with all the work she'd been doing. She'd given Two-Feathers the jars of homemade spaghetti sauce she'd found, since she had given up eating meat long ago.

"We're here," Two-Feathers said, announcing his arrival with Grey Wolf. They had come to replace the fence lines so she could let the horses and cow out of the barn without losing them. A furry ball of energy ran into Emma's legs as she tried to greet the men who stood in the mudroom. She stooped to pick up the mottled, grey-and-white puppy but ended up sitting on the floor, assaulted by a fit of licking, sharp teeth, and puppy breath. With a laugh, she managed to scoop up the feisty fluff-ball. "Thanks for all your help," she said as the dog yanked on her hair and nibbled the side of her face. "What's he on, sugar?" Shifting the dog, she managed to calm it down somewhat.

Grey Wolf laughed. "I hope you don't mind, but I thought you could use the company." His dark eyes gleamed with a bit of mischief. "He doesn't have a name yet, so you can pick one out. He's a Native American Indian dog. He should weigh a good hundred pounds by the time he's grown. "

Emma glanced up, startled by the implication. She shot a look in Two-Feathers' direction. "Didn't you tell him I was here to settle things and sell the farm?"

Two-Feathers raised a hand in protest. "I'm staying out of this."

"I had a vision that you had returned to the mountains." Grey Wolf's eyes focused on the space above her head, as he recalled the memory. "The dog had grown and the two of you hiked through the mountain, searching for something or someone." He shook his head, bringing his eyes to meet Emma's. "You mustn't be afraid. It will be a good thing."

She felt a shiver rush through her body. She didn't know what to say. She wasn't as acquainted with dreams or vision quests as her mother had been, but she knew of Grey Wolf's reputation as a seer. He had always intimidated Emma as a child, but she was glad to see him again.

Slapping Grey Wolf on the shoulder, Two-Feathers brought him back to the purpose at hand. "We have a fence to mend. I know you were heading out for some supplies, so you can leave the dog with us."

Emma hadn't even thought about that. She didn't think the little sharp-toothed creature would enjoy waiting while she ran her errands. She could just picture the new Cherokee with chewed seats and an accident or two on the floor mats. "Thanks. Any requests for supper?" Releasing the puppy, she grabbed her keys and purse as she moved for the door.

Two-Feathers shrugged. "Surprise us."

She shook her head as she overheard Grey Wolf mutter a 'you sure that's wise?' as he scooped the rambunctious puppy and stepped out towards the barn.

"Have a little faith," she called out. She climbed into her car and headed towards the nearest town, an hour down the winding mountain road.

* * *

Lying in bed that night, her thoughts turned to what was still to come. She had four months to sell the farm and head back to the city. Four months to find a new direction for her life since everything was changing there too. Her bedroom window was open even though the night air was cool. She could smell spring waking in the mountains, but it was still too early for her favourite night sounds. The near silence was a welcome break though. She stroked the soft fur as the pup slept soundly at her side. "I think I'll call you Bo," she whispered to the dog. He looked so much like a little wolf, but Grey Wolf had assured her the fluff-ball was all dog.

She smiled when she thought of how surprised Grey Wolf had been when he tasted the thick vegetable stew she'd made. He had a hard time grasping the concept of not eating meat. Her thoughts moved to Grey Wolf's vision, or dream, and she wondered what it meant. One thing she did know was that she couldn't stay here. She had a life to get back to, or did she? Did she need new roommates? Renata had been talking about moving back to Italy, back to her roots. What would happen when Maggie left for Costa Rica, was she supposed to hold on to their condo?

* * *

Two weeks later she sat on an old wooden bench on the front porch, watching the sun rise above the Rocky Mountains as she sipped from a steamy cup of coffee. A smile curled on her lips as she inhaled the fragrant mix of mountain air, pine trees and coffee. Perfect. She closed her eyes and let the warm liquid slide down with a swallow. Her attention was focused on the bird songs that filled the morning air, and on just how peaceful it was out here. She couldn't remember ever feeling this way in the city.

"Kiisuk wi'nam," Two Feathers said, startling her.

Coffee splashed out of her cup as she sat up briskly. "You have to stop doing that, and good morning to you, too." She dabbed at her shirt and the bench, wiping up her mess.

The puppy rolled over and glanced up, only to plop his head back down.

"How about a cup of coffee?" she offered. She knew what the answer would be, so she gestured for him to sit on the clean rocker and headed off to the kitchen. The air was still heavy with the aroma of baking and spices as she took two cinnamon buns from the oven, poured a cup of coffee for her guest and topped hers off. She dug through the cupboard for a serving tray, loaded it up and headed back out into the early morning light.

"I thought there'd be a 'for sale' sign up by now," Two-Feathers said without even turning towards her.

Emma dropped the legs from under the tray and set it in front of the bench. She sat back down, kicked off her shoes and crossed her legs, setting her plate in her lap, not knowing what to say. He was right; there should have been a sign up by now. "It's not as though anyone would see it," she offered.

A slight curl formed on his lips. "Hmm."

Emma shook her head, ignoring him. Pulling a piece from her warm cinnamon bun she popped it into her mouth, expecting the sweet, buttery flavour to fill her senses. Instead, it tasted like sawdust and guilt. She sighed and turned to face Two-Feathers. "I don't know what to do."

"Why don't you stay a while? At least until you're sure about your decision." He took another bite of his bun. "This is really good."

"I can't just 'not go back'. I have a life, responsibilities…" She felt the sting of tears behind her eyes. Oh, God. She'd had responsibilities to her family as well, and look what had happened. The drive through the mountains was too much for her parents, so they had booked a flight on a small plane. Flying through the Rockies was tricky, everyone around here knew that. She just never believed it would happen to her parents. Shivering as she remembered the phone call and the voice at the other end of the line. No survivors.

Two-Feathers put a hand on her shoulder. "How much time do you have before you are expected back in your important life?"

She cringed at the words. "That's not what I meant." Her heart felt heavy as she turned to face him. "I have three-and-a-half months to get everything in order, and then I have to head back." She shifted uncomfortably in her rocker and looked away from his scrutiny, feeling as if he was looking into her soul, seeing all she had been carrying around.

"In the end, it doesn't matter where you live," he said staring out at the mountains. He took a breath and placed a hand on hers. With a gentle touch to her chin, he turned her to face him. Staring into her eyes, he added, "As long as you are truly alive."

She squirmed under his gaze. He was right. She had been going through the motions of life, playing the game, and simply existing. She had things to think about and decisions to make. She wondered how her roommates would react if she was the one who didn't come back. She drew in a shaky breath. She'd call the girls before bed and let them know she'd be taking the time she needed to sort things out, even if that meant not returning to the city. She hadn't spoken to them since she'd landed in Invermere, but now she felt ready to deal with her past, or at least give it an honest effort.

* * *

"Done!" Emma said with a feeling of pride. The last seedling was in the ground. She had worked hard to plant her garden, and she stood back to admire her work. Every row had a ceramic vegetable dangling from a curved metal picket, identifying each crop. She brushed her chin with the back of her garden glove and stretched out the kink in her back.

"You plan on feeding an army?" Two-Feathers surveyed the garden bed with a critical eye.

Emma frowned. "It's the garden bed. I found Mom's notes on which seeds went where, and how many seedlings to plant. I made it the same size as Mom had." She turned to face him. "Is it too big?"

His eyes shone with amusement. "Your mother fed many families with her garden." He squatted down to look at the neatly planted rows. "You'll have your hands full." He straightened a row marker, placed his hands on his knees to stand and faced her. "I came to ask a favor."

A favor, now that got her attention, he'd never asked for anything, not even after having taken care of the animals all this time. "How can I help?"

"Sadie's daughter gave birth early and Sadie dropped everything to go help her daughter," he said. He turned and started walking towards the house.

Did he think that was self-explanatory? She brushed the dirt from her knees and headed after him. "She needs a babysitter?" Surely there were other people willing to take the kids for a while.

He picked up a folder from the stairs. "All the information is in here." He climbed the steps and sat on the bench by the door. Leaning forward, he opened the folder and spread out some of the sheets.

Emma dropped down in the rocker next to the shaman. "What exactly do you want me to do? Am I supposed to know this Sadie?"

He put down the papers, a frown forming on his face. "Sadie, from Dr. Westerman's office." He studied her a moment, then nodded. "Sarah."

Emma laughed under her breath. She'd gone to school with Sadie/Sarah's youngest sister. The memories came slowly back, and Emma remembered how she'd hated her given name, Sadie, and had insisted everyone call her Sarah. She must have gotten over it. What stood out most was the scandal caused when Sarah had gotten pregnant back in her senior year. The graduation robes had barely hidden her huge belly. Then, it dawned on her. "You need a nurse."

With a grunt he pointed to the papers. "Just two days a week for a little while." He lifted his gaze from the schedule. "Do you mind?"

"No, of course not," she said sifting through the papers. Tuesday mornings were set aside for the walk-in clinic, while the afternoon and all day Thursday was for reserved appointments. She frowned. "What's this?" She pointed to the list of names scribbled on a separate sheet. "Do these people come by every week?"

Two-Feathers took the sheet and held it at arm's length. He shook his head. "This is the list of patients he makes house calls to. Though he doesn't expect you to tag along," he paused. "Unless you wanted to…" his voice trailed off.

She laughed under her breath. "I'll start with two days a week and see how it goes." Torn by the sudden desire to be a nurse, and the fear that it might throw the inner calm she'd found in her new life off, she forced a smile. "So, do I just show up Tuesday morning?" She rifled through the papers, looking for an address. "Where is this clinic?"

"It's inside the community center. There's a whole section set aside for the clinic, his office is in there." He stood, leaving her to go over the papers.

CHAPTER 2: SETTLING IN

The only vehicle in the community center's parking lot when Emma pulled up was a black Ford SUV. At six-o'clock in the morning, it had to be Dr. Westerman's since the clinic didn't open for another two hours. Try as she might, she was unable to put a face on the name, and she wondered if she'd ever met him.

She took a moment to calm her nerves before getting out of her Jeep, then squared her shoulders, drew in a deep breath, and headed inside. It seemed like a lifetime ago since she'd worn her nursing scrubs.

The typical smell of antiseptics was laced with something Emma couldn't identify, yet she found it somewhat soothing. Traditional Native American art hung on the walls, making the waiting room cozy and inviting. A far cry from the sterile environment she'd expected. "Hello? Dr. Westerman?" Emma called out, moving cautiously towards the reception area. The place seemed to be deserted.

"Be right out!" a deep voice called from the back of the building. There was a loud slam of a door, some shuffled footsteps, a muffled curse and a crash. Emma let herself through the half-door and made her way quickly down the hall past the reception area.

Three boxes lay on the floor near the back door. A man, the doctor, she assumed, had his back to her as she approached. He was hunched forward, rubbing his shin, muttering under his breath.

"Do you need any help?" She paused a few steps behind him and waited. What if he wasn't the doctor, and had been trying to steal supplies?

The man stiffened and rose to his full height before turning. He was easily six feet tall, and Emma couldn't help but notice his full head of jet black hair. She'd expected an older man, but there

15

wasn't a grey strand visible. This couldn't be the doctor, could it? Wearing jeans, a denim shirt, cowboy boots and a leather belt, the man turned slowly to face her, a look of puzzlement on his face. "It is you." A grin replaced the puzzled expression, revealing two deep dimples in his cheeks.

"Willy? What are you doing here?" She laughed at the sight of Two-Feathers' nephew. Wow, he'd cleaned up nicely. The last time she'd seen him, he had been a long-haired hell raiser, an angry young man that didn't hesitate to take his frustrations out on anyone who dared cross his path.

He stiffened, his expression unsure. "I run the clinic."

"I was expecting Dr. Westerman," she admitted. "Two-Feathers said to show up a little earlier so he could show me around. He never told me you would be here."

His eyebrows knitted together a moment before he started to laugh. He reached to pick up one of the fallen boxes and moved towards a small storage room. Emma followed him with her gaze. She hesitated, then grabbed a box and headed after him. "Do you know what time he usually arrives?" She wanted to get settled before the clinic opened.

He held up a finger for her to wait as he scooted past her, returning with the last box which he stacked against the wall. A quick tug opened a locker and he retrieved a lab coat. Shrugging into it he turned back to face Emma, proudly displaying his nametag: Dr. W. Westerman.

Emma's eyes grew wide and she felt her cheeks tinge with embarrassment. She realized she'd never known his last name. "I'm sorry, I thought I was working with an old man," she confessed. She brought her hand to her mouth and stifled a laugh. "Wow, I can't believe you're a doctor."

He chuckled. "Don't judge me by that summer we met." His eyes danced over her face. "I was angry with the world over the death of my parents. You didn't exactly see me at my best." He shrugged.

She felt an ache in her heart at the mention of his loss, sparking her own pain back to life.

He reached out and laid a hand on her arm. "Hey, I'm sorry. I didn't mean to upset you." His black eyes held hers.

"It's OK. I forget sometimes, and it feels new all over again when I remember." She forced a smile. Would the pain ever fade?

"I know," he said softly.

"Where do I put my stuff?" She swallowed back her emotions and put on her game face. It was getting easier. She could do this.

William, and not Willy, as he'd politely corrected her, took her on a tour of the clinic. Three exam rooms, a storage area, reception area and waiting room had been set aside for his weekly visits. She was surprised at how modern the rooms were, right down to the latest portable ultrasound machine. "We still used the old ones at the hospital," she said, stepping in to get a closer look.

He leaned back against the exam table and crossed his arms, an amused look playing on his features as he watched her. "Come on. There's one last room." He nodded towards the door and headed into the corridor.

Directly across the hall from the third exam room was another room, only unlike the others, the door to this one slid into the wall. The small room boasted a U-shaped counter that ran from her left to her right, with various stations for lab work analysis set up and ready to use. "How'd you get all this? *Where'd* you get all this?"

His soft chuckle made Emma turn back to face him. "It's all legit, if that's what you're worried about."

Her cheeks flamed red. "Well I wasn't accusing you of theft. It's just that this is all new equipment, and for a clinic that's only open two days a week..." her voice trailed off.

"Come on." He slid the door shut and led her to the coffee room behind the reception area. "The plan is to attract more doctors to come out here to give us a day or two of their time."

She nodded in approval. "Great incentive, but what's your excuse for only giving two days?"

Before he could answer, a stout, aboriginal woman came bustling through the door. "You have to come quick!" She waved her arms frantically, trying to urge them towards the door. Emma hurried out after the woman, and William followed a few steps behind, medical bag in hand.

The motor of the faded blue pick-up was still running as the woman yanked open the passenger side door to reveal an ashen-faced man. He was breathing in short gasps, sweat beading on his forehead. He didn't react to the intrusion, barely following the woman with his eyes.

Emma hopped in on the driver's side and killed the engine. Reaching out, she quickly loosened his plaid shirt as William checked his vitals. "Joe," William spoke to the semi-responsive man. "What's going on, Joe?" He pulled the stethoscope from his ears and shot a glance over his shoulder. "Gladys, has he been taking his heart medication?"

The woman sobbed. "I make sure he takes it every day, but I went to visit with my sister over the weekend. He said he would be fine." She let out a strangled sound. "I only got back this morning."

"Joe, when did you last take your meds?" William lifted his coal black eyes from his patient to address Emma. "Get the Stryker from behind reception," he said softly.

With a nod, Emma hurried back inside for the gurney. This man belonged in a hospital, she thought. Lining up the gurney alongside the truck, Emma put the brakes on and waited for instructions. She watched in awe as William effortlessly scooped the man from the truck and laid him onto the stretcher.

He nodded for them to head back inside. Running on auto-pilot, Emma raised the side rail and released the brake. Moving the Stryker across a gravel driveway with a patient proved to be more of a challenge than she'd expected, until Dr. Westerman grabbed his end and helped get Joe to the clinic. "Exam room two," he instructed.

As soon as their patient was inside, William slid open the floor to ceiling doors behind him and wheeled out an EKG monitor. With quick action, Emma slipped the oxygen cannula in place and prepped his chest for the electrodes. "Open a line, I'll be right back." He set the pouch of liquid onto its support above the gurney and rolled the line tray close to Emma.

"I'm just going to start an IV, Joe." Emma spoke softly as she worked. "You're in good hands now."

William returned with Joe's file, flipping through the pages. He reached for the EKG readout, looked at the tracing, and made a face.

"Nurse, would you get the ultrasound from the other room?"

Emma nodded and slipped out the door. "Wait!" Gladys called out. "I have his medication." She held out a dossette as she made her way towards Emma.

Scanning the boxes quickly, Emma noted that if this was any indication, Joe had taken his medication as prescribed. "Are you sure this is up to date?"

Gladys nodded, out of breath. "I fill it for him every week."

With a nod, Emma reached out and gave Gladys' hand a reassuring squeeze. "Your husband is in good hands. I have to get back," she explained. Hurrying to get the ultrasound, she thought she heard Gladys mutter that she still wasn't his wife.

Backing into the room, dragging the machine with her, Emma looked over at William apologetically. "Didn't mean to take so long."

He flashed her a crooked grin and nodded in Joe's direction. "According to the EKG, his heart is fine. I'm checking his enzymes, but my guess is his gallbladder, more than his heart, is the problem here."

"I think the heart has a little something to do with it too," she said to herself, thinking about Gladys.

* * *

By the end of the day, Emma could barely keep her eyelids open. Unable to sleep the night before, too stressed about her first day, and pulling the equivalent of a double shift had taken its toll. At the end of the day she'd accompanied William on two house calls that had been on her way home. The patient contact was amazing, and she felt as though so much more could be accomplished from this type of health care, if only the system had more time and resources.

She smiled wearily, wondering where William got all his energy from. He'd confessed that the two days he spent at the clinic were his days off from the hospital. No wonder he was trying to convince others to join him. She supposed the community was lucky to have those two days.

She gave a grateful sigh of relief when she caught sight of Two-Feather's truck alongside the barn. He said he'd come and collect the milk and eggs on her days at the clinic. Making her way to the house, she drew in a deep breath, filling her lungs with the living smells that surrounded her. She began to question her decision to sell her home. Something about life out here was starting to feel right, but instead of finding reassurance in it, it made her feel restless, like she should hurry to sell and get out.

Stepping into the mudroom, she was assaulted by an anxious Bo. With a weary smile, she dropped her shoulder bag and leaned down to greet her dog before she headed upstairs to shower. She'd heat up something fast and easy for supper tonight; she was too pooped to cook. "Come on, Bo."

The smell of risotto and roasted vegetables greeted her when she stepped out of the shower. With a grateful sigh she threw on a pair of old jeans, a long-sleeved shirt and made her way down to the kitchen. With a sheepish grin she entered to find a steaming plate of food waiting for her. "Thank you," she said to the shaman. "You'll join me, I hope."

Two-Feathers placed another plate on the table and sat across from Emma. He took a moment to look her over. "How was your first day?"

"I was reassured that they aren't all so busy," she exhaled sharply. "I'm tired." She pointed her fork at him. "And you could have told me that *Dr. Westerman* was your nephew." She realized just how much she didn't know about her old hometown, its people and happenings. She could have asked her mother more questions, but the phone conversations were often brief or with her on the run. In the five years since their death, she'd written Two-Feathers, who had reassured her that the house was fine, but she'd never asked about anything. She pushed the thoughts aside.

"I thought you knew." He ate in silence, his attention focused on his food. When he was done he put down his utensils and looked up at Emma. "Do you plan on going back?"

Emma shook her head slowly, closing her eyes. Two-Feathers had been a blessing in her life since she'd come back home, gently guiding her, waking her towards balance and awareness. He'd never asked for anything in return. "Yes, I'll stay until Sadie returns." She lifted her eyes to meet his. "Are you satisfied now?"

He nodded as he stood, collected the plates and rinsed them out in the sink. "You had better get some rest. Morning will be here soon enough."

"Thanks for taking care of the animals for me." Wearily, she pushed away from the table and made her way up to her bed, barely aware of Two-Feathers leaving.

She awoke feeling refreshed after having fallen asleep the instant her head hit the pillow. The clock showed 5:35 am, five minutes before the alarm was set to go off. Stretching slowly, she pushed the covers off and got out of bed. Bo rolled over, barely lifting his head off the ground to watch her, but he made no move to get up. After a quick shower, Emma donned her jeans, pulled on an oversized jersey and headed down for breakfast. She found herself looking forward to her day at home, not that it could be considered a day off.

The animals were waiting for her when she opened the barn door, and she felt a rush of joy at seeing them. Ruby pranced about, anxious to be freed from her stall and she could tell by the sound Tawna was making that she needed to be milked.

Emma found herself living in the moment as she moved from chore to chore throughout the day, feeling a sense of wonder as life blossomed all around and she noticed it. That was the surprising thing. She'd lived here most of her life, but it wasn't until now that she finally took notice of her surroundings. She wondered why neither teaching nor nursing had ever brought her this sense of satisfaction. She stepped out onto the porch and came face to face with the shaman.

"You seem happy," Two-Feathers said as he made his way up the porch stairs.

Emma laughed. "I am. I'm looking forward to my day at the clinic tomorrow as well." She joined the Shaman on the porch swing. "I realized something today," she said in a more serious tone. Pulling a knee up to her chest she rested her chin on top of it. "I'd been missing out on so much." She let out a barely audible sigh and turned to face him. "I honestly believed I was getting so much more accomplished running around all the time." She'd believed that pushing herself to the edge with two demanding jobs made her a better person.

Two-Feathers kept his gaze out on the landscape. "Are you saying you regret what you'd been doing?"

She shook her head vigorously. "No, and don't get me wrong. It's just that I don't see things the same way anymore." She tilted her head. "I feel as though time moves slowly here, allowing me to experience every aspect of my day. Does that sound crazy?"

The shaman's eyes twinkled. "I don't think it is because you are here, per se. I think you have shifted your awareness to just *be* in the moment."

She stared at him for a minute, considering his words. "How was your day? Weren't you teaching that group of tourists today?" Now he was one to talk, he had something different going on every day, and he still managed to come by every evening to pick up the extra milk and eggs. Emma realized he never seemed flustered, never seemed rushed. He really was an example of living in the present.

The phone rang, and Emma frowned. "Be right back," she said to the shaman. She made her way quickly into the house to grab the phone from the kitchen wall, trying to keep her dirty boots in the mudroom. "Hello?" she answered slowly.

"Em, thank God. Are you OK?" Tension eased from the velvety voice.

Emma sank down onto the floor. "Maggie. I'm fine, how have you been?" Her heart constricted. She hadn't spoken to her roommates since she'd decided to stay and she felt a pang of guilt. If there had been internet available, she'd have emailed her friends, but out here, nothing but a land line was available."

"Never mind me, girl. We've been worried sick." She paused. "Why didn't you call?"

She let out a sigh. "I'm sorry, Maggie. At first, I told myself I would call later, that it was too late, I was too busy, or I didn't want to disturb you. I guess I felt bad in the end and didn't know how to explain not having called…" her voice trailed off.

There was a pause. "How are you doing, Hun?" Her voice softened.

"I thought you didn't call because you were mad I'd left."

"I guess we're both guilty," Maggie admitted. "Let's just try and keep in touch."

Emma smiled, she really loved her friends and she should have called. "I'm finally feeling better." She paused. "I'm having second thoughts about selling this place…I don't think I can," she admitted hesitantly, possibly more for her own benefit than Maggie's.

"I'm glad. We were worried you'd regret it. Roots are important, you know." Maggie was probably referring to feeling cut-off from her mother's family and heritage.

"I just need some time to make the right decision." Emma added reluctantly.

"It's not a decision you can rush, but make sure you keep in touch." She stifled a giggle. "Or next time I'll have Renata call."

Emma laughed. "OK, I promise to keep in touch." She paused, thinking about her roommates and life in the city. "Thanks for understanding." Emma hung up the phone with renewed determination. She'd put in for a sabbatical and give life out here a try. How else could she be sure of her decision?

* * *

Emma stood and brushed off the dirt from her knees as she glanced around, satisfied. Only a few pumpkins remained along the far edge of the field, and tomorrow she'd bring them in and cook them. From far, she admired the dark orange shapes. She'd always wanted to grow her own pumpkins. All the energy and efforts put into working the land had brought her a sense of accomplishment, and more importantly, a sense of peace. What remained to see was whether life in the Rockies would be enough. Would she regret losing her teaching position and giving up her job as an ER nurse? She'd have to think about it.

CHAPTER 3: THE CRASH

There was a nip in the October air as Emma made her way up the trail on Ruby's back. The blonde quarter horse moved lazily up the dirt path behind Bo. They were headed up the ridge behind the house to get a view of the fall colors before sunset. Not that the animals would share Emma's appreciation for the beauty that surrounded them. The Rocky Mountains amazed Emma, and she was in constant awe of the splendor found in every season. Drawing a deep breath to savor the earthy autumn smells, she smiled, truly content with the direction her life had taken. She should have forced Two-Feathers to tag along, now that she thought of it, the old shaman would have enjoyed the outing.

A rumble as loud as an avalanche filled the air and Emma lifted her eyes to the mountain peaks. There wasn't enough snow for that. The sound persisted and a shiver ran up her spine. Could it be an earthquake? Pulling on the reins she turned full circle, catching a wisp of smoke that appeared as a broken streak in the sky. Some sort of heat distortion was moving directly toward her.

"What the…" her voice trailed off as she tried to focus on the odd, almost invisible, moving mass. Her blood ran cold. Whatever it was, it was moving fast and heading right at her. A gust of wind almost knocked her off the horse, swirling dirt and leaves all about as the trees whipped around wildly. The ground shuddered, forcing her to turn her back to the wind and horrible noise that seemed to swallow her. A firm grip on the reins and pommel kept her rooted to the horse as Ruby danced nervously, making it clear how easily she could have thrown Emma. The pounding of Emma's heart filled her ears while her legs turned to lead. She hushed Ruby, shakily petting her neck as she tried to steady the horse. Not an easy task since she was as spooked as the mare. Bo chose that moment to run up the ridge through the bent trees. "Bo!" Emma shouted after the dog. "Come on, girl. Let's go find that crazy mutt." Still shaking, she turned the horse and headed up the trail behind Bo. "Maybe it's just some weird weather phenomenon." Yeah, sure, she thought to herself.

A half hour later, Emma still hadn't managed to catch up to Bo through the strangely parted forest. The unearthly silence that had surrounded them since the incident began to fill with living sounds again but the uneasy feeling remained. It looked as if a tornado had passed through, twisting the tree tops and parting the underbrush, yet somehow without causing any serious damage. Agitated barks came from up ahead. "Bo!" Maybe he was stuck.

Emma dismounted, tied the mare to a tree and made her way along the eerie path. The hair on the back of her neck and arms stood on end as she moved cautiously through the trees. "Bo," Emma called out in a hushed voice. After another few minutes she spotted the dog prancing around in one spot, the way he did when his favorite ball got stuck just out of his reach. The dog was wagging his tail and the fur on his back hadn't bristled. What on Earth had he found? Cautiously, Emma made her way to Bo, even though the dog had definitely made their presence known.

"Oh my God." Emma clamped a hand over her mouth. A man lay with his back against the rock outcropping, behind the underbrush. Was he trying to hide? Blood ran from a cut at his hairline and more soaked through the leg of his dark flight suit. Kneeling down, Emma pressed her fingers to his neck in search of a pulse. "Don't try to move," she said. "I'm going to help you." Leaning closer, she noted his breathing was labored and she knew he couldn't be left out here.

Sitting back on her heels she looked around. Where the heck was his plane? She hadn't seen a parachute and he wasn't wearing a harness. How did he get here?

Lifting one eyelid, then the other, she peered into his eyes. She could barely make out their size, let alone see if they were reactive in the fading light. With a tug, she stripped off her jacket, removed her faded jean shirt and tore it. She used a strip to slow the bleeding around his thigh, and couldn't help but notice his leg was a solid mass of muscle. Maybe he was a military test-pilot or something. Tearing another strip for his head, she gingerly wrapped and tied it. Methodically, Emma passed her hands over his body looking for other injuries before attempting to move him. "Can you hear me?" She rubbed her knuckles across the front of his chest but got no more than a slight moan. The strange material his dark jumpsuit was made out of caught her attention, making her wonder about him. And just where was his plane? She hadn't seen any debris, smoke, or anything. There was no name or rank insignia on his suit. In fact, there were no markings at all.

Pushing away her thoughts, she gritted her teeth and put her coat back on, stuffing what was left of her torn shirt in a pocket. He couldn't afford to wait while she tried to figure out what had happened, he needed medical attention now. "I'm going to try to get you out of here." It wasn't as though she had all that many options. Hooking her arms under his shoulders she dragged him back towards Ruby. She struggled to haul the man's dead weight from out of his resting place. She winced every time he hit a rock or bump that made him moan. Laying him down beside the horse, she stood a moment to catch her breath and stretch her back. "Now what?" she asked the animals. She couldn't leave him head down, draped over the horse to ride back to the house, and there was no way she could haul him up onto the horse.

Emma took what was left of her shirt from the coat pocket and put it under his head. She shivered. The temperature had fallen since the sun had dropped behind the mountain and she'd have to hurry before frost set in.

Grabbing a saw wire and rope from her saddle bag, she cut two young trees and stripped off the branches, then took off her coat and buttoned the denim and fleece jacket closed before she slid the trees into the coat and up the sleeves. It looked like her jacket had surrendered with its arms up. So his feet wouldn't have to drag along the ground, she used the branches to make cross pieces for the bottom end of her makeshift stretcher. It took a while for Emma to finish the stretcher, tie it to the horse and get the pilot or whatever he was strapped in with her limited resources. Working by flashlight did nothing to speed things up.

The moon appeared over the Rocky Mountains, casting some light on the trail ahead, and she was grateful for the occasional marker that reassured her she was still on the right path. The last thing she needed was to get lost out here in the dark with a wounded man. An owl hooted and the air seemed thick with night sounds that made Emma's skin crawl. Her blood ran cold when she heard rustling in the woods alongside the trail. What if he hadn't been alone and someone was following them? Using her flashlight, she looked behind the horse first, to make sure he hadn't fallen off. He was still there. Moving the spotlight around them, full circle, she lit the trail and woods, but couldn't see anything unusual.

The rustling grew louder.

"Bo," she called out, but her voice was barely a whisper. She cleared her throat. "Bo!" Her hands started to shake.

Something was definitely in the trees and the dog was nowhere to be seen. She whistled, hoping it was Bo. A flash of white leapt out from the bush and onto the path. Emma stifled a scream, realizing that the wolf in front of her was actually her dog. In the moonlight he looked all wolf, and she shivered. The chilly night air cut mercilessly through her long-sleeve t-shirt. "Stay close, boy." She clicked her tongue to get Ruby moving again and picked up the pace a bit, keeping her patient in mind. Thank God he was unconscious.

When they reached the house, Emma tied Ruby to the porch railing and slid to the ground. "I'll get back to you in a bit." She stroked the mare's soft nose. Looking at the three wooden steps leading up to the door, she had to decide how she was going to get her JD (John Doe) into the house. Stepping beside her makeshift stretcher she quickly untied him and braced her legs as she pulled him to his feet. Bringing his arm across her shoulders, she crouched slightly, tucked herself under his midriff and then passed a hand between his legs and around his thigh. Ok, she could support his weight, fireman style, but now she had to make it up the stairs.

Once inside, Emma made her way down the hall to the guest room. Turning her back to the bed she eased her charge to the mattress with a grunt. Her legs were trembling now. She passed her sleeve across her sweaty forehead and caught her breath while she collected her thoughts. Hurrying back down the hall, she grabbed the first aid kit and a few items she might need. A shiver passed through her, but she was sure it was no longer due to the cold. Gathering her courage as she stepped back into the dimly lit room to face her patient, she instantly reverted to clinical mode.

Unable to locate a zipper to get him out of the jumpsuit she reached for her scissors but the material proved harder to cut than leather. She slid her fingers inside the collar and the material gave way to her touch, opening down the front. Without missing a beat, she eased it over his shoulders and pulled it down to remove it, boots and all, leaving him in what looked like a pair of black bicycle shorts.

The bruising on his ribs was a mottled blue and purple, and she figured he had fractured a few. Her exam led her to believe there were no other broken bones, although he had obviously been violently tossed around. His abdomen remained soft, a good sign that he wasn't bleeding internally.

He moaned and stirred slightly.

"Don't try to move," Emma said in a comforting voice. "You're safe now. Rest while I tend to your injuries." She brushed the golden brown hair from his forehead and cleaned the gash at his hairline. Her fingers trembled as she applied steri-strips to close the wound in lieu of stitches, and she hoped they would do the job. The cut on his thigh was deep and she worried not only about the possibility of infection, but that a gash this deep most definitely required suturing. She considered using the suture kit she had in the barn for the animals, but nothing was sterile.

With gloved hands, she probed around the leg wound. None of the larger vessels had been cut, although it continued to bleed in a slow and steady fashion. With her bottom lip caught between her teeth, Emma cleaned and irrigated the cut as best she could. She'd get Two-Feathers to give him something to stave off an infection. Pulling the edges of the wound together, she taped them shut with the steri-strips, and then wrapped the leg with white gauze. JD hadn't made another sound.

Using a four-inch elastic bandage, Emma wrapped his ribs, knowing it would make breathing easier if they were strapped. She pulled the covers up to his shoulders, leaving his arms under the blankets for warmth. He was pale and cold as he lay unmoving in bed. His breathing was still somewhat labored, but it was more regular than before.

* * *

After putting Ruby back in her stall, Emma tidied up around JD and placed a pitcher of water and a glass on the nightstand. He was definitely going to be in pain when he woke up. She hoped Two-

Feathers would have his bag of remedies with him when he showed up in the morning. This was the first time she felt helpless without a pharmacy of meds on hand. As a nurse, she had always kept a well-stocked emergency kit readily available, but since she'd left her job in the city, she hadn't replaced the basics in her parent's old home kit. She regretted not having built up a selection of herbs and remedies as Two-Feathers had suggested. He wouldn't have to repeat the offer.

Emma wiped the blonde curls from her eyes, grabbed an extra blanket and pillow which she tossed onto the overstuffed chair at the foot of her patient's bed. She would spend the night here, just in case. Exhausted didn't even come close to how she felt, but she needed something to take the edge off, so she headed to the kitchen for a warm cup of tea.

* * *

Sitting in the kitchen with a foot on her chair and a warm cup of tea in hand, Emma replayed the events of the evening, trying to make sense out of them. The herbal blend had managed to steady her nerves, so she took another sip.

Her mind raced. Surely someone would be looking for him. Maybe she should call the authorities, but if he wasn't from around here, then what? She suppressed a shiver. She'd ask Two-Feathers to check and see if he'd heard anything. "Where are you when I need you?" she said to an absent Two-Feathers.

Seeing that her guest appeared to be as human as any of the other patients she'd ever had was reassuring. Maybe he was. She couldn't help but notice how magnificent he looked, even in his condition, almost textbook perfect. Swallowing the last sip of tea, she rose and headed to the sink to wash her cup. Leaning heavily on the edge of the sink, Emma closed her eyes and attempted to stretch out some of the kinks in her neck and back. She passed a hand across her face to wipe away some of the fatigue.

Standing up, she forced a breath then headed quietly down the hall to check on her patient. Before she pushed open the door, she heard the sound of someone's breath catching, of someone in pain.

His eyes were slightly open and he was slowly looking around, barely moving his head.

"I thought I heard something," she said softly. "Just lay back and rest. You were in an accident, but you're safe now. Would you like something to drink?" Her patients were often parched after surgery, or periods of unconsciousness. She reached for the glass she had left on the bedside table earlier. The ice in the pitcher had all but melted, but the water was still cold. She filled the glass without looking at the man in the bed. She could feel him staring at her and she was trying to avoid eye contact, not wanting to feel nervous. "My name is Emma."

In silence, he accepted the straw she brought to his mouth. With her other hand, she reached for the bedside lamp and increased the intensity of the light. He had closed his eyes again, and she returned the glass to the bedside table. He was extremely pale, and his hair was plastered to his head. Falling into clinical mode once again, she checked for fever, which could be a sign of infection. She slid her hand to his shoulder. "You're soaked," she said. She didn't even know if he spoke English. All the military personnel she'd come across had flags on their uniforms, denoting their country of origin.

She walked over to the antique dresser and pulled open a drawer to retrieve a clean set of sheets. She could feel his eyes on her, and avoided his gaze as she placed them on the chair beside the bed. "I'll be right back to change your bedding." She stepped out of the room to get what she would need for a sponge bath. He'd feel better clean and dry.

Arms laden with towels, soap and a bowl of warm water, she moved around Bo who had followed her back into the room. She placed the bowl of water on the floor by the bed so she could work. She hadn't given a sponge bath since nursing school.

His eyes flew open at the touch of the warm cloth to his skin, startling her. He raised an arm, most likely to protest her care, but let it fall back to the bed and closed his eyes again. She needed to get his strength up, but for now, she preferred if she didn't have to fight him while she tended to him.

Remembering how to change an occupied bed, she gently turned him to his side using pillows to support his shoulders and not increase the pain from his cracked ribs. She rolled the dirty sheets up to his back, laid out the clean ones with the excess also against his back and carefully brought him toward her. She passed a gentle hand on his forehead. "Almost done," she whispered. Scooting around the bed she quickly removed the damp sheets and laid out the fresh ones. Bringing him gingerly onto his back she sat on the edge of the bed and checked his bandages. The bleeding from his thigh had finally stopped, but he was very pale, either from blood loss or pain. She'd rummage through her parents' stuff for some clothing later. She covered him back up with the warm blankets and stood to collect the dirty towels and linen.

"Thank you," he said in a weak voice.

Emma froze, her heart pounded wildly in her ears. He spoke English. Ok, so maybe he *was* a military test pilot, flying some kind of top-secret prototype, nothing more. She tossed the dirty linen just outside the door and returned to his bedside. "Let me help you move up a bit in bed, you're sliding down." Shaking slightly, she put a knee on the bed and hooked her arms under his, careful not to cause him too much pain. "Bend your knees and try to push up a little with your legs."

He winced as he moved, but she could see that he was more comfortable now. "Could I have some more water, please?" he asked.

She turned back and looked into his eyes. Not blue. Could they be purple? She smiled and forced herself to remain calm. "Of course." She reached for the water again. "Would you like some soup, or vegetable stew?" she offered. She was unable to take her eyes off of his, until he closed them and nodded. She wondered if he knew what soup was.

Silently, she stepped out of the room, grabbed the laundry from the floor and headed toward the kitchen, her mind racing. Purple, his eyes were purple. Who or what was he? Her imagination was coming up with way too many scenarios. Wait, wasn't there some actress with purple eyes? She headed past the kitchen to the mudroom and dropped the load into the washer. A noise from behind startled her and she spun around, dropping the capful of laundry soap. She clutched at her chest, forcing air into her lungs. "You scared me."

Two-Feathers stood in the doorway and nodded. "I guess that means you found him." Bo danced around his legs, demanding attention.

She tilted her head and her mouth opened to say something but then shut it. Flustered, she grabbed a dirty towel to pick up her mess and tossed it into the machine before looking back at the shaman. "You want tea?" she asked as she pushed past him to the kitchen.

He remained in the doorway. "He is not dangerous." His voice was calm and level. "I came to see if you needed help."

She put the kettle on the stove and turned to face him. "'Could have used a hand to get him down from the mountain." Her eyes met his. She let the reassurance he seemed to send out ease her nerves. "You knew." It wasn't a question.

He nodded then moved to take a seat in an old wooden chair at the table. "How is he?"

The corner of her mouth lifted. "Why don't you tell me?" She was starting to like her friend's mysterious ways. "I was going to heat up some soup for him. Would you like some?"

"If I have a choice, I could really go for some of your stew."

She took out a second pot to warm the stew, set two mugs on the table and filled the inner strainer of the teapot with her own blend of leaves, herbs and flowers. Emma poured the boiling water over the mixture and set the teapot onto the table.

She sat across from Two-Feathers in silence, waiting for him to answer her question as Bo settled at her feet. She hoped the shaman could fill in some of the blanks.

Amusement sparked in his eyes, he'd always liked being put to the test. "He's lost quite a bit of blood, has three fractured ribs, a concussion with a gash at the hairline and a deep laceration on...his right thigh. Nothing too critical." He brought his attention back to her. "How'd I do?"

She shook her head. "Any sane person would run from this place, screaming at the top of their lungs."

He reached out to check her brew as she rose to stir the pots on the stove. She turned down the soup, served two bowls of stew and sat back down at the table. Her mind was all over the place, bouncing between questions and emotions. She hoped he could help with her predicament. She paused a moment to offer thanks for her meal, and her friend, then threw in a silent plea for guidance.

Two-Feathers placed a hand on her shoulder. "You have nothing to fear. He is not dangerous." He took a spoonful of her thick stew.

"I wasn't running screaming from him," she said teasingly. She let out a sigh and lightly chewed on her bottom lip. "And you said that before. I'm just not sure about what to do."

He shrugged. "Do what you can. Do what you would do with any wounded stray."

She made a face. "I'm not sure he'd like to be referred to as a stray." She ate a few bites as she mulled through her thoughts. Was he a guest, a visitor, a patient? She looked over at his 'kit' on the far end of the table. "So what's in your magic pouch today? He could use something for the pain."

He shrugged without looking at her. "Better if you didn't know." He scraped the last of the stew from his bowl and pushed it back. He obviously couldn't help the mischievous grin that formed on his lips.

She swatted him playfully on the arm, picked up the bowls and placed them in the sink. As she spooned some of the warm soup into a bowl for JD she thought about the plants and herbs she had been studying with Two-Feathers. "Are you going to add them into his soup or should we make a tea?"

"Is he strong enough for both?"

Emma could feel his gaze on her as she considered the question. "No. I would imagine he doesn't have the strength to take in too much right now." She watched as Two-Feathers stepped forward to add some finely ground powder to the broth. "What if he is allergic to any of this?" Her programmed response came to life, and she paused to silence it.

He smiled then closed his eyes for a second as he passed his hand over the bowl. He shook his head. "This will be fine." He turned to face her. "Will you be ok, or do you want me to bring it to him?"

Her heart rate jumped up a notch. "You don't intend to stay?"

"I think it would be better if he only had to deal with one person for now."

Emma had to agree. He was injured, vulnerable and probably somewhat apprehensive. "Are you going to hang around while I tend to him?"

"I have to get something from my truck." He clicked his tongue for the dog to follow and headed for the door. "I'll be close by if you need me."

She dipped her little finger into the soup and tasted the modified broth. The pleasing flavour surprised her.

"You should have more faith." He called out from the porch. "I added something for both pain and infection," he said.

She placed the bowl on a tray with a slice of homemade bread. She threw her shoulders back and took a deep breath before heading down the hall.

Emma gently pushed open the door, expecting to find JD in bed, but stiffened when she found it empty. She laid the food on the bedside table and looked around the room. He was nowhere in sight. Movement from under the adjoining bathroom door caught her eye. She wondered if he knew how to use the facilities, but the sound of the toilet flushing answered her question. Maybe he *was* just a military test pilot after all. Maybe she should just ask him, but then, she probably couldn't handle finding out that he wasn't. What if someone came looking for him? She wondered if her life could be in danger.

A crash and the sound of him stumbling brought her out of her thoughts. She rushed to help him. The door wasn't locked so she eased it open, hoping he wasn't behind it.

He was on his knees, leaning against the edge of the antique, clawfoot tub, breathing heavily. His features were twisted in pain.

She dropped down beside him, pulled his arm across her shoulders and slid her arm around him; his spicy musk smell filled her senses. "Let's try and stand, slowly." She kept her back straight as she slowly pushed up with her legs.

He inhaled sharply, but stood with her.

She pivoted and sat him down in the wicker chair beside the tub. "Stay put," she said laying a hand on his arm. "I'm going to get some help to put you back to bed." She squeezed his arm lightly to reassure him before leaving his side.

Two-Feathers stepped into the bedroom before she had taken more than two steps out of the bathroom. He nodded to her but said nothing as he followed her back in to help.

Emma saw JD stiffen ever so slightly when Two-Feathers appeared at her side. His eyes reflected his weakened state, but his gaze followed the tall shaman's every move.

Two-Feathers bowed slightly. "A-kiss-no-haus tsa-a-nam."

She recognized the words. *Star brother.* How did he always know everything? Emma still hung on to a tiny fibre of hope that

John Doe was a military test pilot...from Earth.

Easing past her, the shaman scooped up 'star brother' and carried him back to the bed. With his knee on the edge of the bed, Two-Feathers gently lowered his charge to the mattress where Emma had pulled down the sheets. His eyes were closed and a light shimmer of perspiration covered his trembling body.

Two-Feathers stood over the bed while Emma expertly checked star brother's bandages and vitals. She brought the covers up to his waist. She was going to have to find some clothes for him once he was out of bed. All he had on was a pair of navy sweat shorts. For now, it did the trick.

"Next time ask for help," she said to him.

Eyes still closed, JD nodded.

She wiped his face with a damp cloth and pushed the hair from his forehead, mindful of the gash at his hairline. "I brought you some soup. It will help you gain back your strength and take the edge off the pain." She sat back and watched him closely. "You can trust us."

Two-Feathers moved silently to the door and gestured that he'd be sitting out in the living room. He snapped his fingers for the dog to follow him out.

She nodded and turned back to her patient. She took a silent breath. "Could you tell me your name?" She rested a hand on his shoulder. His skin was soft, smooth, and looked slightly tanned.

"Dthau-Mahsz," he whispered.

Emma strained to make out his words. Did he say 'Thomas'? Well, she'd find out soon enough. "Are you ready for some soup, Thomas?"

He opened his eyes and smiled weakly. "I would prefer to sit up."

"Hold on, I'll get some more pillows." She gathered the extras from the dresser where she had left them, and placed them on the bed. "I'm going to help you slide up. Can you push a bit with your legs like we did last time?" She hooked her arms under his when he nodded. Placing a knee on the bed she braced to move him. "Ready?"

When he nodded again, they moved together to put him in a semi-sitting position. A slight gasp escaped his lips as he shifted.

"Easy," she whispered. She reached back with one arm, still

holding onto him with the other, and placed pillows behind his back. She moved quickly, efficiently. "I'm going to ease you back slowly, but don't tense your muscles, let me do the work." When she felt him relax, she lowered him against the mound of pillows and pulled away.

Taking the bowl into her hands, she felt the warmth of the soup through the stoneware. Emma watched him closely as he took a few shallow breaths with his eyes closed. "This will help get you back on your feet," she said reassuringly. "Whenever you're ready."

His eyelids fluttered open and he nodded.

She brought a spoonful of soup to his mouth. Oh yeah, his eyes were definitely purple, or maybe amethyst, she thought. She forced a smile as she watched him eat, keeping her hand steady. She took his willingness to accept more of the soup as a sign that he liked it.

Halfway through the soup, his eyelids began to droop. Thomas paused a moment and rested as his eyes closed. Beads of sweat appeared on his forehead and Emma reached for a small towel to gingerly sponge his face. Lips pressed together, she waited to see if he would open his eyes again but when his breathing changed, she knew that sleep had claimed him. Returning the soup to the tray before reaching out to support his upper body, she carefully removed the extra padding from behind him, hoping to ease him into a more comfortable sleeping position. Quickly tidying around the bed, she collected the tray and silently left the room.

Two-Feathers, who had been reading quietly in the living room, followed her back to the kitchen. He looked at the contents of the bowl she was carrying and nodded. "You got him to eat more than I had expected. Good."

"It tired him to eat." She stored the leftovers and refilled the kettle. "You having another tea?" She wanted a cup of comfort before she went to bed.

"You sit," Two-Feathers said. "I'll get it, and then I'm going to head out."

All kinds of protests and alarms sounded in her head, but she just nodded. She didn't have to make him repeat that Thomas was not dangerous. It was time to start trusting his, no, *her* instincts.

CHAPTER 4: THOMAS

Emma had slept soundly in the chair at the foot of Thomas' bed, though she could have used a few more hours sleep. The early morning rays of light splashed across the bedroom floor creating a lacy pattern on the polished wood planks. Drawing in a deep breath, she stretched and yawned, passing a hand over her face. Her eyes were drawn to the bed where Thomas lay, awake and staring at her. She felt a rush of heat to her face, uncomfortable that he'd been watching her.

Emma inhaled sharply and gathered her courage. "Good morning. How are you feeling today?" She rose, placed the blanket she'd used over the back of the overstuffed chair and approached his bedside. He seemed to have a bit more colour this morning. She touched his forehead, no fever. His eyes were brighter, respiration slow and steady, and he had a good strong pulse. The steri-strips were holding nicely at his hairline. She smiled. "I'm just going to check your bandages." Her hands moved to lower the blankets but his hands caught her wrists. Her heart pounded erratically in her ears. "It's OK. I'm not going to hurt you."

He held her tight. Emma turned to look into his eyes and forced a reassuring smile. "I need my hands." She waited for him to release her as he searched her face. A strange emotion crossed his eyes. "I'm not going to hurt you," she repeated, her voice almost a whisper. She shuddered inwardly.

Slowly, he loosened his grip. She moved purposely, gently easing back the blankets while trying hard to control the shaking of her hands. She avoided his gaze as she checked the bandage over his ribs. She would tape them later, replacing the elastic bandage. Still in clinical mode, she moved to the gash at his thigh and let out a breath when she saw that it had started bleeding again. "I'll be right back." She covered him up and hurried to the kitchen where Two-Feathers had left some ground concoction he told her to put into the wound to make the bleeding stop. She wondered how he'd known, again. She grabbed the prepared tray from the counter and went back to tend to Thomas.

"Now, let's fix that leg." She sat on the edge of his bed and uncovered his thigh. Pulling her bandage scissors from the pouch on the bedside table, she cut away the gauze from his leg, exposing the steri-strips. Soaking a sterile cloth with amber liquid from a jar, she cleaned the outer edge of the wound, as per the shaman's instructions. The wound had a purple hue to the ragged, swollen edges, but there was no sign of infection. Unscrewing the cap to the mystery powder, she gently sprinkled it over the wound, careful to lightly cover the entire surface, hoping it would work even with the steri-strips. Her eyes widened as the bleeding seemed to stop almost instantly.

She looked at Thomas, watching for any signs of pain or discomfort, but he remained silent. He hadn't so much as moved.

"Are you sure you know what you are doing?" he asked, a hint of humour in his voice.

Emma felt her face turn red. "I'm used to working with the meds and procedures I trained for. Two-Feathers is the local shaman, or medicine man." She pointed to the powder. "He left this for you." She covered the wound with a telfa pad and wrapped his thigh again. Moving the tray to the bedside table, she gathered the courage to face him. Her eyes locked on his and her heart skipped a beat. They were mesmerizing. "Are you hungry?"

He nodded, and shifted uncomfortably. "Could you please help me up?" He nodded in the direction of the bathroom.

"Roll slightly to the side and push up. If your ribs are too sensitive I'll lift you." She watched him slowly roll and move as she had suggested. "Good." She gave him a moment, making sure he didn't show any signs of dizziness before helping him to his feet. They made their way slowly to the bathroom where she had placed a wooden chair for him to use for support. Emma hesitated, not sure if she should leave, since she was not convinced Thomas was strong enough to manage on his own. "Do you want me to help you?"

A flicker of colour rose to his cheeks. "I will let you know if I require further assistance."

While she waited for him to finish, she stripped down his bed and remade it with fresh flannel sheets. "Are you all right in there?" she asked through the door when he still hadn't appeared.

"I am managing well," he answered back. The door opened slightly. He looked down at his shorts before bringing his gaze back up to her. "Could you return my clothes, or give me something other than this to wear?" His face showed distaste.

OK, not what she had expected. She held up a hand and went to fish out a grey t-shirt and a pair of navy sweats from the dresser. It would be easier to look after his injuries if he wasn't in a jumpsuit. She really had to get him some boxers or something. Mom usually had an unopened pack of socks and boxers she'd bought on sale. She'd check later.

Thomas wasn't at the bathroom door when she came back with the clothes, so she gently pushed her way in. He sat in the wicker chair with his eyes closed. They snapped open before her hand could touch his arm, startling her. God, he made her jumpy.

"Let me help you," she said.

He clenched his jaw slightly. She was sure he was going to protest, but he nodded instead. She eased the v-neck t-shirt over his head and he slid his arms into the short sleeves.

"Put the pants on over these," he said, pointing to the shorts. His tone was controlled, yet it sounded almost like an order.

"I changed the sheets on your bed." She tried to make idle conversation to ease her nerves. "You'll be more comfortable with fresh bedding. Let's get you settled again and I'll bring you something to eat." Emma looked at him, watching for a reaction. "I have to step out and tend to my chores, but I'll wait until you're resting."

"I would prefer to not spend my day in bed." He stiffened, staring at her with a stern look, but Emma could see that he was already beginning to weaken from the few efforts he'd made.

She weighed her words carefully. "How about you take it easy this morning, and we'll see how you are doing this afternoon. No sense overexerting yourself and ending up back in bed." She gave him a gentle smile, trying to hide the nervous tremors that ran through her body. It felt as though she was working with an unpredictable, wounded animal.

Stepping out of the room, Bo on her heels, she closed the door and turned to lean on the wall a moment. She let out a breath, straightened and headed back to the kitchen with the empty dishes from breakfast. He was asleep and now she'd head to the barn to care for the animals.

When she opened the barn door, the smell of hay and horses surrounded her, comforted her. She inhaled deeply and remembered a time she'd gone horseback riding with a group from the hospital. It had been a new experience for two of them and she laughed at how they'd gagged from the smell of the stable.

Hanging her coat on a peg by the door, Emma rolled up her sleeves and headed off to feed the animals. She'd milk the cow and collect the eggs next. By the looks of it, she'd have to muck out the stalls as well. She was grateful to have something to keep her occupied until Two-Feathers showed up. He hadn't said he was coming, but she knew he would.

She had worked up a good sweat in the barn and longed for a soothing shower as she made her way back to the house. Her nerves probably needed it more than her muscles. It had been impossible to keep her thoughts from Thomas and his purple eyes. Two-Feathers had called him Star Brother...was he really an alien? Was she in danger?

Heading to the kitchen, she put the egg basket on the counter along with the milk. She stopped and smiled at the sight of Two-Feathers sitting at the table grinding up herbs and roots with an old mortar and pestle.

He continued to focus on his task, not bothering to look up as he spoke. "He is still asleep. I checked on him while you were out." He stopped grinding his mixture and rose from the table. "Go ahead and shower, I'll make tea."

Emma watched him as he filled the kettle with water and set it on the stove. "What did you grind up for him?" She leaned over the table to look at his preparation.

"It's not for him," Two-Feathers explained. "It's for you. You are too tense and he can sense it."

She whirled around to face him. Her heart sank and she was immediately filled with a sense of bewilderment. She needed to get a grip on her emotions. "Did he say that?"

Two-Feathers shook his head. "He didn't have to." He raised a hand and waved her off. "We'll talk after your shower."

A short while later, feeling refreshed, Emma headed back to the kitchen. She wrinkled her nose at the smell from the shaman's brew. The barn had smelled better. She laid some socks and boxers down on the counter. "I'll just run in and check on Thomas." She refilled a pitcher of water and took a clean glass from the cupboard.

"He's still asleep and you need to relax." He pointed to a chair. "It doesn't taste as bad as it smells."

Emma hesitated before taking a seat. Cup in hand, she held her breath before taking a sip. The after-taste wasn't as bitter as she'd expected. She took another few sips before she finally gagged. "Ok, I'm done." She pushed the cup away. "Don't know why I took a shower, I smelled better after having mucked out the stalls." What she didn't say was that even the few sips she'd taken had made a difference. The constant, nervous tremors she'd been feeling were finally subsiding.

"I brought some clothes for him," Two-Feathers said. "I put them on the little table outside his bedroom door." He turned to face her and their eyes met. "You are still worried."

Emma shifted in her chair and let out a sigh. "Do you know where he comes from, or what he is?"

"Try to think of it like this." The old shaman spread his arms as he talked. "Where did your ancestors come from? Was it England, Ireland, Russia, or Italy?" He handed her the cup of foul tasting liquid. "If the brother that had stayed behind was to show up here, today, would you fear him? Even if it's been 400 years since the two lineages had separated?"

She made a face. "Of course not. What's to fear?"

He shrugged. "What if it had been 4000 years instead?"

"Oh," she said softly. "So you're saying that we're long lost cousins or something?" Alien cousin, her mind shouted.

"We can leave it at that." He took the cup back after she had forced another sip down and shuddered. "I'll heat up something for lunch." He waved her off. "He's awake now. Go check on him while I set out the food."

* * *

The next morning Emma left Two-Feathers with Thomas and headed off to the clinic. She had been having a hard time focusing and was afraid William would notice, so she stepped outside for a breath of air.

"You all right?" William appeared from behind her and Emma

screamed.

Shaking, she brought her hand to her chest and forced air into her lungs. She blinked back tears and nodded.

"Hey," William said softly. He moved in and wrapped his arms around her. "What's going on? You've been stressed out all morning."

A strangled laugh escaped her lips. "I thought I'd managed to hide it."

William smiled. "Nope, not even close."

"I've had a few sleepless nights. I'm sorry." She drew in a shaky breath. "I'll be OK." She stepped back and wiped her eyes. "We should get back inside, it's cold."

Arms crossed, William studied her. "Why don't you take the rest of the day off? It's slow today, and it won't pick up either." He pulled open the door and waved her in. "The story-teller arrives tonight for the festival and everyone is busy getting things ready. I can handle a few calls on my own."

She stepped back into the clinic and looked around. It was kind of deserted. "Are you sure?" Maybe she should call it a day before she did more harm than good.

"Absolutely. And the clinic is closed on Thursday. I'll be making a few house calls." He reached out and held her by an arm, his dark eyes searching hers. "You can tell me if there's anything. I'm a pretty good listener."

Emma hesitated. How could she tell William she couldn't sleep because there was an alien in her home? "Have you spoken with your uncle lately?" She had hoped Two-Feathers would have said something to William; she'd be able to confide in him then.

William frowned, shaking his head slowly. "He left a message on my machine the other day, but in all honesty, I haven't had the chance to get back to him. I figured I see him at the festival. Why?"

She forced a smile. "No reason. I think I'll head out now."

He nodded. "Sure. Try to get some rest."

"Let me know if you need help for your run of house calls," she said. "Thanks for being understanding."

A smile lit his face. "It's my finest attribute."

Emma laughed. "Did you invite Krista to the festival?" He'd been hesitating for weeks, trying to decide if or how he should ask her out.

His cheeks flushed and Emma laughed. "Yeah," he said in an unsteady voice.

"Have fun, then. I'll see you next week." She headed to the locker room to collect her coat. The festival couldn't have come at a better time.

* * *

The next two days passed in a blur and Thomas was getting stronger by the minute, though his ribs continued to cause him discomfort. As far as Emma was concerned, this was a good thing, because she was sure her patient wouldn't rest voluntarily. This morning he'd eaten a good breakfast and had finally smiled at something she'd said. It did wonders to alleviate the tension she felt every time she was near him. Now she had planned on getting him out of the house, even if it was only to tag along while she tended to her chores since he'd been curious as to why she would disappear twice a day.

"Ready for a bit of fresh air, Thomas?" Emma poked her head into his room. She had a folded pile of clothing from Two-Feathers in her hands. "I'll just leave these here for you." She placed them on the dresser and backed out of the room, closing the door behind her, and then sat in the living room, in her grandmother's armchair, while she waited. Bo settled at her feet, but his posture told her he was anxious to get out.

Thomas hadn't been very talkative but he would answer her questions with a brief response. He always seemed to be observing and analyzing his surroundings. She wasn't sure how she felt about that, but she'd finally agreed with Two-Feathers, Thomas wasn't a threat to her. Now if only she could relax around him.

He stepped out into the living room a short while later, wearing jeans and a t-shirt. The dark blue flannel shirt was open, and he stared at the buttons. "I am not sure..." he started as he lifted the ends of the shirt up.

Smiling, she stepped closer and showed him how to slip the buttons through the holes. "Just like that," she said. She paused and stared into his eyes. They took her breath away every time she looked at them. They almost seemed to be lit from behind, and that intrigued her.

He nodded. "Now what?" He looked around the room.

"It snowed a little last night. I have a coat for you." She held up a winter jacket, a wool hat and pair of mitts. "It's cold out there." She nodded towards the door. She showed him how to zip the jacket and handed him a pair of moccasins. She quickly dressed and opened the door to the winter wonderland that awaited them. She took a deep breath as a smile spread across her face. "Isn't it beautiful?"

A light dusting of snow covered the outside world, a promise of things to come and Emma's heart soared, filled with delight. She couldn't suppress the giddiness she felt as they headed for the barn.

He followed her in silence while she tended to her chores, and she showed him around, explaining what she could. "You have a nice home," he said as he collected the eggs.

Emma watched him a moment as he gently removed the eggs from the nests, careful not to startle the hens. As she turned back toward the cow and began milking, she watched him from the corner of her eye. He spun around, obviously trying to identify the milking sounds and she bit her lip in an attempt not to smile at his reaction.

For a moment he just stared, unmoving. A slight frown formed on the rugged features of his handsome face. "I thought all these things were available in provision centers and that they were accessible to everyone."

She smiled openly now, but kept on milking. "I kept my father's farm and his ways. Well, since I've returned." When she was done, she stood with a bucket of fresh milk and spoke to the cow. Turning back to Thomas she said, "I keep enough to provide for my needs and share the rest. Over the summer, I grew what I could in my garden." She avoided his gaze.

"Why would you give yourself such trouble?" Thomas asked.

She laughed. "Believe me, it's no trouble." She went to feed the animals but was uncomfortable with him watching her every move. "Here." She handed him a scoop of oats and pointed to the horses. "Fill their buckets with feed. I'll get the cow and chickens." As soon as they were done they bundled up and headed back towards the house. The wind was cold and cut through their layers of clothing. "Let's go put some more wood on the fire and warm up."

About an hour later, they sat quietly in the living room, watching the fire dance as they ate warm apple crisp. "You may not believe or understand it, but it's almost as though time has stood still in this room," Emma explained, pointing with the handle of her fork. "The furniture is still in good shape, even though it dates back to my grandparents." She paused, letting the smell of the wood smoke and apple crisp fill her as she remembered how she used to get on her mother's case for not upgrading the room. "I feel at home in here, and couldn't bring myself to change a thing." She shrugged at the irony.

Thomas watched her closely, a look of curiosity in his eyes. "Why would you live here by yourself?"

Her expression became more serious as she thought about her life and all the changes that had come over it in the past few months. "Don't you have people who live alone?"

"No, we are part of a community." His tone was abrupt. "You should not be out here alone."

She looked at him and swallowed the lump forming in her throat. "When my parents passed away, I couldn't bring myself to come back, so I buried myself in my life in the city. That was five years ago. I only came home to close up and sell the farm, to deal with my responsibilities, because my life in the city was about to change." She took a moment to compose herself. She didn't react well to change. "Instead, I fell in love with it all over again. I had forgotten what life was all about." She took another bite of apple crisp and tried to push back the mix of emotions. Not an easy feat under his constant scrutiny, and the last thing she wanted was to appear even more emotionally unstable.

"Don't you miss being around people? What about nursing or teaching?" He prompted as he sipped his tea slowly, keeping his eyes on Emma.

"Oh, I'm still quite active in our community." She put her plate down and stood to refill their cups. "I've continued to work part time as a nurse, making house calls with Dr. Westerman, and I study as well. I have been learning about Native American healing from Two-Feathers. You met him, though I'm not sure you were lucid enough to remember."

"I remember."

That surprised her, because he had been so out of it at the time. She continued, trying to appear calm. "He is the shaman of a nearby Ktunaxa Tribe." She sat down and took a sip of tea. "I just feel so alive here." She smiled openly and took a deliberate breath.

"It is interesting." He said. His eyes panned the room.

"What about you?" She asked. It was her turn to get some answers. She had not pressed him for information on his origin at all, and she had to admit, she wasn't sure she wanted to know. This might be one of those situations where ignorance was bliss.

He stared at her. "What would you like to know?"

Great, Emma thought, he's going to make me ask. She avoided his gaze and spoke with clinical detachment as she tried to keep her heart rate steady. "I saw you crash. Well, the brief streak your craft made as it went across the sky. The clothes you were wearing were not like anything I had ever seen..." She raised her head slowly and looked deep into his eyes. Her stomach lurched as he held her gaze.

"Does this frighten you?" he asked. He put down his cup and leaned slightly forward.

She took a long, slow, deliberate breath. Her eyes never left his. "Should it?" A slight shudder passed through her.

"I am not a threat to you, or anyone else." He watched her closely.

She took a moment before speaking, to hide behind her clinical facade. "Where are you from?"

"Have you heard of a legend that tells of the forefathers, who came from a planet around the Dog Star *Sirius*?" He watched her for a sign of recognition.

She nodded. "The Indians out here have told me about it. They also claim that the Egyptians and some African tribes also have a similar legend." She moved to the edge of her seat, her curiosity overpowering her uneasiness. "Are you one of our forefathers?"

"No." A hint of amusement lit his eyes. "My people are from the first planet the forefathers had seeded in this galaxy. We were entrusted with the survival of all subsequent colonies." He studied her closely. "How do you feel about this?"

"I don't know." She stood and walked around the room a bit, holding her teacup and saucer to give her hands something to do. So much for the test-pilot theory she'd been holding on to. She swallowed a sip of tea, trying to ease her dry mouth. She turned to face him and spoke slowly. "Are your friends coming?" Her cup rattled as she returned it to its saucer. "Do they know where you are?" She swallowed. "Can you even get home?"

"No," he said softly.

She sat on the window ledge, staring at him. "Then I guess you've left the city too."

They sat in silence for what seemed like an eternity. Calling on all her inner strength to keep calm and rational, she managed to focus on her breathing until the shaking stopped. She felt a pang of sorrow for him, remembering how disorientated she'd felt when she had come back after her parents' death. He'd truly lost everything, and if what he said was true, he was stuck here. Adaptation for Thomas would most likely be more difficult than it had been for her.

Emma cleared her throat quietly. Her blue eyes met his amazing amethyst ones. "How do you feel about this?"

CHAPTER 5: *No Way Home*

Emma awoke with a start. Her dreams were haunted by aliens. They were there, watching her. Everywhere she went, every time she turned around, they, no *he* was there. She tried to shake off the unease, but ended up tossing and turning, unable to fall asleep again.

She hadn't had a good night's sleep since their discussion last week because her mind kept repeating the obvious -Thomas was stuck here, with no way home and nowhere to go. Her dreams were haunted by him. Every time she turned around, no matter what the dream, there he was, watching her. Although they had spent most of their days together without incident, she was still wary about what he was and her overactive imagination certainly didn't help. Sighing, she sat up and passed a hand over her eyes. The clock's blue lights glowed a steady 2:57AM. With a moan of protest, she shoved the covers aside, pulled on a pair of wool socks and slipped into her tattered, blue terrycloth robe. Bo rolled over to watch her, stretched and moved to her side.

Cautiously, she headed down the stairs, trying to remember where to put her feet to avoid the squeaky spots so as not to wake Thomas. Her hair was a mess and the robe dangled open as she made her way to the kitchen to brew a cup of Two-Feathers' foul tea. She hadn't dared ask what he'd put in it, she was learning. She smiled wearily, it was definitely a lesson learned at great expense. Of course, had it been for someone else, she'd have hounded him for the list of ingredients.

The kitchen was dark, except for the moonlight that streamed in from the window above the white enamel sink. Emma filled the kettle with water and set it on the stove while she reached into the cupboard above her head for the jar of Two-Feathers' sleep-promising, vile-tasting concoction. Spooning some of the powder into a cup she turned to place it onto the table. "Oh my God!" she exclaimed. The cup fell to the floor and shattered, sending bits of ceramic and powder everywhere. Thomas had been sitting at the table, watching her. Shaking, she dropped to her knees and began to pick up the sharp pieces as tears streamed down her face. Her nerves were shot. She'd been struggling to keep it together since she'd first seen the streak in the sky.

She stiffened at his touch on her shoulder. He took her by the arms and lifted her to her feet, drawing her close. She remained stiff and panicked.

As some unexplained sense of reassurance surrounded her, Emma slid her arms around his waist, rested her forehead on his chest and let him hold her until the flow of tears ebbed.

"I am so sorry; I did not mean to frighten you," Thomas said in a hushed voice. He didn't move to touch her in any other way. He just held her.

After a long moment, Emma stepped back and wiped her eyes. "I'd better pick this up," she said shakily, avoiding his gaze as she went to get a broom and dustpan. Dropping the shattered pieces into the trash, she turned back to Thomas. "Would you like a cup of Earl Grey?" She had changed her mind about Two-Feathers' blend.

"I do not know what that is, but I will try some." He pointed to the glass of water in front of him. "I could not sleep, either. I came in for some water and was watching the moonlight through the window when you arrived." He tilted his head and smiled wearily. "I was sure you had not seen me and was trying to figure out how to announce my presence without scaring you." He looked into her eyes. "You are nervous enough around me. I did not want to add to your discomfort."

Emma could see the sincerity in his eyes. "My mother would have told me I got what I deserved." She felt defeated as she turned to make the tea.

"I am not sure I understand." He remained standing near the table.

She sighed. She could feel his eyes on her. "Deep down inside, I know you are not a threat. Unfortunately, my overactive imagination and lack of trust in my instincts seem to have the upper hand right now." She answered honestly and wondered if he understood her explanation. She poured the boiling water into their cups and let the tea bags steep.

"As a nurse you must have relied on your instincts." He sat down on his chair.

Emma set the cups on the table and put the milk next to the sugar bowl. She sliced two pieces of the pumpkin-date bread and handed one to Thomas. "You're right. There were times my gut screamed that something was off, and when I listened, things usually turned out for the better."

"But not this time," he said. He took a bite of the cake and nodded in approval.

She fidgeted. "No, for some reason, not this time. I have had a lot to deal with since I left Vancouver; maybe my ability to deal with stress has been overloaded." She had to admit that aside from a total turn-around in lifestyles, finding an *alien* was cause enough for her jumpiness.

"Would you prefer if I left?" He showed no emotion while he waited for a reply.

She dropped her fork. "No, God, no. I couldn't just put you out." She wiped her hands on a napkin and placed a hand on his forearm. "I'm sorry. Please forgive my reaction." She felt a sinking in the pit of her stomach. Why was it so hard to control her fears? "I think it has more to do with a disruption in my quest for balance or inner peace." She let out a breath. The feeling of comfort she'd felt before was back, slowly easing its way over her nerves. "Let's just take this one day at a time." She looked at him, forcing a smile as she waited for a reaction.

He nodded again. "One day at a time."

Emma took a sip of tea, letting the warmth comfort her from the inside. "I was wondering about something, though." She had been thinking about this for a few days, not sure if she should bring it up.

He held her gaze. "You were wondering if I wanted to return to my ship to collect things I might need."

Her mouth dropped suddenly and she clamped it shut just as fast. "Yes, that's exactly what I was wondering." Damn, so much for finding peace around him. Maybe she was the transparent one, since Two-Feathers always seemed to know what she was thinking as well. For some reason, Thomas being able to read her mind was beyond disquieting. She felt exposed and very, very vulnerable.

"I have no way of locating it without your help. Though by now there would not be much of it left." The expression on his face was unreadable. He reached for his cup and inhaled the aroma before tasting it. "You added milk and sugar to yours."

Emma nodded. "Here, try mine and decide how you like your tea." She handed Thomas her cup.

He took a sip, holding the liquid in his mouth a moment before swallowing. "I like this," he said, handing Emma the cup.

They sat in silence, sipping tea and Emma let herself get lost in the torrential current of her thoughts. When Thomas laid a gentle hand on her arm she jumped. Her eyes lifted to meet his and her heart rate kicked up a notch as she stared into his eyes, mesmerized. She swallowed her tea. "Do all of your people have eyes like you? I mean the same colour as yours?"

He sat back in his chair and watched her for a moment, obviously debating something. "No. Amethyst eyes are rare, even amongst my people."

A wave of frustration passed through her. It would be nice if he could just offer some information, she thought. She had so many unanswered questions and hated to probe.

He smiled in an amused way and leaned closer to her. "What exactly would you like to know?"

She stiffened. "What are you willing to tell me about yourself, aside from the fact that you have a rare eye colour, cannot go home and are not a threat to me?"

He let out a breath. "First of all, my name is Dthau-Mahsz, and not Thomas." He waved a hand in dismissal. "You may, however, call me Thomas, if you prefer." He shifted in his seat and clasped his hands together on the table. "I...was the commander of the Phoenix. A crisis intervention vessel, charged with the transfer or establishment of colonies."

Emma blinked. She wasn't quite sure what that meant, but she didn't dare interrupt.

"The role of my people is to oversee the wellbeing of our sister colonies. Some observe and evaluate, some are actively involved with planetary governments, others evaluate uninhabited planets for possible colonization and my vessel acts in crisis situations."

She shook her head. "Which means what, exactly?" Her mind

raced. Were all these people here on Earth right now? No, that couldn't be, otherwise he'd be able to get home.

"It means that my ship is out of a commander." He clenched his jaw, and looked away.

"Yeah, well, I guess they'll have to find a replacement now," she said absently, thinking about the jobs she'd left behind. She caught an odd look as it crossed his face. "What, don't tell me you thought you were irreplaceable?" She almost laughed, but his face told her there was nothing funny about the situation.

"At the time, I was." He passed a hand over his jaw. "Suffice it to say, that we do not apply for our positions. Selection is based on the mental, physical, emotional and psychological aspects of the individual. We do not randomly choose our place." He reached for his cup, but it was empty. He set it down and pushed his chair back. "I am ready to retire for the night."

Emma looked at the time on the stove. "What's left of it." She gathered up the cups and put them into the sink. To her surprise Thomas was putting the milk in the fridge. They quickly tidied in silence and headed off to their respective rooms with barely a nod good night. Too tired to even think, she fell asleep before her head hit the pillow.

* * *

The warm rays of the sun covered Emma's bed, and she stretched slowly, keeping her eyes closed as she relished in the warmth. Realizing that the sun didn't cross her bed until mid-morning, she sat up abruptly and looked at the clock. She'd overslept, way overslept. Hurrying to the bathroom, she brushed her teeth then pulled her hair into a quick ponytail. She shrugged off her terrycloth robe, slid into her jeans and pulled on her work shirt before hurrying down the stairs. She realized that Bo wasn't around, turned back to look over her shoulder to search for him and slammed into Thomas as he stepped out of the kitchen.

He grabbed hold of her arm to steady her and laughed softly. "Good morning." His eyes were filled with gentleness.

She let out a forced breath. "I'm sorry, I overslept and wanted to get the chores done," she rambled. Before she could continue Bo stepped out from the kitchen and shoved his snout under her hand. She looked at Thomas, realizing the dog must have been with him. "Traitor," she mumbled to Bo.

"I have already tended to the animals." His tone was uncertain. "As best I could."

Emma's eyes widened. She was sure she caught a slight flush of colour to his cheeks. "Thank you." She watched him for a moment, imagining all sorts of incidents. "How did it go?"

"It took me a while to figure out how to get the milk from the cow," he admitted. He gestured back toward the kitchen and followed her in. He pointed to the bucket on the counter that contained only half the usual amount of milk.

Emma bit the inside of her lip, unsuccessfully trying not to smile. "She kicked the bucket over, didn't she?" Emma tried to imagine him struggling with Tawna. She was dying to ask how he'd calmed her down, but couldn't bring herself to do it. She didn't want to make him feel uncomfortable.

"Yes, she kicked it over. I found out that if you talk to her it helps," he answered her unspoken question and they both laughed.

"I'm sorry I missed it." She tried to imagine him talking to the cow. She poured the milk into glass bottles and put them into the mudroom's small fridge for Two-Feathers regular pick up. She stored the eggs in the fridge and turned back to him. "What do you feel like eating for breakfast?"

He shrugged. "I am not familiar with your selection beyond what has been provided for me." He frowned slightly at the amusement on her face. "What?"

"Nothing, it's just..., nothing." She waved a hand and giggled. She put a hand over her mouth and started to laugh. "I'm sorry. You have the strangest way of speaking. It's kind of amusing."

"Apparently," he answered back, seemingly unflustered. "Can I help with the preparations?" He pointed back to the stove.

"Sure. Do you want tea or coffee this morning?" Her eyes narrowed. "Do you know what coffee is?"

He shook his head. "I might as well try it."

* * *

Emma watched as Thomas ate his blueberry pancakes in silence. He seemed to be enjoying them as much as the coffee.

He put his fork down and looked up at her. "Have I done something wrong?"

She brought her eyebrows down into a slight frown. "No, of course not. I was just wondering if you ever spoke during meals, that's all," she confessed.

He shook his head. "No, meals are usually taken in silence." He watched her reaction closely.

"Oh." She didn't know what to say to that. She had always enjoyed good dinner conversation, and up until Thom– Dthau-Mahsz had arrived it was all one sided with Bo.

He reached out to touch her arm. "I am no longer home, and I would welcome the conversation." His eyes met hers and lingered a little.

She swallowed the lump in her throat. You'd think his eyes would no longer have an effect on her by now. "Ok, then, what would you like to talk about?"

"Tell me about yourself." He put down his fork and wiped his mouth with his napkin. "From what I have gathered, you have no siblings." He stood to refill their coffee cups as he continued, "Your parents lived here and you lived in the city. You changed your mind about selling the place and have since made it your home." He sat back down.

She nodded. "That pretty much sums it up." She paused to take a sip of her coffee, inhaling the aroma. She smiled inwardly and let the flavor take her back to another time and place.

"What were you just thinking about?" Dthau-Mahsz asked. He tilted his head to watch her.

His voice brought her back to the room, and she turned to face him. She studied his expression as she considered her answer. She shrugged. "I just got carried away with my thoughts." She put her cup down, realizing that she hadn't really answered his question, something that she found annoying when he did it to her. "I was just enjoying my coffee and the way it's made."

He frowned. "Is there another way?"

She smiled nostalgically. "Every Sunday, my father insisted on making his coffee with the sap collected from our maple trees. My mother used to get upset when he stored bottles of it in the freezer, saying it took up too much place. The rest of the week, he used water and the drip coffee maker, but on Sundays, he used the old percolator." She felt silly discussing this with him. Like he knew what a drip coffee maker was if he'd never even had coffee. She pointed to the pot in question and watched as his gaze followed.

"Emma." He brought her out of her thoughts once again. "For

now, I have to assume that this is my home. I would like to know as much about it as possible."

A sudden realization washed over her, leaving a heavy feeling in the pit of her stomach. He must have had a family too, maybe even a wife and child. "Were you married?" she blurted out. She felt her cheeks flush and looked down. "I'm sorry. You don't have to tell me anything." She raised her head so their eyes could meet.

His expression was unreadable as he drew in a long breath. "I leave behind my parents, a sister and her young son. My sister had returned home to our parents after her husband died on duty." He paused, looking lost in thought. A flicker of an unnamed emotion crossed his eyes. "I do not have a wife."

"What about someone special?" she ventured.

He stood abruptly. "No." He gathered the plates from the table and proceeded to fill the sink with soapy water.

Emma stayed sitting a moment, trying to understand his reaction. He'd said 'no', so why did he seem so distressed? "I'm sorry if I upset you." She rose to dry the dishes, watching him out of the corner of her eye.

"You would not understand and I would rather not discuss it." He put the last dish on the rack, turned and walked out of the kitchen without another word.

Once the dishes were put away, Emma started preparing the vegetables for the slow cooker. Going over their conversation, she looked for something, anything to explain his reaction. She heard footsteps behind her and turned to apologize, but stopped short when Two-Feathers walked into the kitchen.

"Kla'as sawsaqa'ni," he said from the doorway.

Emma shook her head. He'd have to stop assuming she understood him all the time. "He's what?"

"Outside." He pointed behind him with his thumb. "I'm going to saddle the horses and show him how to ride. I think he needs to clear his head." Without waiting for her response, he turned silently and left.

Emma sighed. "I guess it's just you and me," she said to Bo. She looked around the kitchen, but her dog was nowhere to be seen. "Or not," she said to the empty room.

CHAPTER 6: COMING TO TERMS

It was almost dark by the time the men returned from their ride. Emma had to busy herself not to run out and greet them, fighting her curiosity to see how Thom– Dthau-Mahsz had enjoyed his ride. Having been alone all afternoon had given her the chance to sort through her demons and put her overactive imagination to rest. The fact that Two-Feathers was at ease around Dthau-Mahsz helped a lot. She had bravely faced her irrational fears created by one too many sci-fi movies and laughed at the thought of government officials charging into her house to capture and quarantine them, or better yet, of seeing him in his 'true alien form'. It was almost a disappointment to accept that he was just like her, especially without his technology.

"We're back," Two-Feathers called out from the porch.

"Go wash up," Emma said. "Supper's ready." A sense of peace filled her as she laid the food out on the table. She would let Dthau-Mahsz know he was welcome to stay as long as he wanted and she hoped he would accept her offer.

After the meal, the three of them retired to the living room. Emma watched from her grandmother's armchair as Dthau-Mahsz lit a fire, fascinated at how he moved with balanced strength and grace, in total control of his every move. She let out a calm breath and eased back comfortably in her chair. It was the first time she'd been this relaxed since the crash, and it felt good to be able to breathe freely again. Having Dthau-Mahsz around was nice when she wasn't a paranoid jumble of nerves. She'd wait for him to sit before making her offer.

"Emma," Two-Feathers cut into her thoughts. His face was solemn.

The feeling of well-being drained from her and her stomach knotted. "Is something wrong?" She rapidly searched for scenarios, but her mind came up blank.

The shaman drew a ragged breath. "I have offered to let Dthau-Mahsz move to my community." His eyes searched her face.

Dthau-Mahsz stood and brushed some woodchips and dust off his jeans. He looked from Two-Feathers to Emma. "I understand that my presence is a strain on your well-being." He sat on the couch across from Emma with his elbows on his knees, and rested his chin on his clasped hands. "Maybe it would be better for you if I left."

Emma shook her head. "No, please. I'm so sorry about the way I've been acting." She shifted in her seat and wrung her hands. "I was going to ask you to stay. I've finally managed to sort through my irrational fears." She felt heat in her cheeks and gave a crooked smile. "I really let my imagination get away from me, but I think I can handle the situation now." She glanced at Two-Feathers, noting that his expression remained unchanged. Slowly shifting her eyes to Dthau-Mahsz, she caught a flicker of relief on his face. Surprised and pleased by his reaction she kept watching him in silence. Maybe he didn't want to leave after all. Why did that delight her?

Dthau-Mahsz lowered his hands and nodded. "If you are comfortable with your proposition, then I accept." He turned to Two-Feathers who stood.

"I'll leave you two to work out the details." The shaman put a hand on Emma's shoulder. "Take it one day at a time. My offer stands if need be." He walked out of the living room without looking back.

"I am grateful for your offer," Dthau-Mahsz said to her.

Emma looked down, trying to hide the colour rising on her cheeks. He was grateful for her offer. This made her feel a little giddy. The thought of him leaving had disturbed her more than she cared to admit. Thinking about all the emotions he seemed to evoke in her would give her something else to reflect upon, other than her imagined sci-fi horrors.

They sat in silence for several minutes, just staring at one another. Emma felt calm, and embraced the renewal of the sense of peace she had felt earlier. Having put her irrational mind to rest, at least for now, allowed her to see Dthau-Mahsz in a different light. He was definitely handsome, and although she had admired his body through detached, clinical eyes, she couldn't help but notice how magnificent he really was, and her heart skipped a beat.

"Could I ask you something?" Thomas spoke in a cautious tone, jarring her from her thoughts.

She nodded. "Feel free to ask me anything." She shifted in her seat, drawing her feet up under her.

He sat back, resting his ankle over a knee. He passed a hand through his hair, as if to buy time. Drawing a determined breath, he looked deep into Emma's eyes. "What was it that made you uncomfortable around me?"

Wow, OK, he didn't beat around the bush. She blushed openly now. Damn her fair skin. How could she tell him what had haunted her thoughts and dreams. "I was uncomfortable knowing you were not from around here." Now that sounded silly. She shook her head and sighed rather loudly. "I had all sorts of ridiculous thoughts running through my head."

"Such as?" A slight curl appeared on one corner of his mouth. His eyes moved over her and back up to meet her gaze.

She pursed her lips, closing her eyes for a moment. A slight moan escaped her lips, she'd might as well fess up.

A loud crackle from the fire caught their attention. A burning log had split, rolling away from the grate, and spewing a continuous wisp of smoke into the living room.

Before Emma could react, Dthau-Mahsz had already reached the fireplace to tend to the burning log. He had moved swiftly, silently. Every move precise and calculated as he returned the piece of wood to the grate and closed the old chain link curtain to keep sparks from flying into the living room. Her eyes followed him, wondering about the training, or lifestyle that had produced such a man.

"Did you play sports back home?" Emma ventured as he returned to the couch opposite her.

He cocked his head slightly and studied her face. "My people do not play sports of any kind. Why do you ask?" He eased back in his seat and lightly crossed his arms over his chest, raising a hand to his chin.

She shrugged. "You just look like someone who works out a lot. Just guessing here though, I would think your job doesn't qualify as a physical one."

His eyes widened with a subdued hint of amusement. "True that on a daily basis my role as commanding officer does not call for constant exertion. However, endurance training is practiced by all my people on a regular basis."

She felt the expression on her face drop. What the heck was 'endurance training'? She imagined young and old being sent on forced walks with heavy packs and no food.

Dthau-Mahsz coughed into his fist, as though he was swallowing an outburst of laughter. "Endurance training can be compared to…" his eyes went off to one corner as he searched for a word. "Think of it as an obstacle course with endless combinations and levels of difficulty, allowing each person to develop, maintain or surpass their personal abilities."

"An obstacle course," she repeated. "You mean ropes and bridges, tunnels and balance beams?" She pulled an image from one of her favorite movies, where an advertising agent ends up teaching Shakespeare in the army. To earn their respect he had gone through their obstacle course trying to explain himself. She smiled.

"On a basic level, yes." He leaned closer to her, resting his elbows on his knees.

"You have yet to answer my question." He waited a moment before reminding her. "What was the source of your discomfort?"

She hopped up from her chair and paced quietly around the room. She could feel his eyes on her, watching her, waiting. Without looking at him, she took a deep breath and gathered her courage. "I guess I was afraid of the unknown. I didn't know if someone would come looking for you." She turned slowly to face him. "I'm not sure if I feared someone from your world or mine. I don't know if you're just you or if you're hiding something." She shivered outwardly.

"Are you asking if I change form at night?"

Ok, now he was teasing her. She could hear the amusement in his voice. Her eyes met his and for the briefest moment, time stood still. She nodded. "Yeah, I guess I am."

A weight lifted off her shoulders and breathing suddenly became effortless.

His expression was calm, reassuring and held a spark of amusement. "I can assure you," he said calmly as he stood and turned his arms out towards her, "that this is all there is to me."

"No magic powers?" she whispered, holding her ground.

"No magic powers."

She could feel him standing inches from her. It was almost like some subtle source of electrical current popped into existence when they were close to one another. She wondered if a light bulb held between them would glow, betraying the existing current. Her whole body tingled and she turned to face the window, still able to watch his reflection in the glass pane.

"Well, you know, that's kind of a disappointment," she said lightly.

He raised an eyebrow. "Is it?"

He laid a hand on her shoulder and turned her gently to face him. She could hear her heart pounding in her ears as she lifted her eyes to his. "It's getting late." She cleared her throat. "We can continue this in the morning." With her stress level falling, she felt tired, but more than sleep, she needed to sort through her feelings.

He let his hand drop down to his side and took a step back from her. "Very well. I trust you will have a good night's sleep."

She smiled optimistically. "I hope so. Good night, Dthau-Mahsz." She turned away and headed toward the kitchen and the stairs. She heard him add more wood to the fire. Maybe he wasn't going to bed after all.

After her shower, Emma sat in the corner of her room, looking out the window into the darkness and could smell snow in the air. She thought about the fears she'd let mount inside her and shook her head out of disgust. She wasn't normally prone to paranoia and found it difficult to understand how it had come to that. True, she'd had a lot to deal with since her return, and she still had to decide what she'd ultimately do with her parent's house. She sighed, the formal details surrounding the latter had yet to be dealt with.

She glanced down at the book in her hand, closed it on the bookmark and set it beside her chair. She had been rereading the same sentence over and over, unable to focus.

Bo tumbled in and danced at her feet. Emma could feel the cold from having been put outside by Dthau-Mahsz. It must have started snowing, because tiny droplets glistened on his thick fur coat. "What are we supposed to do now?" Emma asked Bo.

Pushing his snout under Emma's hand to be pet, his wolf eyes looked up at her. She stroked the top of his head and then scratched behind his ears. "Do you think he'd like to take a trip into town?" She stopped petting the dog for just a moment and he nudged her hand again. She smiled down at him, giving a quick pat as she rose to her feet. She thought about how graceful Dthau-Mahsz looked when he did it. Indulging, she sat back down and attempted to rise in a smooth, fluid fashion without the use of her hands. "Hmmm, not as easy as it looks," she admitted as she watched herself from the mirror across the room.

CHAPTER 7: OUT IN THE OPEN

By morning a thick blanket of snow covered the world around Emma's house and everything glowed with the magic that the first snow brings. It was a lovely surprise after a good night's sleep. Emma felt better than she had in a long time and she inhaled deeply, taking it all in. Sipping her coffee, her whole body felt tingly as she sat on the porch in her pyjamas, a wool blanket draped loosely over her shoulders. Bo lifted his ears and rolled over to stare at the door. Dthau-Mahsz stepped out of the house carrying a cup of his own. "Good morning." He paused momentarily as he took in the view. His eyes widened slightly but his expression remained in check.

Emma's face lit up, a childlike exuberance filling her. "Isn't it beautiful?" She patted the space next to her on the old wooden bench and he joined her. She could see him watching her from the corner of her eye, but her attention remained on the spectacular display. The fir trees were heavy with snow, looking absolutely picture perfect, and every once-bare tree branch was intricately highlighted under its snowy deposit. Chickadees, Blue-Jays and the Pine Nuthatch's knocked the snow from the branches as they hopped around the suspended feeders while they awaited their turn.

When Dthau-Mahsz turned his gaze outward and deliberately panned his surroundings. Emma watched him more openly, trying to read his expression. "Did you have snow back home?" She followed his eyes across the landscape.

He shook his head. "The climate on my planet is not as varied as your own." He took a sip from his cup and a flicker of surprise crossed his face.

Emma smiled, reading his reaction. "I know it's not Sunday, but the magic of the first real snow calls for maple-water coffee," she said lightly. Turning back to face him she set her cup on her knees.

"Why don't you talk about where you're from?"

He stiffened so slightly Emma barely caught it before he brought his amethyst eyes to meet hers. He let out a controlled breath. "The less you know the better."

His answer shook her calm. Her mind raced, opening the door to her fears. When he placed a hand on her arm she jumped, and she couldn't help but wonder what he was hiding.

"Emma," he said softly. "I am no more than what you see. My eyes are different, even amongst my people." He searched her face, sliding his hand down her arm to take her hand in his. "I am part of your world now. Unless my people find me by some stroke of fate, this will be my home until I die."

The finality of his statement sobered her. She nodded, pulled the blanket tighter around her shoulders and swallowed back the hard lump in her throat.

* * *

Emma spread the last of the straw in Ruby's stall and put the feed buckets back in. Dthau-Mahsz led the horse back to her place. Hanging the pitchfork back on the wall, Emma looked down at her faded overalls. They were going to need a washing, but not as much as Dthau-Mahsz's jeans. She had to get him some clothes. "Would you like to go into town with me this morning?"

His head appeared from around Ben's stall where he was brushing the dark brown quarter horse the way Two-Feathers had shown him. His eyes lit up and he didn't hesitate to answer. "I would enjoy that very much."

Emma hung the pitchfork on the wall with the other tools. "Good, now let's go get cleaned up and we can have lunch out after we finish up our errands."

* * *

Though the mountain roads had been plowed, it still took Emma an hour-and-a-half to get into town. Almost thirty minutes more than usual. Dthau-Mahsz hadn't complained. He watched her drive about as much as he had watched the trees go by. She had laughed when he asked if she was alone on the mountain since they hadn't crossed any other houses along the way. The only two roads that cut across their path looked as isolated as the one they were on.

"It's still a bit early for lunch, so I suggest we take care of our errands first." Emma said as she parked the car in front of a strip mall. She turned back to release his seat belt for him and pointed to the door handle so he could get out of the Cherokee. She giggled when he did a double-take at the chirp from her alarm system. "Habit," she said apologetically. "It was necessary in the city, but not so much here."

Dthau-Mahsz looked at her, unable to conceal the fact that he had no idea what she was talking about. Or maybe she was beginning to read his expressions more. "What was necessary?" he finally asked.

"The car alarm. It's to deter thieves." They walked towards a man's clothing store. A few people passed them going to and from the mall and she was relieved that they paid little attention to Dthau-Mahsz. "Don't you have something similar back home?"

He paused by the door and held it open for her. "We do not use personal transportation devices, and one does not usually covet the possessions of another." He stopped just inside the door and took in his surroundings. Clothing was displayed on circular racks across the floor, and floor-to-ceiling shelves covered two of the walls. The store was divided up into various sections from formal to sporting wear.

Emma linked her arm through his and led him toward the casual and sporting clothes section. "Don't tell me you don't have clothing stores." She nudged him playfully. She stopped at the face he made. "Oh, come on now…" her voice trailed off.

He smiled slightly. "None like this," was all he said.

She sighed. One day I'll get you to talk, she thought to herself.

"Clothing is issued in accordance to function occupied."

She thought about that for a moment. "So your wardrobe consisted of what, exactly?" She stepped closer to a shirt rack, sized him up and pulled a few from the rack. She held up a navy t-shirt to size it against him, reached back and took a few more in different colours as well as a mix of short and long sleeved ones. "Here, hold this." She dumped the pile in his arms so she could examine a knit sweater more closely. "What do you think about this?" She held up the blue and charcoal, thick wool sweater. Something about it reminded her of the jumpsuit he had been wearing when she'd found him.

He looked it over before he nodded in approval. A slight grunt escaped his lips as he turned away to look around at the people shopping.

"What?" She laid a hand on his arm and tugged him towards the pant-racks where she selected two pairs of jeans and two pairs of Dockers. He followed in silence but Emma could sense something was up. She ushered him toward a changing room to try on his clothes.

He stopped suddenly and Emma slammed into him, barely managing to keep her balance. "Forgive me. Are you all right?"

Emma nodded. "What's wrong?"

"There is nothing in here." He pointed to the small room. "Why-" He paused at her laugh.

She recovered quickly and pointed inside the changing room. "Go inside and try on the clothes." She placed his clothes on the wall hooks and unbuttoned the shirts. "Here, try on these pants with this t-shirt. If this t-shirt fits, they all will. Try on one of the shirts over it." She handed him a blue chambray shirt and a pair of wranglers. "Call me when you're dressed. Oh, and don't bother putting on your shoes in between." She thought it prudent to say so, just in case.

About an hour later they tossed the bags of clothes into the back of the Cherokee. Dthau-Mahsz looked a little worn. She couldn't help but think about the typical male anti-shopping stereotype. Maybe there was some truth to it after all. "You should like the next stop a little more." She pointed him in the direction of the home and hardware store across the parking lot. Ok, so maybe she was pushing the stereotype thing, but it was funny.

Mimicking his earlier behaviour, he stood close to the entrance and took in his surroundings. "Why are we here?"

"I want to buy some lights to replace my parents' old Christmas lights. The sets are so old, if one light burns, they all go out. They had refused, saying it made no sense to throw out perfectly good lights." She tugged him forward and grabbed a shopping cart. "We can run quickly through the aisles, there's always something I need." She was looking forward to the decoration-section, but they'd do that one last.

"I'm starving," Emma said as they dumped their bags in the back of the Cherokee along with the others. It had taken more time in the hardware store than the clothing store because Emma had to explain what just about everything in the store was for. She thought it was cute and so she went along with it, but now, they had to eat. "How do you feel about a pizza and some pasta?" She looked at him for confirmation as she climbed into the driver's seat. "There's a little place that makes wood fired pizza, and you don't know what it is…" her voice trailed off. Her eyes met his and found amusement in them. "Do you trust me?" she asked teasingly.

"With my life."

She felt a pang of emotion. He might have been joking, but it wasn't funny. For a second she wondered if it was a good idea to drag him around in public.

Dthau-Mahsz placed a hand on her arm. "I did not mean to cause you any distress. However, having to wait any longer for food will be even more difficult." He smiled openly. Teasingly.

Heat radiated from his touch, awakening Emma's senses and sending a tingling wave of energy up her spine. A familiar sense of calm followed, filling her and she relaxed. Nodding, she pulled out of the parking lot and headed toward the little restaurant. She watched him from the corner of her eye, enjoying the comfortable silence as they drove.

"Do you eat meat?" Emma's question broke the silence and she heard him shift in his seat. She stole a glance his way. "I'm not sure if I had even bothered to ask you about it."

"No. None of my people do." His tone was a little abrupt.

Emma sighed. "Does it bother you when I ask you questions?" She turned off the main road into the parking lot of the Old Stone Oven pizza parlour. She put the Cherokee in park, removed the keys and shifted to face him. She pressed her lips together before speaking. "I need more. I need to be able to feel at ease around you." She raised a hand to prevent him from interrupting. "I can understand that you will not tell me things, things about your technology, for instance. Things that might somehow cause me more trouble than necessary, but I need you to trust me." She let out a breath of frustration. "I'm not interrogating you! I'm just trying to get to know you." She felt tears well up in her eyes and bit the inside of her cheek to keep them from spilling.

Reaching across the seat, Dthau-Mahsz took both of her hands in his and drew her into an embrace. She stiffened momentarily before allowing herself to lean on his chest. That sensation of comfort and reassurance surrounded her again, easing her nerves and dissolving her guard. Eyes closed, she was acutely aware of his beating heart, of the gentle, yet powerful strength in the arms that held her, of his masculine scent. She inhaled the subtle mixture of soap and the great outdoors.

The sound of people laughing and car doors slamming snapped her from the place she had drifted. Pushing away from him she was mortified. She couldn't seem to get her head around her feelings or her actions when she was near him. "Let's go eat," she said. She forced air into her lungs, quickly pushed her hair into place and reached for the door handle.

Dthau-Mahsz followed her into the small restaurant. Red and white checkered table cloths covered every table. The light from burning candles, set in portly wine bottles that were barely visible through the layers of melted wax, flickered on the wooden-planked walls. The air smelled of wood smoke and oregano. She was hungry again.

"For two?" A young woman with dark eyes and a long black braid collected their menus and waved for them to follow. Her white blouse was pulled a little tight over an expanding belly. Emma didn't recognize her, a reminder that she'd been away from her hometown for a long time.

The momentary strain Emma had felt seemed to have been left behind and she was grateful. She served up a piece of three-cheese vegetarian pizza to Dthau-Mahsz and slid one onto her own plate alongside the grilled vegetables and pasta-bows in a vodka-rosé sauce. She glanced up optimistically at Dthau-Mahsz as he examined his plate. "I hope you like it." She thought of offering a toast to a new friendship but realized that if he wasn't aware of the custom she would be putting him in an awkward situation. She took a bite of her pasta and watched as he followed suit. She wondered if he had done this at home. She picked up her pizza and took a bite, waiting to see if he would use his utensils or his hands. A smile tugged at the corner of her mouth and spread as she watched him wrestle with obvious reluctance to pick his slice up. "You can use utensils," she reassured him. "I just think it tastes better like this."

He stopped to stare at her, presumably to consider her words. "How can that be?"

She shrugged. "You'll have to try it yourself to find out." To her surprise, he tried both ways but settled on using his utensils.

After a few bites he lowered his knife and fork, sat back in his chair and looked around at the other families and couples talking and eating. Slowly, he brought his gaze back to Emma. Their eyes locked for a moment and Emma felt her pulse quicken. She was sure she could drown in the endless depths of his eyes. She reached over and placed a hand on his forearm. "I enjoyed our outing, it was a welcome change."

He covered her hand with one of his and nodded slowly. "It has been enlightening."

Emma frowned. Enlightening, well at least it wasn't bad.

"What did you have planned for us this afternoon?" He picked up his fork and took another bite of pasta.

Emma's eyebrows lifted slightly. Was he making conversation? She cleared her throat. "I was kind of hoping to spring it on you at the last minute." She wiped the corner of her mouth with her napkin before reaching for her water glass. "I had planned on hanging the Christmas lights." She watched him for a reaction.

He raised his head in acknowledgement. "The ones we just purchased."

She gave him an uncertain smile. "Do you mind?"

"I have never had the opportunity to do so. This too, should prove interesting."

* * *

Once they had made it home, Emma let Bo out, unpacked the boxes of coloured lights and hauled out a few extension cords so she could plug in the new sets. "Ready?" she asked, excited about the project. "Oh! Wait." She hurried back into the house and turned on a classical rendition of Sleigh Ride, loud enough to be heard from outside. Grinning from ear to ear she showed Dthau-Mahsz how to wrap the lights around the railing.

They had almost come full circle around the porch when Dthau-Mahsz stopped again. He hadn't seemed to grasp the idea of decorating for the season. "Why are we doing this again?"

"You know, you might not be from around here, but a man is a man." She handed him the end of another string of lights. She started to wind the lights along the railing, slowly moving away from him, but turned back when she thought she was stuck. "Very funny."

"I believe I have been insulted," he said flatly, holding the string of wire tight.

She burst out laughing. "Oh, the universe is so doomed," she said playfully. Putting her lights down, she took a handful of snow and tossed it at him.

He dropped his end of the lights and lunged toward her. She screamed, jumped down the steps and headed around the side of the chicken coop for cover. She could hear him following in the snow so she dropped down and quickly started scooping up snow. She poked her head around but he was no longer in sight. Cautiously, she stood and took a step forward, but screamed when he grabbed her from behind. She wiggled around enough to drop her handful of snow on his head.

Surprised, he let go to brush the snow from his hair and she made a break for it. He reached out to grab her wrist when she bent hastily to scoop up some more snow. He shut his eyes as she tossed the handful towards his face and they both went down. Bo barked and jumped around them frantically.

The snowball fight ended with them both on their backs in the snow, panting and laughing. "Hardly productive," he commented, "but enjoyable."

She sat up and brushed the snow off her jacket. "You're hopeless." She stood and offered him a hand to get up, slipped on an icy patch underfoot and somehow ended up in his arms. "Thank you," she whispered as she stared into his amethyst eyes. Her heart rate skyrocketed.

Time seemed to slow and the falling snow appeared to hover as he leaned forward and kissed her tenderly.

Emma melted into his embrace, allowing warmth and well-being to fill and surround her. Everything but the moment faded away. Unaware of the passage of time, they were brought back to the present by the sound of an approaching vehicle. Slowly, reluctantly, she drew back and he stood, helping her to her feet in turn.

As they rounded the corner into the yard, they saw Bo dancing around as he waited for Two-Feathers to step down from his truck.

Emma, a little embarrassed, let Dthau-Mahsz reach Two-Feathers first. She stopped and shielded her eyes from the sun that peeked through a break in the clouds. "Coming in for something to drink?" she asked, keeping her distance. Coward, she thought to herself. Taking refuge in the kitchen she couldn't seem to focus on the task at hand. Her mind kept wandering back to the kiss like a giddy teenager. She couldn't help herself, it was an amazing kiss. No, it wasn't just the kiss, it was the connection. She felt as though her world, her very essence, had merged with all that he was.

The slamming of the mudroom door snapped her back to reality. She hurried to finish preparing the pot of tea and set some warm scones on a tray. "You coming into the kitchen or would you prefer the living room by the fire?" She wiped her hands on a tea towel and reached for the milk and butter. She set them onto the tray along with the sugar and antique cups.

"Living room will do," Two-Feathers answered. Emma knew by the tone of his voice that something was wrong.

Dthau-Mahsz stepped into the kitchen to pick up the tray. His eyes twinkled as he looked her over. She felt his energy touch her and inhaled sharply. She turned to find some napkins, anything to hide her reaction from him. Somehow she knew she was already exposed to the soul. Drawing on her inner strength, she composed herself and headed after him.

Her stomach lurched at the sight of the grim expression on Two-Feathers' face. Sitting beside Dthau-Mahsz on the couch, across from the shaman, she waited for him to speak. "Yesterday, two hikers came down from the mountain with unknown debris they had found." He looked at Dthau-Mahsz. "Is there any chance it could be from your ship?"

Emma's heart raced. Oh God, please no. The nightmares she'd had when she had first found Dthau-Mahsz of men in black storming the place came back full force.

"The structural damage from the ship may have hindered the disintegration of the vessel, but by now there should be no traces of it left." He showed none of the worry Emma was feeling. He covered her hand with his and squeezed it reassuringly.

Swallowing the lump lodged in her throat, Emma asked, "Is there some way to find out?"

Two-Feathers shifted in his seat. He pulled out a folded map from his shirt pocket and leaned closer to show Dthau-Mahsz. "According to the GPS reading the hikers took, they would have found the pieces here." He pointed to a spot on the map.

Emma moved in closer. She hadn't seen any kind of ship when she'd found him, but he couldn't have been too far from it. She frowned. "Can I see that?"

Two-Feathers handed it to her. "Is it possible smaller pieces landed around the crash site?" He was watching Dthau-Mahsz for a reaction.

Emma focused on the map. She located her house and the trail that brought her up the ridge. Difficult to say...

"Upon impact some parts of the ship may be scattered, however the electromagnetic discharge retrieves any debris within a 30km range. This process assembles the parts to allow a systemic regression of all matter to its molecular state."

Two-Feathers nodded. "Is there any chance that a piece might have, nonetheless, gone overlooked?"

Dthau-Mahsz took a moment to consider the question. "There is always a chance. No system is ever perfect. There could be variants in the planet's magnetic field, hindering the process."

Emma closed her eyes and took slow, deliberate breaths. He had purple eyes, for Pete's sake. If anyone saw him while holding some strange piece of metal...how could they not put two-and-two together?

"Even if a piece had been scattered further from the crash, the ship's components are designed to return to their molecular state," Dthau-Mahsz repeated slowly.

"Then how does it keep from coming apart in space?" Emma couldn't seem to grasp the concept.

Dthau-Mahsz chuckled. "Trust me on this one."

* * *

The next two weeks felt like a living nightmare. Emma watched as groups of men parked in her yard and climbed the cliffs behind her house in search of the mysterious debris. Two-Feathers was here every day to greet the men, answering questions and keeping them away from Dthau-Mahsz. She had argued with the Shaman that it would be best if he'd keep him on the reservation, but neither man agreed.

Her nerves were shot, again. Dthau-Mahsz came to sit in the living room next to her. He offered her a cup of cocoa and stared at the fire. "You must stop worrying, Emma. None of this has to do with me."

She whirled around to face him. "How can you be so sure? No system is perfect. What if it is from your ship? What if they come looking for you?" Her voice rose.

He calmly searched her face.

"Say something! Aren't you the least bit worried?" She wanted to scream, to throw something.

He let out a slow breath. "They will not find anything. I am in no danger. Unless you throw that cup at me." His mouth quirked into a slight smile.

Anger flared within her. "There's nothing funny about this."

He sobered. "Trust me, please."

"You, I trust." She pointed sharply at the window. "It's them, I don't trust."

CHAPTER 8: SPRING

The Holidays came and went peacefully. Nothing more had come from the strange metal debris found in the mountains, and the group of searchers faded away. She wasn't sure if they'd come back in the spring to resume their search or not, but she rarely thought about it much anymore. What bothered Emma most was that not much had come of the kiss they'd shared either. On occasion he would hug her, or touch her while talking, but the passionate kiss had not been repeated. However, they seemed to have settled into a comfortable routine.

As the cold winter days died away, spring grew in confidence until the leaves and flowers had finally awakened. While Dthau-Mahsz tended to the animals and the chores in the barn, Emma had been cleaning up the garden bed. She looked up and caught sight of Bo chasing a squirrel and shook her head. It was still too early to think about planting anything, but no harm getting a head start on the work. She paused a moment to stretch her back, leaned on her garden rake and filled her lungs with fresh mountain air. Pine and cedar were dominant since no wild flowers were out yet, but add the smell of fresh turned soil and you couldn't ask for a better spring mix.

Emma was startled by the ringing of the phone. She propped the rake against the fence and ran awkwardly for the house in her rubber boots.

When she answered the phone she was chided by a female voice. "I was going to let it ring. I hope you didn't bust anything getting to the phone."

"Maggie? Oh my God! How are you?" Emma pulled up a chair and sat against the wall where the phone was. She wiped the back of her hand across her forehead to push a stray strand of hair from her eyes.

"I'm good, and so is Renata." Emma could hear another voice in the background but couldn't understand what was said. "Here's the thing. You've been gone a whole year and we really miss you." Emma felt a pang of guilt but let her friend continue. "We want to come out and spend a week with you. What do you think?"

Joy bubbled inside bringing a smile to Emma's lips. "You really want to come out here for a week?" She ran through a list of things to do to prepare for guests. How would she explain Dthau-Mahsz? Maybe he could go try one of Two-Feathers' vision quests or something. "That would be great, when do you think you'd be able to visit?"

There was a pause at the end of the line. "How long did it take for you to drive into town again?" Maggie's voice hesitated.

"Are you telling me you're already in Invermere?" Emma looked down at herself. She was covered in dirt and in desperate need of a shower.

"We landed fifteen minutes ago." There was a pause.

"We took a chance because we miss you and really wanted to see you," Renata's voice came over the line. "Besides, the travel brochure says there are some pretty nice things to visit out here."

Emma laughed. "OK, but I really need a shower. Grab a bite at the snack bar and I'll be down within two hours."

"Where are we going?" Dthau-Mahsz asked. He came into the mudroom carrying milk and eggs which he deposited on the counter before closing the door behind him.

"It looks like we've got company for the week." She pulled off her rubber boots and stood, biting her lower lip. "I'm going to grab a quick shower before I go."

He reached out and laid a hand on her shoulder before she could escape. "Would you prefer if I spent the week at Two-Feathers' home?"

She let out a breath and held his gaze. That's exactly what she'd been thinking, but she couldn't imagine being away from him for that long. "No, I'd like you to meet my friends." She yanked off her pants, pulled off her grimy sweatshirt and dropped them into the laundry basket before hurrying upstairs, still wearing her oversized t-shirt.

Twenty minutes later she made her way down the stairs in a flowing skirt and wrap-around cotton sweater. Emma realized she'd been cooped up far too long and she was looking forward to going out; she just hoped her friends felt like Italian tonight. The apprehension about having her friends meet Dthau-Mahsz was not as intense as she'd imagined, she was more worried about the fact that she'd never mentioned him.

Dthau-Mahsz watched her from the bottom of the stairs. His eyes roamed over her in a far from discrete manner and Emma had to admit, she liked it. "You look beautiful," he offered.

Her cheeks pinked. "Thanks, I thought it'd be nice to take advantage of the trip into town and eat out."

He offered her an elbow and escorted her towards the entrance. "Should you take a jacket then, in case the temperature drops tonight?"

She smiled and nodded. He was gorgeous in his navy Dockers and tan button down shirt. He'd rolled his sleeves, exposing the highly detailed muscles in his forearms and his broad chest filled out the shirt to perfection.

"So," he began to speak a few minutes into their drive. "Who will be coming to the house?" It was nice to let him drive and not have to worry about the road.

A smile blossomed on Emma's face just thinking about her friends. "Maggie and Renata, the two girls I lived with back in the city." Emma filled him in on trivial details about her roommates as they drove into town.

Without turning towards her, Dthau-Mahsz nodded. "Tell me more about them."

She shot him a glance. He was serious. What kind of details did he want? "Renata came over from Italy with her parents when she was four. She's spunky, big hearted and has a tendency to blurt out whatever comes to mind." She stifled a laugh when she thought about some of the things her friend had said over the years.

"And the other one is Maggie?" He kept his attention on the road.

Emma nodded. "Yes. She is lovely, with perfect milk chocolate skin and eyes as black as night. She carries herself with such an air of dignity, she seems almost regal. Her mother was born in Namibia, but her father is Canadian." She clasped her hands on her lap and drew in a deep breath. She was getting a little nervous about the meeting. On some level she felt guilty for not having stayed in touch much since she'd returned to the mountains, but she knew they'd understand.

Dthau-Mahsz reached over and gave her hand a reassuring squeeze. "Do not worry yourself. I am sure the reunion will be good for you all."

She looked from her hands to his face. He always seemed to know or sense how she felt and she still wasn't sure whether she found it reassuring or not. But then again, with Two-Feathers around, she should be used to it by now. "I guess, and since they went to the trouble of coming out here must mean they really do miss me."

He laughed openly now. "Yet the fact that you have said this to them the few times I've heard you talk to one another does not count?"

She pursed her lips. "I suppose. I feel like I abandoned them, you know, like I just up and left. Here they were talking about moving on and I ended up leaving first." They would be at the little airport shortly and she'd know where she stood.

"You did 'up and leave' as you say, but I do not think they felt abandoned. I am quite sure they understood." The Cherokee stopped at a red light and Dthau-Mahsz reached over to touch her cheek. "It will be fine."

When they pulled into the parking lot Emma hesitated. She wasn't particularly fond of this place or its memories, but then she saw her two friends waving madly from the little patio deck and felt anxious to greet them. Dthau-Mahsz opened her door and offered her a hand down.

"I told you it was a man keeping her from us," Renata blurted out as she rushed forward.

Dthau-Mahsz put a steadying arm around Emma as she stumbled getting out of the Jeep. They exchanged glances but aside from a twinkle in his eye and an awkward grin from Emma, no words were uttered.

Stepping forward to embrace Renata, Emma couldn't help but notice the look on Maggie's face as her dark eyes lazily skimmed over every inch of Dthau-Mahsz. Her mouth quirked in approval seconds before she stepped into the group hug. "And to think we were worried about you, girl."

Renata, the shortest of the three pulled back first. "Yes, you had us sick out of our minds with worry." She shot a sidelong glance at Dthau-Mahsz and lowered her voice. "And you better not leave out any details."

Feeling a giggle erupting, Emma fought it down and turned to introduce the girls to Dthau-Mahsz. She watched how he reacted with charm as he accepted Renata's crushing embrace and Maggie's half hand shake and peck on the cheek.

"So I was thinking," Emma said once they were all seated in the Cherokee. "Why not go out for an early supper before heading back to the house?" She looked over her shoulder at the women in the back seat.

"Oh I love shopping!" exclaimed Renata.

Maggie tapped her on the shoulder. "How did you get shopping from supper?" She looked at Emma and the three of them burst out laughing. Some things never changed.

By the time they pulled into the driveway at home it was dark. Dthau-Mahsz stepped around the Jeep to open Emma's door and help her step down. "Go on inside with your friends, I'll tend to the animals." He cupped her chin and passed his thumb across her cheek. "Let me go change and I will take care of it."

Emma dropped her gaze. "Thanks." She felt a little uncomfortable over his touch in front of her friends.

Emma had barely entered the living room when her girlfriends ganged up on her. Renata pulled her onto the couch with a little too much enthusiasm. "Oh, Dio! Where did you find him?" She bounced giddily, shaking her hands in front of Emma as if she was trying to milk information from her.

"Let the poor girl talk," Maggie said smoothly, holding Emma's gaze. "Now spill."

Emma pressed her lips together, an onslaught of images passing through her mind of Dthau-Mahsz since he'd arrived.

Renata leaned in closer and looked over her shoulder. "Did the two of you…" She gestured figuratively and raised her eyebrows. "You know, get together? I mean, is he any good?"

Emma's mouth dropped in mock horror. "Renata! No, we didn't."

"Why, is there something wrong with him?" Maggie asked, almost disappointed.

Turning her head, she shot Maggie a look of admonition.

"Why don't you just tell us the whole story?" Maggie coaxed.

Chewing on her lower lip Emma wrestled with her desire to share the truth. "We met last fall." Emma fell silent. How was she supposed to explain having 'found and kept' him? The whole thing seemed incredulous.

"Where?" Renata prompted.

"Where what?" Emma tried to follow.

Renata sighed, the drama queen that she was. "Where did you meet him?"

"I found him when I was out horseback riding. He was injured and I helped him out." There, that sounded believable.

Maggie nodded slowly. "It's amazing that you don't have a whole house full of strays with those cliffs out back." She waved a hand in the air.

Emma furrowed her eyebrows. "What are you talking about?"

"Oh come on. We see it all the time on the news. Hikers lost in Rockies, two wounded in cliff climbing accident, tourists mauled by grizzly…" her voice trailed off.

Emma laughed. "You have way too much imagination."

She cocked her head. "And you forget I still work in Emerg. I have seen it all."

"Seen it all, huh?" Emma thought about Dthau-Mahsz's crash landing.

"And then some," Renata added.

Sighing, Emma settled back into the couch. She couldn't tell them. It wasn't her story to tell.

"OK, so you found him, then what?" Renata laid a hand on her forearm to get her attention.

"He was hurt and I cared for him." It was the truth.

"Who fell in love with whom?" Maggie asked, a wicked grin spreading across her full lips.

"I don't know," Emma thought about it. Did she love him? Did he love her? Was it even possible?

"But you kissed, right?" Renata badgered. "I saw the way he looks at you, the way he takes care of you." She sighed. "I wish I had someone like that."

Maggie nudged her "Oh come on, spill already!"

"OK, yes, we kissed. There, are you happy?" Emma blurted out.

Renata clasped her hands together loudly. "Oh, I just knew it!"

She reached over and pulled Emma into a too tight embrace. "So why haven't you slept with him?" She whispered into Emma's ear.

"Stop!" Emma pushed back from the embrace.

"What are you trying to hide?" Maggie asked. "He's not married, is he?"

"To his job, maybe," Emma said, bending the truth. Yeah, that would explain if he had to disappear suddenly. She drew in a breath and sat up stiffly. "I can't tell you too much, and you can't say anything to anyone." She looked from one set of eyes to the next. "Promise?"

Both women nodded and gestured for her to get on with it.

Emma bit her lip. Here goes. "He crashed into the mountain." She held up a hand to silence Renata. "He's a military test pilot, top secret planes and stuff." She leaned in closer. "You can't say anything to anyone. Even I don't know the whole story." Her voice was almost a whisper. "He can't say anything to me and he can up and leave in a moment's notice…which is why I am hesitant to get too involved."

Maggie pulled back offended. "You can stop lying to us now." She crossed her arms and turned away. "You are so far gone in love with him; a blind man could see it."

CHAPTER 9: TRUTH

'So far gone in love'…Emma weighed the words. Maggie was right and it was time to face it. She was hopelessly in love with the man…or alien, and where would that leave her? "You're right. I do love him, I'm sure of that. But how can I be sure he feels the same way?"

"You are sad, you know that?" Maggie said, shaking her head. "He has been the sweetest thing all day."

"Is he always like that?" Renata interjected.

Nodding, Emma thought about how he paid attention to every little detail. Nothing ever felt awkward or forced either, it seemed as natural and effortless as breathing. A silence settled amongst them, broken only by the ticking of the clock on the mantle.

Maggie sat up and turned to Emma. "So, when you found him, you said he was injured and you took care of him, right?"

Emma nodded, her eyebrows furrowing slightly. "So?"

"Was he awake or unconscious?" she asked in a detached clinical voice.

"What do you want, his medical history?" Emma asked.

Renata stifled a giggle. "She just wants to know how much you got to see."

"Maggie!"

"Well come on, girl. You say you two haven't gotten down to basics, and let's face it, he is one fine specimen." Maggie nodded slowly, her eyes growing wide.

"Which specimen are we talking about?" Dthau-Mahsz asked casually as he entered the living room.

Maggie and Renata burst out laughing, but Emma dropped her head, trying to hide.

"Ah," Dthau-Mahsz replied in an un-offended tone.

Taking hold of her courage Emma raised her head and met his

gaze. She knew he'd be watching her, but she was surprised by the twinkle in his eye and the lazy smile on his lips. He winked before looking at the others. "Would you like to be left alone?"

"No, of course not," Renata said patting the tiny space on the couch next to her. "You come sit right here.

Everyone laughed this time, and Emma stood to take a seat in her grandmother's chair across from her friends, hoping Dthau-Mahsz would sit beside her. Her heart skipped a beat when he moved in closer and planted a kiss on her neck from behind. "I am going to shower and change." He lifted his gaze to their guests. "Ladies." With a curt nod he left the room.

Emma's face flushed several shades brighter. The only thing she was aware of was the tingling in her neck that seemed to spread to every nerve ending.

"I'm so happy for you!" Renata blurted out.

* * *

The girls managed to remain civilized through breakfast the next morning, but when Emma stepped out of the house she found her friends sitting on the side porch, Renata's feet propped up on the railing in a most unladylike fashion, while Maggie sat, chest puffed out, watching Dthau-Mahsz chop wood. "Would you two knock it off," Emma hissed. "What's wrong with you?"

Maggie smiled, pried her gaze away from Dthau-Mahsz and gave a little shrug. "We're just watching the natives."

Renata giggled. "Come on, Emma. We have seen more naked men than we can remember."

"Hmm, and some I wish I could forget," Maggie added.

"Fine, but aside from that injured black belt, I don't remember either of you ever drooling over a patient. And besides, he's not your patient." Emma wasn't sure she wanted to go through a week of this. She was surprised at how territorial she was beginning to feel. Life with Dthau-Mahsz had been so simple, so easy, she hadn't even noticed how close she'd grown to him, or how domestic things had become.

"Damn shame," Maggie said. "You sure you don't want a second opinion on anything?"

"Why doesn't he take off his shirt?" Renata asked. "He must be getting hot by now?"

"OK, that's it. Inside, both of you." Emma was getting a little short tempered. "Let's make a pitcher of iced tea and prepare a snack." She tugged on her friends' shirts and ushered them inside.

Once the door closed behind the group Emma let out a breath. "Honestly, you two, I don't know if I should send you to your rooms or send you home."

"Well, good," Maggie said. "At least you're acting possessive. Now what are you waiting for to let him know how you feel?" She pulled out a chair and eased herself into it, clasping her hands on the table in front of her.

Renata was rummaging around the fridge, dropping things onto the counter. "Yes! You don't want him thinking you're not interested, do you?"

Emma couldn't believe she'd lived with these two and remained sane. She searched for the lemons through the pile of vegetables Renata had dumped on the counter and then set water to boil to make the tea. "What's the rest for?"

"Snack, I'm feeling creative," Renata said with a shrug. "Maggie won't let me do this at home anymore."

Emma raised an eyebrow and turned to look at Maggie.

"There's too much of a mess to clean up afterwards." She straightened in her chair. "Have you looked at his eyes?"

Emma felt the hairs at the back of her neck prickle. "What about them?" She swallowed the dry lump in her throat.

The fridge door slammed shut and Renata whirled around. "What are you, dead?" She laid a hand on her heart and drew in a dramatic breath. "He has Elizabeth Taylor eyes…Oh, they are magnificent."

Emma felt a wave a nausea followed by a wave of relief rush through her. Thank God.

"Yeah, if he can't go back to his work maybe you can get him a gig as a male model," Maggie suggested.

"Oh sure," Emma said lightly. "I hear Grizzly Folk Modeling Agency is all the rage out here." She shook her head and took a seat next to Maggie as Renata went to work making a mess of the kitchen. "You had better clean that up."

Maggie laid a hand on Emma's forearm and when Emma turned to meet her gaze, she only searched her face, not saying a word.

"What?"

Maggie held Emma's eyes. "Are you afraid to get involved?"

The sincerity in her voice touched Emma. "No, I don't think so..." she let her voice trail off. Could she be afraid?

"Well, you lost your parents in a plane crash," Renata said, making the sign of the cross.

Maggie shot her a look of warning. "And you did find him after he crashed," she said softly.

Emma pressed her lips together in thought. They didn't know the truth about Dthau-Mahsz, but their theory was a good one.

* * *

Later that day Dthau-Mahsz came into the living room carrying a tray with tea and cake. "I am not sure if you have any preferences, but if this is not to your liking I can prepare something different."

Emma smiled appreciatively as she reached for the teapot and began pouring. She hadn't asked her friends if they'd wanted any because this had been a weekly ritual when they'd shared a condo. She passed a cup and plate to each of her friends, then served Dthau-Mahsz and herself before settling into her grandmother's chair next to him.

"So you got the animals all settled for bed?" Renata asked.

Maggie looked over at her friend. "Settled for bed? They aren't children." She looked over at Emma, a slight frown on her face. "What do you have in there anyway?"

Resting her antique cup on its saucer she looked quickly at Dthau-Mahsz before answering. "We have two horses, but I have been thinking about getting another one. A cow and some chickens." She took another sip of tea.

"That's it? I thought your parents had all kinds of creatures in there." Renata stood to help herself to another piece of coffee cake.

"Creatures?" Dthau-Mahsz asked.

A look somewhere between sympathy and hopelessness crossed Emma's face. "My parents used to have goats, turkeys and pigs as well, but I don't eat meat and I don't like goat's milk."

Dthau-Mahsz nodded. "You do not like animals?" he asked Renata.

"Not much, no. I have enough with the human animals to deal with."

Maggie snorted. "She won't even touch the house cat."

As if on cue Bo barreled into the room, still chewing on his last bite of kibble. He paused to raise his snout and sniff the air for more food. He moved closer to the coffee table but when Dthau-Mahsz snapped his fingers the large dog paused and obediently made his way to lie between Emma and Dthau-Mahsz.

"I can't believe you have something so big in the house, and that looks so much like a wolf." Renata shook her head in disapproval.

"I bet you'd bring the cow inside if you could," Maggie teased.

"Tawna is the sweetest thing. You two have to come out and meet the animals tomorrow, and I thought we'd all go horseback riding. Two-Feathers will bring us another horse for the day." Emma stared at Renata, waiting for a reaction.

"I'll stay home and wash your windows."

A mischievous grin spread across Emma's face. "And if I decide to hold you to that, then what?"

"Come on, Renata," Maggie coaxed. "You agreed we'd experience Emma's life out here to try and understand what has stolen her from us."

"Pshaw," Renata snorted, waving a hand. "He's right there." She pointed across the room at Dthau-Mahsz.

Emma felt her cheeks heat.

"Finish your tea," Maggie instructed. "It's bed time." *Sorry,* she mouthed to Emma. She stood and motioned for Renata to do the same. "We'll see you in the morning, thanks for everything."

Dthau-Mahsz and Emma stood to bid them good night, but both remained in the living room. She hesitated a moment before sitting back down. "I'm sorry," she said softly.

Still standing, he eyed her. "Sorry for what?"

"She really is harmless." Emma looked at him and started to laugh. She covered her mouth with her hand but was unable to stop. She was tired and now that her initial fear over her friends meeting Dthau-Mahsz had passed she'd be able to concentrate on having a good time with her friends, if they could behave.

"Would you like to go sit outside on the porch for a while?" he asked, still rooted in place. "Of course if you prefer to retire for the night –"

"No, I could use a bit of fresh air." She cut him off. Emma slowly rose to her feet and accepted his outstretched hand. "Thanks." She wondered what he thought about her friends, and all

EMMA... TO BEGIN AGAIN

their nonsense.

He settled onto the porch bench and wrapped the warm blanket around Emma's shoulders as she sat next to him. With an arm around her shoulders he drew her in closer, allowing her to rest her head in the crook of his shoulder. "Are you comfortable?"

"Hmm, yes." She let out a long breath and she felt him chuckle softly. "What was that for?"

"You cannot control everyone's reactions, and you should not feel that their misconduct is in any way your fault." He planted a kiss on the top of her head.

"Is that what you think I'm doing?" She strained to look up at him, feeling a spark of anger. She pushed off, wanting to stand but he brought her right back to where she was in one gentle motion.

"I am not trying to anger you." He brushed a wayward strand of her hair from her forehead and passed the back of his fingers across her cheek.

She leaned back into him, enjoying his touch. "I know, and I'm sorry. I was just so worried about them meeting you."

"I trust I caused you no grief."

She shook her head. "No, you I can take out in public." She thought about her girlfriends and laughed softly. This was going to be one crazy week.

* * *

True to her expectations, the girls had a fun, event-filled week. Standing outside the little airport as Dthau-Mahsz removed their luggage from the back of the Cherokee, Emma embraced her friends.

"We're going to want to come back out here, you know. I had the best time," Renata said. She hugged Emma heartily and whispered in her ear, "Is it OK if I hug your man, just once more? I don't think I can resist any longer."

Emma laughed and nodded. "Try not to scare him." She kissed her friend on the cheek. Maggie moved next to Emma to watch as Renata had Dthau-Mahsz bend down for his bear hug. Emma was sure his cheeks tinged slightly but she returned her gaze to Maggie when he looked up at her.

"I'm glad to see you're doing OK." Maggie wiped a lone tear with the back of a finger. "Keep in touch with us." She moved her eyes to point towards Dthau-Mahsz without turning. "And don't you dare leave anything out." She squeezed Emma gently and moved towards the entrance, turning back to wave to Dthau-Mahsz and usher Renata forward. "Take care, and thanks for everything."

Emma waved one last time as her friends boarded the old Cessna. She offered a prayer to carry them safely home. Dthau-Mahsz wrapped an arm around her and she leaned in heavily against him. Somehow he had become more demonstrative during her friends' stay and she couldn't help but wonder if it was to keep Renata at bay.

He held her a little tighter then kissed the top of her head. "Can I invite you to dinner?"

She twisted her gaze upward. "You paying?" she asked surprised.

"Of course."

She pulled away from him. "You have money?"

He laughed. "Yes, though I think I should find a better way of storing it." He pulled back and studied her face. "This surprises you?"

"Well, yeah." She knew he helped Two-Feathers and his community often, she just never realized that they paid him. A smile bloomed on her face at his thoughtfulness. "OK, take me to dinner." She laughed, feeling carefree.

Dthau-Mahsz watched her reaction with amusement.

"What?" She finally felt comfortable under his scrutiny.

He reached for her hand to lead her away. "You are very beautiful when you smile."

Hand in hand they made their way back to the Cherokee. "You make it sound like a rarity."

He opened the car door and waited for her to tie herself in. He paused, shifting his weight onto one leg. "When we first met you were burdened with great sadness. Over time this seems to have dissipated, but you rarely seem truly happy.

She shifted slightly in her seat, her movement restrained by the seatbelt but she needed to look into his eyes, to see the truth. "You're right."

He reached out and cupped her face in his hand. "I wish to make you happy." He let his hand fall away, winked and closed the door.

Emma sat there for the few seconds it took him to walk around the Jeep and climb in, allowing the energy from his touch to pulse through her. If this was the feeling from a simple touch, she wondered what would come of a more intimate encounter...

"Where would you like to have dinner?" His question intruded on her thoughts. "We never made it out for your wood-fired pizza."

"That's what I was thinking. Would you mind?" She had hoped to bring her friends there the day they had landed, but Renata had refused go near anything remotely Italian. Nothing but homemade was good enough for her.

The smell of the wood smoke and oregano greeted them as soon as Dthau-Mahsz opened the car door. Emma inhaled deeply. "This smells almost as good as snow," she said with a smile.

He paused and tilted his head slightly. "Snow?"

She nodded, feeling giddy. "There's this smell in the air, just before it snows and it's wonderful."

He helped her down from the Jeep. "You will have to point it out to me," he said with sincerity.

"I love this place," Emma said as she stepped inside the dark wood-paneled restaurant. This is one of the few places that had never renovated since it opened back when she was a little girl. Taking a seat she nodded a 'thank you' to the waitress and inhaled deeply. The mix of wood smoke and food cooking was simply the best.

"Are you sure you like your meal?" She looked at his half-eaten plate of pasta. "You can have some of my pizza."

He sat up straight. "I am sorry. Everything is fine, I was just thinking."

"Did you want to talk about it?" She hated uncomfortable situations, and had the bad habit of thinking it was somehow her fault.

He let out a long breath. "I wish to apologize if my behaviour was in any way inappropriate this week." He reached out to stroke the back of her hand that rested on the table.

She dropped her eyes, disappointed. "I didn't find your behavior inappropriate," she said softly, blinking back tears. Did he regret his actions?

"I do not want to hurt your feelings with what I am saying." He shifted uneasily. "We have never discussed our relationship, and I do not want to make you uncomfortable. I do not want to take liberties or to mislead you…" His voice trailed off.

Emma shook her head, confused. She lifted her eyes to meet his, feeling a jolt in the pit of her stomach. "I'm sorry if I don't seem to get it, but are you telling me you do or do not like me?"

He let out a breath, almost a laugh. Taking both her hands in his, he brought them to his lips and kissed them. "I believe I have fallen in love with you."

She was mesmerized as she watched his lips on her fingers. How could a simple touch, a simple kiss make every cell in her body come to life. His words registered…he had fallen in love with her. She stared into the depths of his amethyst eyes, searching his soul. He was serious. Drawing in a sharp breath she forced herself to face her own emotions. She was definitely attracted to him, on many, many levels. Did she want more? Did he?

"I need to know if you would be interested in pursuing this with me." His voice was level, controlled.

Emma's heart began to beat wildly. He was interested, he must be or he wouldn't be asking. "One day at a time?"

A smile spread across his lips and lit his eyes. "I cannot ask for more." He reached out and cupped her cheek.

"Are you done here?" the waitress asked, breaking the moment.

"No, not yet. Thank you," Dthau-Mahsz said. "We should eat before it gets too cold."

Nodding, Emma picked up a piece of pizza. She loved pizza, and it didn't matter if it was hot or cold. She caught the last of Dthau-Mahsz's comment as he muttered under his breath. "That's an interesting idea, a plate that keeps food warm. I know a lot of moms and emergency care workers who'd love that," she said.

A strange look crossed his face, but he only nodded and took a bit of his pasta primavera.

"Can I bring you the dessert menu?" their teenage waitress asked. She shifted onto one leg and waited for an answer. The dark circles around her eyes led Emma to wonder if she was juggling studying for finals and work.

"Bring us each a Tartufo, and I'll have a decaf." She looked at Dthau-Mahsz. "Did you want something to drink?"

"I will have tea, thank you," he said. He waited for the waitress to leave. "What is Tartufo?"

EMMA… TO BEGIN AGAIN

Emma felt herself smile in anticipation. "You're going to love it. It's kind of like a small ball of vanilla ice cream inside a ball of gourmet chocolate-almond ice cream, covered in a fine cocoa powder." Her mouth watered just thinking about it.

Lying in bed that night Emma couldn't help but wonder about what Dthau-Mahsz had meant when he talked pursuing their relationship. He had kissed her goodnight and retired to his own room without even hinting that he might want to spend the night with her. Granted she'd decided long ago to wait until she was married, but at her age she was getting anxious, and honestly, she longed for more.

CHAPTER 10: TRUST

"Are you all right?" Dthau-Mahsz asked. "You have been fidgeting non-stop all day."

Emma threw the last of the hay onto the floor of the stall. "I'm feeling restless today. I need to get out for a ride. What do you think; do you want to come with me?"

Dthau-Mahsz frowned. "It will be dark soon. Is it wise to go out at this hour?"

She wrung her hands as she looked around the barn. "Come with me. We'll go slowly; I just need to get out." She went to get a bridle for each of the horses from a hook on the wall next to the saddles. He waited a moment before taking down the saddle blankets.

As they walked the horses out of the barn, Bo on their heels, Emma pointed to the moon through the trees. "You see, it won't be so bad tonight. We'll have some moonlight to guide us after dark." She also knew horses had great night vision.

He shook his head. "I think it would be more prudent to return before dark."

Stepping into the stirrup, she swung her leg over the horse and settled into the saddle. She urged the mare forward, not bothering to wait for Dthau-Mahsz. She had been feeling antsy all day and needed to move. This didn't happen often, but when it did she needed to feel the wind in her hair and her heart pounding in her chest.

Moments later she heard the sound of hooves growing louder as the other horse caught up to her. She knew he was at her side now, but she had to concentrate on climbing the trail that rose up behind the house. She wanted to make it to the top of the ridge before nightfall.

The moon shone through the leaves, casting strange shadows

across the hard packed trail as they made it to the top. The smell of the moist soil and thick vegetation didn't comfort her as she had expected, as it usually did. Something wasn't right, but she couldn't put a finger on it.

Bo began to growl and the mare sidestepped. "Hold up a moment, Emma," Dthau-Mahsz called out to her. "There must be something in the woods spooking the animals."

Pulling on the reins Emma brought Ruby to a halt, but the mare was beginning to fuss and protest. Emma strained to listen for a clue, but aside from the sound of the wind in the trees the night had grown quiet. "She wants to go back down." Emma stroked the horse's neck, trying to soothe her. Bo's growling was getting more guttural and the hairs on the back of Emma's neck and arms lifted.

"Move behind me," Dthau-Mahsz instructed. "Head back down. Bo!" He clicked his tongue for the horse to turn around and fall in behind Emma as she turned back towards the house.

The eerie growl went through to Emma's bones. It sounded like a mountain lion. "Go home, Bo!" Emma instructed as she nudged Ruby with her heels to get her to increase her pace. Not sure what happened next, Emma saw a flash of fur and heard the scream of the cat as Ruby reared, jerking her front legs off the ground, throwing Emma from the saddle.

Air rushed out of her lungs as she slammed roughly into the ground. A sharp pain to her head and arm caused her to cry out as a wave of nausea hit.

"Don't move," Dthau-Mahsz said. She felt his hands pass over her body, quickly examining her. His methodic verification was somehow reassuring.

Everything became fuzzy and Emma felt like she was drifting. Something warm enveloped her, it was so strange. His life force energy, his very essence somehow flowed through her, supporting her, keeping her afloat the way you would keep someone from drowning.

"Rest," he said to her. "I have you." She heard him exhale as he lifted her and nestled her into his arms. She loved the way he smelled, so fresh and masculine. Surrounded by his embrace, his warmth and energy, she let herself slip off into oblivion.

Before she opened her eyes she knew she was home. The distinct smell of an old house, along with line-dried sheets told her so. The sharp pounding in her head assaulted her, preventing her from trying to move, and she heard herself moan.

"You're home," Dthau-Mahsz said softly. "Two-Feathers is preparing something for you, it won't be long now." He touched her forehead lightly.

She heard him let out a breath, felt him take her hands in his, spreading warmth from his touch. His voice sounded close, almost as though he was in her mind, soothing her, comforting her, until the pain ebbed.

Over the next few days Dthau-Mahsz tended to Emma and all of her needs. At first, she was too sore to even think about protesting, and the slightest movement had brought the overpowering pounding in her head to life, but today she felt stronger and her mind was clearer. She pulled herself stiffly from her bed while Bo raised his head from the blankets and watched.

"What are you doing?" The sharp tone caught Emma off guard. She was leaning against the wall, making her way to the bathroom. After three days without a proper shower or bath, all she could think about was a long soak in a hot tub.

"I'm going to take a bath." She faltered, bringing him instantly to her side.

"All you had to do was ask; you could have hurt yourself." He scooped her easily into his arms and brought her back to the bed. "I will run your bath, and you will wait here."

She closed her eyes and nodded, trying to hide the shaking caused by her efforts.

"Your bath is ready," he said softly, laying a hand on her thigh. She must have dozed off a moment, because his voice startled her. He lifted her from the bed before she could protest and carried her to the chair beside the tub.

He proceeded, without asking, to unbutton her nightshirt and her breath caught. "I'll do it," she said.

Leaning forward he kissed her on the forehead. "Let me care for you, as you had once cared for me, as you have done for so many of your patients."

She closed her eyes and nodded. She hated having to rely on someone else for her own personal care, but as a nurse, she knew he was right. It's just that he'd never seen her without clothes before and that made her both nervous and uncomfortable.

Gently, he slipped her nightshirt from her shoulders and freed her injured arm. Keeping his gaze locked on hers he lifted her again, easing her slowly into the antique tub. She sank down into the bubbles, so very grateful for the bubbles, and felt the water begin to draw the tension from her body. "Thank you," she said. She let her head rest against the towel he'd draped over the tub's high back and closed her eyes. "I'll let you know when I'm done."

"I have no intention of leaving you alone. I will wait." His tone was gentle but firm.

She opened her eyes enough to watch him as he settled into the chair and picked up a copy of 'Everything You Ever Wanted to Know,' a fat, colorful book filled with all sorts of trivial information. She closed her eyes again and allowed herself to relax.

"You should get out of the tub now," Dthau-Mahsz said to her softly. "Your water must be getting cold."

Emma opened her eyes with a start. She'd been dreaming that she'd left a window open and had started to shiver. Realizing that her bubbles were all but gone, and that there was nothing to protect her intimacy, she pulled the plug and crossed her good arm over her chest. He slipped his hands under her arms from behind and lifted her to her feet. He quickly wrapped her in a towel and lifted her from the tub. She leaned her head against his chest as he toweled her off in such a way as to keep her covered. "Thank you," she said. At the hospital, nurses didn't have time for stuff like that, and for the first time she knew how her patients might have felt.

He held out a clean night shirt, helped her get her sore arm through and draped it across her back before he turned away. She dropped the towel, slipped her other arm through and pulled the shirt closed.

She let out a breath as he turned back and began doing up the buttons. "How are you feeling?" he asked as he turned his attention to her face. He gingerly moved her golden locks from her face and examined the side of her head.

She gave him a half-smile. "I feel as though I fell off the mountain. What happened?"

"Do you remember anything about that night?" he asked. He settled her back against the pillows into a semi-sitting position and brought the old, handmade quilt up around her.

She winced and adjusted her position. "Not really. I remember the growl, and seeing the cat pounce, but it happened so fast."

Dthau-Mahsz sat on the edge of her bed and took her hand in his. "Do not worry too much about it. Everyone is fine. Ruby made her way back down to the barn with Bo. By the time I got you home they were waiting in the front yard."

She closed her eyes a moment, grateful her animals were safe and that she was only stiff and sore. "I guess I won't be able to convince you to take anymore night rides."

He kissed her fingers. "Not unless it's in the field along the side of the barn."

A tap of the door sounded, and Two-Feathers entered carrying a tray. Bo, tail wagging, followed the shaman happily into the room. Emma sighed. "Please don't tell me you have anything bitter for me to drink."

Two-Feathers grunted as he placed the tray on her bedside table. "For a nurse, you make a lousy patient." He picked up a small cup, stirred the ingredients and handed it to her.

Dthau-Mahsz laughed from the other side of the bed, but helped steady her as she drank from the cup. She handed him the cup and grimaced as she swallowed the last of her sip.

"Hey, you're supposed to be on my side." She huffed and stiffly crossed her arms over her chest.

Two-Feathers took away the cup. "Good girl," he said in a teasing tone. He set a bed tray in front of her and arranged the bowl of stew so she could reach it easily.

Dthau-Mahsz stood. "I will go tend to the animals while you are here," he said to the shaman.

Two-Feathers nodded and turned back to Emma. "How are you feeling today?"

"Better, still sore though." She savored her mouthful of stew.

"Well you're lucky he went with you, or things might have turned out worse." He picked up her arm to examine the bruises and swelling. "When you are done eating I'll make a poultice to reduce the swelling and take some of the ache out."

"Don't suppose you have anything for my head?" she asked, forcing a smile.

He brushed the hair from her temple and looked at the side of her head. "Hmm. You drank it. It should start to feel better soon enough.

Emma's brain was slow to keep up, but the shaman's words finally registered. "What did he do?" Other than the horse getting spooked and her fall from it, Emma didn't remember any other incident.

"He wouldn't tell me exactly what happened, but the scratch mark on his forearm says a lot." He began mixing the clay, mashed pumpkin and oils to make the poultice.

She wrinkled her nose at the smell and took one last mouthful of stew. "Did he fall from his horse too?" She watched as he spread the strong smelling mixture over a rag. It actually smelled good. "What is that smell?"

"Birch. And no, he did not fall. It looks more like he was clawed." He laid his preparation down. "I need to free your shoulder and upper arm to apply the poultice."

She nodded. She couldn't get the buttons easily undone on her own anyway. Clawed. "Is he OK?"

Two-Feathers nodded as he applied his bandage to her arm and wrapped it up. "He had me tend to it, so there shouldn't be any infection, and William stitched it up." "Oh no!" Emma exclaimed. "The clinic." She made a move to push the blankets aside but was assaulted by a wave of pain and dizziness.

Two-Feathers settled her back down. "Sadie's back, remember? Everything is fine, though I think William wanted to talk to you about handling the house calls with him. Sarah never cared for them." He finished covering her arm and examined his work. "Do you want to put your arm back through the sleeve or leave it out?"

She looked at herself. "How long will you leave it on?" Her eyes watered from the vapours, but the warmth had already started to soothe her.

"A good twenty minutes," he said, picking up his stuff.

"Just leave it. I'll rest in the meantime." She nestled back against her pillows, feeling herself begin to doze. She'd forgotten about Sadie coming back. She was a little sad her time at the clinic had come to an end.

"I'll be downstairs."

"Thanks, Two-Feathers." She let herself drift away.

The gentle touch on her shoulder brought her slowly from sleep. She expected to see Two-Feathers, but smiled at the sight of

Dthau-Mahsz bent over her. "Sleep well?" he asked her.

She nodded. "I feel much better too." She started to sit up.

"No, don't move yet," he said, a second too late. The blanket that had been covering her slipped down, exposing her and this time he didn't look away. Slowly, he lifted his gaze as he brought the blanket back up.

Her heart beat faster as their eyes locked. She wished he would kiss her. She really wanted him to kiss her...and he did.

She melted into his embrace, relishing in the feel of his mouth on hers and her heart skipped a beat as he slowly trailed kisses down her neck. He'd kissed her before, but not like this, and his mouth had never left her lips.

Much to her dismay, he pulled back. Tenderly he kissed her lips, nose and forehead before easing her back down. "I do not wish to hurt you," he said lovingly.

She drew in a deep breath and felt her heart swell. She wanted him, all of him and she didn't want to wait.

CHAPTER 11: THE BONDING

Summer passed in a blur. Every day Dthau-Mahsz had showed his affection for her as they worked and lived side by side one another and every day Emma hoped for more. She tried to focus on being grateful for what she had with him rather than torment herself with what she still hoped for. Fortunately, this summer had been busier than the last, and each night Emma collapsed into bed, tired but content with all she had accomplished. The storeroom shelves were laden with canned fruits, vegetables, jams and other prepared foods. Her freezer was also filled to the brim with all she had grown and harvested.

The weather had turned colder, and soon the pumpkins would be harvested for cooking, marking the end of all her hard work in the garden. Dthau-Mahsz had chopped and stacked wood for the winter, and the evenings had become so cool that he made a fire every night.

"I can't believe you've been here a year already," Emma said. "Time just flew by." She felt serene, and happy with the flow of her life. She had come to accept their loving friendship and let go of her expectations. He surely had his reasons for holding back.

"I would like to discuss something with you," Dthau-Mahsz said. He put the load of wood he had been carrying down by the fireplace and moved the burning logs around with the poker before adding a new one.

She relaxed on the couch with her feet tucked under her, sipping tea. She patted the cushion beside her. "Come sit. What would you like to discuss?" She leaned forward and handed him a cup of tea from the coffee table, while waiting for him to tell her what was on his mind rather than make up her own stories. That was something she was still good at.

He took a sip and set the cup back down. "I have enjoyed every moment spent with you since my arrival. You have never been anything less than kind, generous and loving. I cannot imagine spending my life with anyone else." He paused a moment as he seemed to collect his thoughts. He looked into her eyes. "It is just..." He paused.

"Is something wrong? Are you leaving?" She turned, her blue eyes searching his face. She could not imagine life without him. They had formed a symbiosis, complementing one another in such an easy way. Of course, if he had been planning to leave, then that would explain why he'd been holding back.

He smiled softly. "No." He took her hand in his. "I want to spend the rest of my life bonded to you."

She pulled back a bit. "Bonded? You mean Married?"

He shook his head. "It is more than just married. My people choose a single partner for life." He held her gaze. "We share all our thoughts and feelings. We are completely open with one another and over time complete one another."

She smiled. "It sounds too good to be true." On some level she felt they already had that. He always seemed to be in tune with her.

"Will you bond with me?"

A strange burst of energy filled Emma's abdomen and her breath caught. Eyes wide, she lifted them to return his gaze. "What do I do?" she whispered. It felt as though she had swallowed a ball of static energy, and with every breath it grew within her.

He stood, took her by the hands and led her to the floor. He sat cross-legged on the floor and had her sit in the cradle of his legs with her legs wrapped around his waist. She felt heat rise in her cheeks, but she did not resist. He gently brought her forehead to his and held her hands in his hands, close to their hearts. "Close your eyes and breathe with me," he whispered.

The static feeling vanished and she felt herself fall into his warmth. He was soft and inviting, yet strong and safe. She felt his heart beating inside her and saw herself through his eyes. "Oh my..." she said in her mind and knew he heard her. She knew his thoughts and began to explore his feelings for her. She saw her world through his eyes, and he let her in deeper. Abandoning herself in his energy she felt it change and vibrate with renewed strength and love, as it became 'their' energy.

Emma felt him move gently, curiously through her thoughts,

and he now knew that she had been terrified when she'd first found him, but had cared for him anyway. She felt his reaction to that and knew it touched him deeply. He watched her feelings for him grow over their time spent together, and now, thanks to this incredible link they shared, she finally had answers to all her questions and felt safe enough to abandon herself to their relationship.

They met somewhere within, finding total truth and pure emotion. She loved him, and he loved her. She felt how scared he'd been when she'd been thrown from her horse, and felt his realisation that how much or how little time they had together was unknown. He chose to take every moment he could to be with her, no longer looking for excuses to keep her at a safe distance. She admitted to her fears as well, and rose above her insecurities to embrace him with all that she was. They were one.

When they pulled apart, the intensity of the experience diminished, but didn't vanish. A connection remained in the form of a reassuring presence and Emma smiled. She felt complete, safe.

"Hold tight with your legs," he said as he wrapped his arms around Emma's bottom, lifting her slightly.

Emma let out a gasp of surprise when he stood in one fluid motion without putting her down. She released her ankles and brought her legs to the floor, but remained in his arms.

He scooped her up and made his way to the couch, settling her onto his lap as he continued to hold her. She rested her head on his chest and closed her eyes, breathing in his scent. She loved how good he smelled.

He laughed softly and planted a kiss on the top of her head. She would have to get used to him knowing her thoughts. She now knew that he could sense her emotions, but not read her thoughts as she had sometimes wondered. She felt a shift in his mood and lifted her eyes to meet his. "What is it?"

"Your traditions when it comes to joining a couple are different." He paused a moment. "Would you want to have a traditional joining ceremony?"

She understood what he was asking, and she appreciated it, but the truth was she didn't have any family left to share this with. There were her friends, but somehow the whole white wedding thing didn't matter. She had all she'd ever hoped and waited for right here...besides, they'd never come up with the legal documents needed.

She kissed him on the cheek and shook her head. "This was perfect, I don't need anything more."

He pulled back a little to examine her. "Perfect? Then tell me, why a kiss on the cheek is all I get?"

She grinned. "What did you have in mind?"

The link expanded and Emma's body came alive. He cradled the back of her head as he leaned down and kissed her. Electricity flowed through every nerve, making her acutely aware of her entire being. "Oh, what are you doing to me?" She slid her hands into his hair and pulled him closer, and her breath hitched when his hands slid beneath her shirt.

He paused, pulling away. He looked into her eyes, searching their depths. "Are we going to be sharing a room now?" His face was all serious.

She frowned. He was stopping for this? "Well, yes, if you like."

He nodded. "Yours or mine?"

"Mine is bigger," she offered.

Again, he nodded. "Fine, but would you be terribly upset if, just for tonight, we went to my room?" He caressed her cheek with the back of his hand. "Mine is closer…"

She laughed nervously but felt her desire flare. "Take me wherever you please."

He stood with Emma cradled lovingly in his arms, and carried her to his room.

* * *

Later on that night Emma lay curled on her side, nestled safely in his arms. She listened to the sound of his breathing and of his heart beat as she felt the rise and fall of his chest against her. She had seen his world, parts of his life through their exchange, and she knew how difficult the adjustment was for him. She supposed it would be like her going back a few hundred years in time, but even then, the difference was still greater for him.

Although she didn't quite understand all she saw, she realized that many people owed their existence to him. She had caught a glimpse of his ship, his quarters and the people he worked with. She liked what she saw of him, she liked it a lot. She smiled, letting out a sigh of satisfaction and felt his arms tighten around her. He nuzzled her neck and kissed her, sending waves of delight through her body.

"So you like what you see of me?" he teased.

She tried to sit up but he brought her right back to where she was, effortlessly, giving her an idea of just how strong her man was. "You are not supposed to be reading my mind," she protested.

He flipped her over to face him. "Would you mind telling me where you got the images you were broadcasting?" His eyes twinkled with mischief.

She felt her cheeks flush. She wasn't sure if there were any ground rules to this bond.

A smile spread across his face, highlighting a small scar on his upper lip. She reached out and traced it with a finger. "Where did you get this?" she asked.

"You are changing the subject."

She saw a scene flash in her mind; he was carrying a child to safety as burning debris fell all around. An explosion rocked the area and pieces flew. He turned his back to shield the child but as he looked over his shoulder a scrap of metal made contact with his face.

Emma heard her breath catch as she felt the impact of the piece and pulled back. The image vanished and Dthau-Mahsz came into focus. He was watching her.

"I'm sorry," she stammered. "I don't know how to turn it off."

He brushed a lock of hair from her face. "You cannot turn it off. It is a part of us now." He brought her hand to his mouth and lightly kissed the back of her fingers.

"So you are always going to know what's going on inside my head," she gasped, horrified.

He laughed softly. "No. On a day to day basis we will simply sense one another. But when we become intimate, He let his gaze flow across her body, barely hidden by a sheet and she felt the link burst to life.

I truly love you, he said through the link.

CHAPTER 12: *Unto Us This Night*

Emma listened to Christmas music softly in the kitchen, not wanting to wake Dthau-Mahsz. They had spent Christmas day alone by choice, after spending the previous evening with Two-Feathers and a few friends and members of his family. She smiled as she thought about all the questions Dthau-Mahsz still had about the holiday.

With her hair pulled back in a ponytail, and her sleeves rolled above her elbows, she rolled out the last of the cookies and laid them on a baking sheet. A light dusting of powdered sugar covered her cheek as she wiped the back of her hand across it. Her girlfriends would be spending a few days with them over the Christmas break and she couldn't wait to see them. She felt guilty, not having told them about her wedding, but then it wasn't a wedding, but a bonding and she didn't know how to explain that.

One of her favorite songs began filling the room with its upbeat melody and holiday cheer. She sang along with the music as she finished making the last of this particular batch of cookies. Slipping the baking sheet into the oven, she wiped her forehead with the back of her sleeve. Emma didn't need to turn around to know he was there, watching her. The barely perceptible tingling that flowed along her spine, reaching out to every nerve ending announced his presence. She took a deep breath before she turned to face him, intending to offer him a cup of coffee and a taste of the warm Vanillekipferl cookies. Instead, she turned to find him a scant distance from her.

"Good morning," he said as he drew her into a tender embrace, surprising her.

She slid her arms around his waist and leaned into him, letting his scent, mixed with cedar and fresh air, surround her. The link sparked inside her and she gasped, pulling back. Sometimes she forgot about it, and its intensity took her by surprise. The flicker dimmed down to a comfortable hum. Drawing in a shaky breath Emma felt his finger on her chin as he gingerly lifted her head so their eyes could meet. Amethyst eyes stared back, and she was sure he could see into the depths of her soul.

The stove timer dinged and she stepped out of his arms to slip on her snowman oven mitts. She could feel his eyes still on her. Setting the tray of cookies down, she began placing them into the bowl of icing sugar, but stopped to offer Dthau-Mahsz a warm bite from the previous batch. "Just open your mouth," she said as he made a face at the little crescent-shaped cookie. She smiled openly at his delight in tasting the warm offering. Bo whined for one too and Emma broke off a small piece for him.

Dthau-Mahsz turned and held one out for Emma. "Why didn't you let me help?"

Emma frowned. "You want to help me make Christmas cookies?" She studied his expression, but he seemed serious.

"Yes, why not?" he reached for another cookie.

"Well because you made such a fuss about hanging Christmas lights, I assumed you wouldn't be any more interested in baking." She wiped her floured hands on her snowman apron. "You're serious, aren't you?"

He nodded, picked up her cookbook and leafed through the pages. He frowned. "Where are the cookies you just made?" He handed her back the book and waited.

"You won't find them in there. My girlfriend from Austria showed me how to make them. I was going to start in on the Spitzbuben now, if your offer to help still stands..." Emma pulled out a folded paper from the pocket of her apron and handed it to Dthau-Mahsz. "These are Ursula's recipes." The paper had yellowed over time, and there were stains and spatters on it but there was no way she would even consider tossing it for a neatly rewritten, cleaner version. As long as the recipe was legible, she'd keep it.

"How should I go about this?" He held up the stained paper.

Smiling softly, shaking a lock of hair from her eyes Emma smiled. "Make sure all the ingredients are out. Then we'll go through the steps to prepare them."

Nodding, Dthau-Mahsz studied the list of ingredients again.

By the time the baking was done and the kitchen restored, the two of them retired to the living room to rest and sample their work. Silence between them had become not only comfortable, but comforting. She looked up from her cup, about to comment on their cookies only to realize he was watching her and dropped her gaze. Feeling her face flush, she drew in a deep breath before facing the depths of his eyes. The effect was just as powerful as ever.

He was still watching her when she lifted her head. He smiled reassuringly before taking another sip of his tea. Setting his cup down, he straightened. "When do your friends arrive?"

"Their plane lands at seven tomorrow evening, they confirmed the time this morning. Two-Feathers is going to be in town and he offered to bring them back. I hope the weather won't cause them too much trouble. It's snowing pretty hard out there." She was anxious to see her friends again. Now that she and Dthau-Mahsz shared a room she'd have some explaining to do, since she'd been on Maggie's case to wait for the right man and all. She'd just have to tell them that she'd gotten married, without them. Hopefully they wouldn't be too upset.

Dthau-Mahsz frowned. "Would you not prefer to meet them yourself?" He shifted in his seat and leaned closer to her, taking her hands in his. He passed his thumbs over the backs of her hands.

"It doesn't make much sense to go down if he's already going to be there, not in this weather." She did want to meet them, but they already knew Two-Feathers, so it wasn't as though she'd be sending a stranger. She sighed. Now he had her doubting her decision.

"Why don't we head into town tomorrow afternoon? The storm will have passed by then. We could do some shopping and eat out before meeting them." He squeezed her hands tenderly before releasing his hold, and reached for his cup.

Chewing her bottom lip, Emma considered his offer. She loved the after Christmas sales, and dinner out would be nice, not to mention a change of scenery. She nodded with enthusiasm. "OK, let's do it."

"Maybe you should inform Two-Feathers," he said.

She nodded, swallowing a mouthful of tea. "You're right." She stood and turned to reach for the phone, slamming into Two-Feathers who reached out to steady her.

Dthau-Mahsz laughed softly. "I never said on the phone."

"Does this mean I can't come over and have cookies with the girls tomorrow night?" Two-Feathers asked in a serious tone.

Emma swatted the shaman playfully on the arm. "Did you really have business in town or was your offer just another way to get extra cookies?" She shook her head and burst out laughing. "You're terrible. You could have just asked for some more." She tilted her head in thought. "Wait a minute; don't you usually complain sometime in January that you still have baked goods coming out of your ears?"

He reached down for a cookie from her plate. "Hmm, yes, but you're the only one who gives me this kind." He popped it in his mouth and closed his eyes a moment while he chewed. He looked down at her, reached for another cookie and paused before consuming it. "And with the extra guests, my portion will be even smaller."

Emma stared at him. Was he serious? She shook her head and stepped to the side to give him full access to the plate. "Would you like some tea with that?"

He smiled. "Milk, please."

She heard the two of them talking as she made her way to the kitchen. Pausing over the sink she took a moment to watch the large flakes float lazily down in the fading afternoon light. This was already the second Christmas here, and years without her parents. Time went by so fast. The reality of her loss came back like a slap in the face, as fresh as the first time it had hit her. Sorrow rose up within and she blinked back some tears. Taking a shaky breath, Emma tried to calm herself and push the sadness away. Swallowing hard, she cleared her throat and turned to get the milk from the fridge.

Dthau-Mahsz was standing there. Without saying a word he drew her into his arms and she rested her cheek against his chest. He gently stroked the back of her head in a soothing manner.

Grateful for the comfort Emma let herself be drawn in. She felt safe in his arms and let her guard down. Everything about him surrounded her, comforted her, and soothed her. She drew in a breath and let the smell of wood smoke, and spicy musk that was him fill her. Time seemed to stop in the comfort of his arms, giving her the chance she needed to regain her composure.

"You had better bring more cookies," Two-Feathers called from the living room, breaking the moment.

Dthau-Mahsz kissed the top of her head and gave her a gentle hug before releasing her. "Let me help you," he offered, wiping a tear with his thumb.

Emma forced a smile and tucked a loose strand of her wavy hair behind her ear. "Thanks," she whispered, and not for the offer to help. Having the comfort of the link was an amazing gift, and she couldn't imagine going a day without it.

Dthau-Mahsz followed her back to the living room, and she could feel his gaze on her as she straightened her shoulders and drew in a steadying breath.

Two-Feathers looked up as Emma walked into the room and smiled sympathetically at her, almost as if he knew how she felt, but he didn't say a word. "OK," she said, handing him a festive tin filled with his favourite cookies, "these are just for you." She laid out a fresh plate of the sugar coated treats and handed him his glass of milk.

As she turned back to offer Dthau-Mahsz more tea he laid a hand on her forearm. "Allow me," he watched her settle into her grandmother's armchair and turned back to the teapot.

Two-Feathers wiped the powdered sugar from his fingers. "I do have business in town tomorrow with Grey Wolf," he explained.

Emma stopped him before he could continue. "We've decided to go down tomorrow as well, so we'll pick up Renata and Maggie when their plane lands." She paused, a smile tugging at the corner of her mouth. "But you could still stop in for some tea and cookies after you're done in town."

He nodded, satisfied. Standing, he wiped the last of the powdered sugar on his jeans and leaned down to hug Emma. "Give it time," he said as he squeezed her shoulders. He nodded in Dthau-Mahsz's direction and let himself out.

Easing back into her chair, Emma sighed. She'd made it through Christmas without her parents, so why was she so emotional today?

Dthau-Mahsz turned his attention to Emma. "Did you want to talk about it?"

She shook her head, not trusting herself to speak. Bo made his way over and wedged his snout under her arm with insistence. She stroked him absently and pulled her hand back, but he persisted, nudging her with his damp nose as his backside danced to the rhythm of his wagging tail. In spite of her sudden drop in mood Emma smiled. Looking over at Dthau-Mahsz she asked, "Do you feel like taking a walk?"

In that smooth, seamless fashion of his he rose to his feet and collected the dishes. "I could use the exercise," he said, making his way to the kitchen.

Emma paused and turned to face him. "What are you talking about? You never stop." There was nothing he couldn't do once he learned how and Emma marvelled at his strength. Grey Wolf had teased him when they had mended the fences, saying he should partake in the summer warrior games, a test of speed, strength and agility. She paused by the door as she zipped her coat closed. "Don't suppose you'd feel like riding the horses up the ridge?"

Dthau-Mahsz opened the door and quickly stepped aside, just in time to let Bo barrel out past him. Emma made her way onto the porch next to him and he looked her over closely, concern on his face. "I would prefer if we went for a walk today," he said to her. "I do not think you would be up for such a strenuous ride."

She hesitated as she took in the yard. Giant snowflakes were still falling and a good rate, and everything was blanketed by several inches of fresh snow. "You may be right, and the snow is still coming down hard, it would probably be safer." She forced a smile. Truth was that since her accident she was a little more cautious when it came to both horses and the mountain. In the end she just wanted to get out and clear her mind a bit.

Arm in arm they made their way through the deepening snow, Emma's emotions were about as unstable as the weather. Yes, she was upset about her parents not being with her at Christmas, but there was something more. Maybe it was the unease at not having told her friends about Dthau-Mahsz and herself.

Dthau-Mahsz's presence came through their link and she relished in the sense of security it brought. Lifting her face to the sky she let the snowflakes come down all around her and inhaled deeply, letting the crisp coldness of the pure mountain air fill her lungs. "Sorry if I'm a little moody, I think I just needed to get out," she admitted.

He moved behind her and wrapped his arms around her, pulling her against him so she could lean back and stare at the sky. "I don't mind. You have had enough to deal with since before my arrival. I can let you lean on me." He dropped a kiss on her forehead.

* * *

Stepping out of the bathroom after a hot shower, Emma toweled off her hair. "The walk really did me good," she said.

Dthau-Mahsz looked up from the bed. He had several wilderness books and outdoor magazines spread across the quilt that he'd been studying. "You do look better." He smiled, then quickly picked up his books and cleared off the bed.

She draped the towel over a bar behind the door and exchanged her bathrobe for a delicate cotton nightie. "I think the link has a lot to do with it." She propped her pillows against the headboard and sat down next to him. "It's too bad we don't have that here."

He draped an arm around her shoulders and let her settle against him. "You do, you simply choose to ignore it."

She looked up at him. "No, we don't." She'd never experienced anything like this connection with him in her life.

She felt him laugh. "It is there. You just have to open to it."

"OK, give me some examples." She sat up and turned to face him, sitting cross-legged.

Amusement colored his eyes. "You seem to forget that we are essentially the same." He studied her a moment. "Have you never thought of someone only to have them call or show up on your doorstep moments later?"

She nodded. "Sure. It happens to everyone." She propped her elbows on her knees and leaned her chin on her hands. "And that is nothing like the link."

He smiled openly, shaking his head a little. "It's exactly the same. It is the link at its most basic level."

Emma snorted. "Yeah, with the difference being caveman to spaceman level."

He raised an eyebrow. "Actually the cavemen relied heavily on the link for survival against predators."

"Oh, now you're just making that up." She was caught off guard by a yawn. "I'm sorry, I guess I'm more tired than I realized." She stood and tossed the extra pillows onto the chair in the corner of her room before turning down her blankets. She suddenly felt drained.

Dthau-Mahsz rose, leaned over her to give her a kiss and padded towards the bedroom door. "I will let the dog out and be right back."

She had wanted to discuss the link more, but she was so exhausted she barely noticed when he crawled into bed next to her.

* * *

"Good morning, sleepyhead," Dthau-Mahsz said as he entered their room. He was carrying a tray with coffee and French toast. And it smelled wonderful.

Emma stretched and smiled. "You're up early." Sunlight spilled into the room and the realisation that the weather would be clear for their drive into town lifted her spirits...almost as much as being brought breakfast in bed.

He laid the tray across her lap and went around the bed to settle down next to her. "It's ten-thirty." He kissed her before handing her a cup of coffee. "Relax, you were tired and needed the rest."

Emma had to agree. William had taken two weeks off from the hospital, which meant two weeks of house-calls and patient follow-ups. Emma could barely keep up with him, but she loved the way they were able to help people.

"I finished the chores early this morning so all you'd have to do is rest until we left for town," Dthau-Mahsz said, bringing her away from her thoughts. He took a sip of his coffee. "We both know that once your friends get here, you will be kept quite busy."

Emma winced, the other whirlwind in her life. She hoped Renata would control herself, at least until she told her friends he was taken. She giggled as she thought of the look on their faces. They'd be happy for her. She took a bite of her French toast and grimaced.

"Is there something wrong with your breakfast?" he asked. He reached over and touched her forehead.

She shook her head and forced a smile. "It's fine, I'm fine." She forced another bite down and made a mental note to be up early enough to cook breakfast in the future. "Thank you for doing this."

He ate heartily, obviously enjoying his food. "Have you planned any activities for your friends?"

With a slight nod she took another sip of coffee and returned the empty cup to the tray. "I thought we'd go for a sleigh ride, and we're having a small New Year's Eve party, but aside from that, no." She looked over at him, taking a moment to get lost in his fathomless amethyst pools. "Should I plan out the week?"

He cut a piece of her French toast and offered it to her. "I think we can decide all together once they get here." He watched her as she dutifully took the offered bite. "You really don't like it, do you?"

"It's not the food, I think it's me." She raised a hand to cover her mouth and paused a moment. "I think I'll go take a shower."

Dthau-Mahsz lifted the tray and deposited it on the floor at the foot of the bed. He watched her as she climbed out of bed. "If you are not up for the trip into town it's not too late to have Two-Feathers pick them up."

"Do I look that bad?" She paused a moment to do a quick self-assessment. She felt a little tired, but that was all. She raised her eyes to meet his gaze and felt a slight rush when they made contact. "You might want to shower too..." She dropped her gaze as she focused on the link. It took him a moment to catch on, but she felt desire swell within him and then reach out tentatively to touch her.

She didn't hear or see him cross the room to her, but when she felt him take her into his arms, she tilted her head up to kiss him. Her heart beat faster as she laced her fingers behind his neck. The shower could wait.

CHAPTER 13: WE'RE MARRIED

"Why does it bother you to tell your friends about us?" Dthau-Mahsz asked as he turned the Jeep's engine off. He shifted in his seat to face her, obviously waiting for an answer. "Do you regret what we have done?"

"No! Oh, I have to get used to us sharing thoughts…or should I say 'half thoughts'?" She tried to explain her feelings and felt the link swell inside her and come to life.

Show me, he said through the link.

Emma wasn't sure she understood, but she pushed her uncertainty aside and focused on her friends, on how she felt and her fear of disappointing them. She couldn't bear having them feel left out.

I see, I understand how you feel, but from what I've seen of your friendship, they will be happy for us. We can make the announcement together if you like.

She let out the breath she hadn't realised she'd been holding and reached out to touch his cheek. "Yes, I'd like that very much."

He smiled reassuringly. "Good, now let us face the whirlwind." He winked at her and opened his door.

A second later he opened Emma's door and leaned in to kiss her on the cheek. He didn't give her the chance to move before he scooped her out of the car and deposited her on the ground. She laughed out loud, feeling reassured about telling her friends.

"You see!" Renata exclaimed as she scurried from around the airport building and hurried to greet them, slipping on a mound of snow. "They are so happy together." She shot a look back towards Maggie who made her way elegantly towards the group.

"Renata." Dthau-Mahsz nodded. He moved forward to help her with her suitcase.

Maggie moved in to hug Emma. "You look good, girl. Love

suits you."

Hugging her back, Emma smiled. "Good to see you. Come on, let's head for home." She shivered. "It's cold out here."

The trip home passed quickly as the group talked and laughed, getting caught up on recent events. "So what about you two," Maggie asked. "You were cute when we last saw you, but something has changed." She looked right into Emma's eyes. "You gonna tell us, or do we have to guess?"

Emma shot a glance of panic towards Dthau-Mahsz who winked. *Go ahead. Don't be afraid. Have faith.*

Emma looked from Renata to Maggie.

Renata slapped Maggie on the hand. "I told you there was something!"

"Well if you let her talk, then maybe she will tell us what that is," Maggie exclaimed. She turned her attention back to Emma. "Go on, Honey."

Emma smiled uncomfortably, her burst of certainty gone. She drew in a sharp breath as the link expanded, but then the reassurance she'd felt so many times since he'd come into her world comforted her, guided her. She glanced nervously at Dthau-Mahsz before looking back at Maggie. "We're married," she blurted out.

"Oh Dio!" Renata exclaimed. She turned to Maggie, hands clasped over her mouth. "I told you they were going to get married! Oh, I am so happy for both of you." Tears sprang into her eyes as she began to mutter in Italian.

A wave of emotion crossed Maggie's face. "Congratulations, to both of you."

Emma reached back for Maggie's hand and gave it a reassuring squeeze. "We had a private ceremony, no celebration, no family." She blinked back tears. "I don't want you to get upset…" her voice trailed off.

"Oh, Honey," Maggie said. She gave Emma a forced smile. "I am happy for you, and I understand. I would have liked to have been there, that's all." She rooted around her handbag for a tissue.

"You did not have a celebration?" Renata cut in. "Then we will celebrate!"

Emma and Dthau-Mahsz exchanged glances.

"Renata, give them some space," Maggie said. She turned her

gaze towards Emma.

"Since a small group of us will be gathering for the New Year, we could celebrate our joining as well," Dthau-Mahsz offered. He raised his eyebrows and shrugged in Emma's direction.

Emma scrunched up her forehead and shot him a weary smile. He just got them into a heap of trouble.

Renata squealed with delight. "Let me handle everything!"

"No!" both Maggie and Emma exclaimed. "You're not shutting me out of this," Maggie proclaimed, giving Emma an apologetic look. Renata meant well, but sometimes, she needed a mentor.

* * *

"Did you want a snack or some tea?" Emma offered her guests once they'd arrived home. She opened the door wider to let Bo out.

"We had to work a double just to get time off," Maggie said. She turned towards Renata who was leaning heavily on the railing, just about ready to head upstairs to her room.

"I am exhausted. I had planned on being asleep by now," she smiled half-heartedly then frowned at Maggie. "You are not coming upstairs?" Renata shifted on the step.

Maggie's face lit up, looking quite proud of herself. "I'm taking the downstairs guest room. Goodnight." She straightened, pivoted on her heel and waved over her shoulder as she made her way down the hall.

* * *

Emma's shoulders slumped slightly. "To tell you the truth, I'm a little tired myself. Maybe a good night's sleep will do us all some good." She waved to her friends but headed towards the mudroom to grab a work coat.

Dthau-Mahsz took her by the wrist and turned her to face him. "Are you feeling all right?" He gave her a once-over before settling his gaze on hers.

She nodded and nestled into his arms. She loved to feel his heartbeat, his breath, his life force. "I've just been obsessing about telling them about us, and I haven't slept too well these past few nights." As if on cue she yawned. "Not to mention trying to follow William on all the house calls. I'm just going to tend to the animals and I'll be right up."

He held her gently, massaging the back of her head. "Go to bed, I won't be long."

She shook her head stubbornly. "No. You did the chores on your own this morning, and had I found myself baking and entertaining, then OK, but everyone's off to bed and I have to do my share of the work too."

He slid his arms tightly around her waist. "You will go to bed and rest." He lifted her head and searched the depth of her eyes, before he leaned in and claimed her mouth with his own. "I won't be long." He kissed her again quickly, and then turned her towards the stairs to send her on her way.

Emma let out a sigh but headed slowly up the stairs. She'd beaten herself up after her friends' last visit, having let him practically wait on them hand and foot. So much for breaking that pattern…. Maybe after a good night's rest she'd be able to pull her weight.

Renata's door was open just a crack, and the light snapped shut just as Emma passed by. "Sleep well," she said softly.

She stepped into her bedroom and began to undress, leaving her clothes draped over the back of her reading chair. She'd put them away tomorrow. Barefoot, she padded to the bathroom to get ready for bed, deciding to skip her nightly moisturizing ritual. Reaching for her nightshirt that hung behind the bathroom door, she slipped it over her head and crawled into bed.

Propped up against the antique headboard she took a critical look at the large room. A little sprucing up couldn't hurt, and she could redecorate in a way that would reflect the two of them. Now it looked like a B&B's antique-themed room. She'd never even asked him if he liked it. Well, with the oncoming winter months, a little indoor project might be fun. She'd pick up some magazines next time they were in town and get some ideas.

A gentle kiss on her cheek brought a smile to her lips and she opened her eyes to see her husband leaning over her. She stretched, yawning. She must have dozed off. "Are you coming to bed?" She patted the spot next to her, and to her surprise, he laughed. Pushing herself up on her elbows, she frowned. "Why is that funny?"

He sat on the edge of the bed and reached out to stroke her cheek. "It is morning. You were already asleep by the time I came in last night."

She looked over and checked the time. The blue numbers glowed brightly, showing her that it was now 05:45 AM. She bolted upright. "I'll be up in a minute." She tucked a strand of hair behind her ear. "I'll be right with you."

"Why don't you take care of breakfast, and I'll tend to the animals. I do not think your friends will be up any time soon." He took her hand as she stepped out of bed and shivered. "Would you like me to make a fire before I head out to the barn?"

"No," she said, stepping into her jeans as she headed to the bathroom. "Once the oven is on, the kitchen will be warm. "How cold is it outside?"

"Cold. It's -30C this morning." He stood and straightened the covers on the bed and tossed the pillows back against the headboard.

Emma pulled her hair back into a ponytail, dressed warmly, and followed her man down the stairs to the kitchen to make coffee. A jug of maple water stood in the sink. "You thought of it," she exclaimed.

He leaned back in from the mudroom and smiled, drawing her to him for a hug and kiss. "I won't be long."

By the time Dthau-Mahsz returned, Emma had an orange-cranberry loaf baking alongside a fluffy omelette. She laid a plate of sliced fruit on the table and prepared some cheese slices. "Smells wonderful." He nodded towards the stairs. "I am going to shower."

"Your coffee will be waiting." As she turned back to the stove, she heard the familiar sounds of Renata's heavy steps moving about upstairs. Good, they would be able to eat soon.

Even before Maggie entered the kitchen, Emma caught a whiff of her flowery perfume as it wafted in from the hallway. Emma wrinkled her nose. It wasn't the greatest mix with breakfast. "Hey, Hon," Maggie said as she glided into the kitchen. "Now that's a great way to wake up." She sniffed the air. "Need help?"

"Just have to set the table, everything is ready." Emma said. She was looking forward to spending time with her friends.

* * *

"Breakfast was amazing," Renata said, pushing her plate back.

"Would you care for more coffee?" Dthau-Mahsz asked. He refilled her cup when she held it up and topped off his own.

Renata took a sip and savoured it. She shot an accusing glance at Emma. "How come you never cooked like that when we lived together?"

Emma snorted. "When? Between working at the hospital, lesson plans and teaching, I barely had time for sleep." She picked a few pieces of fruit from the serving dish and added them to her plate.

Two-Feathers entered through the mudroom. "Morning ladies, sorry for disturbing you." He shifted his attention to Dthau-Mahsz. "Xma kin kqsamunałap?"

Emma stiffened as she watched Dthau-Mahsz nod curtly and stand. Two-Feathers needed his help. He deposited his plate in the counter and leaned in close to Emma. "I will be back as soon as possible."

Emma nodded, accepted the quick hug and kiss, and watched him run upstairs, only to return a moment later wearing the jumpsuit she'd found him in. He pulled snow pants on over it and grabbed his parka. "Please forgive me, ladies, but I must take my leave of you."

Emma shot a warning glance in Two-Feathers' direction. She didn't want anything to happen to her husband.

"We should not be too long," the shaman promised.

"Be careful!" Renata called out as they left the house. As soon as the door shut she whirled to face Emma. "What did he say? What does that mean?"

"Xma kin kqsamunałap? Means *can you help me* or *I need help*, I think. My Ktunaxa is not very good."

Renata waved an arm towards the door. "And yet your man understands?"

Emma shrugged. "He seems to, although I've never asked him."

Maggie stood and started clearing the table. "Don't even think about it," she said to Emma as she got up to help. "It's the least we can do." She waved for Renata to get up. "Why don't you go make a fire and we can all go hang out in the living room this morning?"

Emma paused. "It'll only take a minute if we all chip in; besides, I have to put the slow cooker on." She reached for the ceramic pot she had prepared yesterday, set it into its base and turned it on.

Maggie waved her off with the back of her hand. "Good, now get out of here, you have a fire to build."

Emma let out a breath. "Fine, but if you don't know where something goes, just leave it on the counter.

* * *

Dthau-Mahsz had been gone a little over three hours and there was still no sign of the men. "Quit worrying, girl," Maggie said. "They probably went to dig some poor guy out of a ditch."

Emma looked out the frosted window. The sky was a beautiful, cloudless blue, and the occasional gust of wind shook last night's snow out of its resting places. "I suppose."

She felt the link swell up inside her and she barely stifled a gasp. Dthau-Mahsz stood in snow to his thighs. He and a small group of people were searching for someone, someone that had been buried in the snow. She felt him focus his attention, creating a virtual image of his surroundings in his mind. Slowly, one by one, the people surrounding him appeared as shadows in his image. After a moment, one more form appeared and Dthau-Mahsz turned instinctively towards the shadow. He motioned for Two-Feathers to join him and the two began digging frantically until they found him.

"Emma, what's wrong? Are you OK?" Maggie was talking to her.

Forcing a smile she nodded. "I'm fine, sorry about that."

"Did you have a seizure?" Renata blurted out.

"I did not have a seizure, I just got lost in my thoughts," she offered, shaking her head.

CHAPTER 14: SOME GIRL TALK

"Stress can do some nasty things to the body," Maggie said. "You might want to have that checked out."

"I assure you, I'm fine." Emma stifled a laugh. Better take it with a grain of salt. "I just got carried away worrying about my man, that's all."

Renata eyed her with close scrutiny. "And where do you think he might be?"

"Helping someone stuck in the snow, or looking for lost hikers or skiers..." Emma's expression matched her grave tone.

Making the sign of the cross Renata offered up a silent prayer. She reached out and squeezed Emma's arm. "He'll be OK."

Silence filled the room and they sat there a while, each lost in her own thoughts. Finally Renata slapped her thighs as she leaned towards Emma. "I need to know something."

Uh-oh, Emma thought. This didn't sound promising.

"Why did you get married so fast? Are you pregnant?" She held Emma's gaze.

Emma's eyes widened, but she didn't have a chance to answer before Maggie jumped in. "What's wrong with you? This isn't the old country where a baby out of wedlock is a crime."

"No," Emma reassured Renata. "I am not pregnant. He asked me to marry him and I did." Please don't ask for details, she silently pleaded.

She looked around the room and frowned. "No pictures?" Renata asked accusingly. "Are you just pretending to be married?"

Lord, give me strength. "No pictures, just a simple, private ceremony."

Renata scoffed. "Now I suppose you're going to tell me he doesn't believe in God either?"

Maggie shook her head slowly before drawing in a breath. "Let it go, Renata. Weddings are personal."

"And we are her best friends!" She sat back against the old settee and crossed her arms in a huff.

"Look," Emma started, without even knowing what to say. "It was the most beautiful, most intimate exchange ever." Tears welled in her eyes and she brought her hands to her chest just thinking of it. She drew in a steadying breath, suddenly feeling self-conscious.

"Oh, Hon." Maggie reached out to touch her arm.

Emma forced a smile and sat up straight. "He asked me if I wanted a traditional wedding, but what we shared was just so beautiful, so perfect, I didn't need anything more." She cleared her throat and dropped her eyes. "Without my parents, I couldn't bear to have such a wonderful celebration be yet another reminder of my loss." Her voice was barely a whisper.

After a long silence, Renata spoke up, "Forgive me, Emma. I was out of line." She paused again. "Now, could you tell us about this magical experience?"

Maggie moaned and Emma laughed feeling her cheeks flush. Some things just never change. In all honesty, she wouldn't even know how to describe the experience.

"Give it a rest, Renata. You wanted to make sure she was happy, and from what I've seen there's no doubt in my mind about that." Maggie stood and wandered over to the window. Pushing the drapes aside she looked out across the yard. "What I don't get is why you'd live out here in such an isolated area."

Emma shrugged, and shifted to tuck her feet up under her. "I grew up here. It's fun to be in the city with all that goes on, but I get so much more out of life here."

Maggie turned away from the window to face her. "You were an ER nurse, saving lives. How does that compare to milking a cow and growing a few vegetables?"

A slap across the face would not have hurt Emma any less. "I have learned so much about the healing properties of plants and herbs. I see my role in a different way now, and I get to work on a more personal level with the patients I help. They're not just cases or injuries, they're human beings." She didn't feel like talking anymore.

"Where do you think your man ran off to?" Maggie asked.

"Definitely a lost hiker," Emma answered without thinking.

Maggie and Renata exchanged glances. "When did he say that? Turn on the television and see if they're talking about it," Maggie waved towards Emma's old television. "Does that thing even work?"

She shrugged. "I haven't tried turning it on. I think you have to let it warm up before the image appears," Emma said with a frown. "I'm not sure if the antenna is still good."

Maggie and Renata exchanged glances. "Girl, what's come over you?"

Emma was going to say something about a change of pace but Renata burst out laughing. "A man," Renata said. A grin spread across her whole face, as she laughed some more.

Her friends settled back down and refreshed their cups of tea while Emma added another log to the fire. She felt a wave of relief rush through her and knew that Dthau-Mahsz had found the missing hiker, or hikers. She was sure she caught a flash of their faces.

"Are you OK? Did you burn yourself?" Maggie asked.

Emma closed the metal curtain to prevent sparks from flying out of the fireplace and turned to face her friends. She shook her head, forcing a smile. "No, came close, though," she lied. She must have made a sound when she felt the link. She'd have to ask Dthau-Mahsz about it later.

"So there's no way of telling how long your man will be gone?" Maggie asked.

Cup in hand, Emma sat back down and took a soothing sip. She glanced over at the mantle clock. "I don't think they'll stay out much longer. They usually work in shifts." In reality, she had no clue.

Renata leaned closer and swatted her on the knee. "OK, so now you tell me if he's any good."

Emma's face turned bright pink.

"Ooh, I'll take that as a yes," Maggie teased. She waved Emma on. "Come on, girl, you've got to give us something."

"Don't you two have any men in your lives?" Emma retorted. She watched Renata's cheeks flush. "Oh, I saw that! Come on, spill." She pointed to her friend.

* * *

The girls were laughing at one of Maggie's hospital fiasco stories when Emma felt a tingling in the pit of her stomach. Her heart rate quickened with anticipation as she took it to mean Dthau-Mahsz was home. Bo perked up and trotted out of the living room. Sure enough, Grey Wolf, Two-Feathers and Dthau-Mahsz entered in the living room, still wearing their jackets. Emma stood to greet the men. "You must be hungry," she said. "Everything is ready, we just have to serve."

Emma stayed back as the group filed out of the living room, leaving her alone with Dthau-Mahsz. Her heart swelled and she smiled, relieved he was home safe. "Love you," she said. He drew her into a tender embrace and Bo squeezed in between the two of them. Dthau-Mahsz laughed and stroked the rambunctious dog before leading Emma to the kitchen.

Emma sat down and offered thanks for the safe return of everyone involved in today's search, and for the meal they were about to share. She shook her head as Renata barely let the men get a bite of food into them before she bombarded them with questions. "But why would anyone in their right mind go out in this weather in the first place?" Renata asked.

Grey Wolf raised his head to consider the answer while Dthau-Mahsz and Emma exchanged glances. She felt the now familiar tingle in her stomach and accepted the contact Dthau-Mahsz offered. Emma dropped her head and smiled, marveled by the exchange.

"I don't think these boys had any notion about how quickly weather can change out here, or how cold it really gets," Grey Wolf said.

Renata waved him off. "They do not go out in the winter?"

Two-Feathers dropped his head to hide the smirk on his face, busying himself as he reached for more food.

"They drove up from Southern California," the seer continued to explain patiently to Renata. "They wanted to spend their Christmas holidays in the snow, hiking, and sleeping in a quinsy."

"A what?" Renata asked with a frown.

"It's a type of snow shelter," Two-Feathers offered.

Renata muttered something in Italian, shaking her head. "I hope they had on more than their surf shorts."

Everyone laughed. Leave it to Renata to come up with that.

"Who's ready for dessert?" Emma stood and collected the plates. Dthau-Mahsz got up to help her, offering ice cream to go with the warm pudding.

"What is it?" Grey Wolf asked, eyeing the cake in the rectangle pan.

Emma shook her head. "Still don't trust me, do you?" She scooped out a serving and flipped it over on his plate so the warm apples and strawberries were now on top. "Now, did you want ice cream and caramel sauce on top of that?"

* * *

Later that night while lying in bed, Emma snuggled against Dthau-Mahsz's chest and sighed in contentment. "I felt it when you found the boys," she said. "At least, I think I did."

He kissed her head and pulled her a little closer. "I had never used my ability for such an endeavor. Somehow Two-Feathers knew that I could sense the presence of the people around me." He went silent a moment.

"So they are safe because of you?" She said, not quite sure exactly *how* he found them.

"They are safe because of us all. The shelter they had made was buried under last night's snowfall."

She turned over to face him. "How bad are they?"

"They were both suffering from hypothermia, but they should be fine." He traced her lips with his thumb.

"How come I felt it?"

He smiled, and then leaned in to kiss her. "Because we are forever linked. We are joined in a way lost to your people so long ago."

She pushed up on one elbow. "I still find it hard to believe Humans could do that too."

He smiled. "You must remember that we are from the same source."

She laid back down, lost in her thoughts. She was barely aware that he was watching her, and she lifted her gaze to meet the fathomless depths of his amethyst eyes when she realised the awareness had come from the link. "Do you ever hope to go back home?"

He let out a sharp breath, startling her. Hundreds of images flashed through her mind, showing her a life left behind. "There is no way for me to go back." He stared off into space, absently running a hand along her arm.

"But what if there was?"

"Then I would have to go." He trailed kisses down her neck, distracting her from his revelation. She wanted to pursue the comment, but the link flared and every nerve ending came to life as they changed modes of communication.

* * *

Feeling lightheaded, Emma rose early and headed down to the kitchen to make some tea. She had slept on and off all week, replaying what Dthau-Mahsz had said about having to go back if they found him. Where did that leave her? Was she expected to let him go and simply forget about him, or would she be expected to leave her life behind? The thought of either turned her stomach. She wanted things to stay the way they were, now that they were good.

Her friends had left last night and she'd hoped to finally get a good night's rest, but it hadn't happened, and now the lack of sleep had finally caught up with her. "You are still unable to sleep?" Dthau-Mahsz asked her from the doorframe. His eyes looked her over carefully.

There was no point in trying to hide it. "I even tried drinking Two-Feathers' brew," she confessed.

He held out a hand for her, and when she took it he led her back up into their room. He pulled down the sheets of the freshly made bed and scooped her into his arms. Sitting with his back against the headboard he continued to cradle her. "Lean against me and close your eyes," he instructed. The link flared, and she gasped. "Shh, just relax."

A familiar sense of well-being filled her, soothed her, and she realised he'd been doing that for months. She felt her mind still and her body relax. Her breathing levelled out and she slipped away.

Emma awoke feeling relaxed and energized. She dressed in her jeans and wool sweater and headed downstairs to look for her husband. Stepping into the kitchen she found Dthau-Mahsz, Grey Wolf and Two-Feathers sitting around the table in silence. She frowned. "Is everything OK?" she asked. She moved to sit next to Dthau-Mahsz and brought her attention to the link, to try and see if she could sense what was going on.

Dthau-Mahsz reached out and gave her hand a squeeze. "They want me to be part of the search and rescue team for the area," he explained.

"Really? Well that's good, isn't it?" She looked from one face to another. "Why do you all look so miserable, then?"

"Because he turned us down," Grey Wolf said sharply.

Emma nodded slowly. "Well maybe he needs some time to think about it."

"That sounds like a good idea," Two-Feathers said. He stood and motioned for Grey Wolf to follow. He turned his attention back to Dthau-Mahsz. "All I ask is that you give it some consideration."

Emma watched them leave, and leaned her head on Dthau-Mahsz's shoulder. "Is there a reason you would not want to do this?" She was curious as to why he had turned them down.

He kissed the top of her head and wrapped an arm around her shoulders. "You appear to be much better."

She nodded. "I feel great, actually. I don't suppose you'd feel like taking the horses for a ride?"

He nodded and stood, but frowned when Emma stood as well. "Not until you have eaten something."

She shifted her weight onto one leg, thinking. "I'll grab a slice of banana bread." She turned to face him. "Would you like some?"

Sitting back down with two plates of banana bread and two cups of hot cocoa, Emma studied his tense expression. "Why did you turn them down?"

"There is enough work to keep me busy around here." He sipped the cocoa and made a face. "I hope I have the chance to let you taste our chocolate one day," he said.

Emma ignored the comment. "Would it suit you if it was only part time?"

He frowned. "I do not understand?"

"Well, what if you go out only for S&R missions, and not have to patrol the park on a daily basis or anything."

He scoffed. "How would that be possible? You either do a job, or you do not."

Emma shook her head slowly. "No, you could just go out on rescues." She watched as he visibly relaxed and took a bite of his banana bread.

"And this practice is acceptable?"

She raised her eyebrows and nodded. "Yes."

"Then I accept." He turned to her and smiled. No trace of tension remained. She was even more curious to learn about his world, especially if the concept of part-time didn't exist. She wondered about the structure that governed work. After all, he'd said that he'd have to go back if ever they found him.

She cleared the plates and handed her last morsel to the waiting Bo. His wolf eyes hadn't left her the whole time she'd been eating. Emma turned to her husband with a smile. "Our horses a-wait."

* * *

"Welcome back!" William called out from down the hall. He hurried over to give her a hug. "Thanks for coming in on such short notice. Sadie really wasn't feeling well this morning."

"I don't mind," she said as she moved to the locker room to hang up her coat. "I've missed working here."

"We have a pretty normal day ahead of us," he said as he shrugged into his lab coat.

Emma paused and looked at him. "Didn't anyone ever tell you to *never* say things like that?"

He paused and frowned. "I'm not sure I understand."

She pursed her lips. "Hmm, we'll talk about it again at the end of the day."

William laughed. "I never took you to be superstitious."

She shook her head and walked out of the locker room, making her way to check the patient list. She smiled, glad to be back. Too bad Sadie hadn't taken more time off. She walked into the waiting room and called the first patient in, nodding at Rosie, the receptionist.

A young mother, carrying a red-cheeked infant followed Emma to exam room two.

* * *

By lunch time William began to tease Emma outright, since their morning had been slow and uneventful. "So, are you going to tell me when we should expect this mad rush?"

Emma raised an eyebrow. "You're only going to make it worse." She spooned a mouthful of vegetarian chili into her mouth.

He chuckled. "Well, I guess we'll just have to wait and see."

Rosie charged into the lunchroom holding a paper. "S&R just called in. They have two small boys that went down the rapids. One had to be resuscitated on site, the other suffered multiple scrapes and contusions. They splinted a leg." She brushed a lock of dark hair from her eyes. "ETA is a little over ten minutes."

"Don't say it," William said to Emma and hurried out toward the trauma room. "How old are they?" he asked Rosie.

She handed him a paper. "This is all I have."

William studied the information and handed it to Emma. "We'll take them both in here. Get the room ready, I'm going to talk to them." He followed Rosie out of the room and Emma pulled out the trauma kit.

Minutes later the door pushed open and Dthau-Mahsz came in, cradling a small boy of about four or five. He was murmuring softly to the shaking child, who held tightly to his rescuer. Emma pointed to the exam table and Dthau-Mahsz eased his charge down, keeping a hand on the small chest. With his other hand, he caressed the boy's cheek, still speaking softly to him. Emma watched as the boy relaxed and she began her initial evaluation, exchanging a brief glance with Dthau-Mahsz. William tended to the older, unconscious child.

When the medevac lifted off with the boys, Rosie stepped out to wave William back in. Emma and Dthau-Mahsz followed close behind, hearing the screams from inside. "We tried calming her down, but the poor thing is hysterical." Rosie said.

Without a word, Dthau-Mahsz moved closer to the child and laid a hand on the small of her back. She fought her mother wildly, trying to free herself from the woman's grasp. Dthau-Mahsz said something to the woman and transferred the girl to his arms. Speaking softly, the girl stopped fighting and began to listen. He followed William to the exam room and Emma came in behind them, leaving the mother with Rosie, to fill out forms.

Surprised to see Dthau-Mahsz sitting on the exam table, holding the brown haired girl in his arms, Emma watched as the girl nodded and slowly held out her arm for William to examine. "Get me the bandage scissors," he asked Emma. He had to remove a makeshift layer of blood-soaked gauze.

She nodded and pulled out the suture tray, wheeling it to William's side. Rosie let the mother into the room and settled her in a chair across from the exam table, and then handed Emma the girl's, Clara's, file.

"No allergies," Emma said to William, who nodded.

"You don't have to look," Dthau-Mahsz said to Clara as William froze the arm and prepared to suture the wound. The little girl nodded and hid her head in her protector's chest. Emma couldn't describe the mix of emotions at seeing her husband handle the children today. He would make a good father.

CHAPTER 15: FAMILY

The door opened and Dthau-Mahsz entered with a gust of cold air on his heels. You wouldn't know it was spring. Emma rushed to greet him, thrilled to have him home, especially since this rescue had kept him away for three days. He dropped his equipment bag and gathered her into an embrace. "I missed you," she said, a little more emotional than necessary.

He held her before pulling back to get a look at her face. "Are you OK?" Concern filled his voice as he opened the link to steady her.

She nodded, and moved back into his arms. "I just needed to know you were safe."

He released her with a kiss, and picked up his equipment bag. "Let me store my gear and have a shower. We can talk then."

"Are you hungry? I can prepare something while you shower." She covered her mouth as a yawn escaped.

He nodded gratefully. "All the others went out to eat, but I wanted to come home to you." He flashed her a grin, then set about putting away his stuff.

The food had been laid out and as soon as Dthau-Mahsz came down from his shower, they'd eat. She hadn't factored in the two hour drive back from the rescue site, and could barely keep her eyes open as she waited at the table. It was late and she'd already been in bed, but once she sensed the rescue over, she knew he'd be on his way home.

A headache threatened to take hold and she slouched a little in her chair. Controlling her breathing wasn't helping, and at this point she wasn't even sure she was hungry. She hadn't eaten much of anything while Dthau-Mahsz had been away, and she understood her mother now when she'd said that cooking for one was no fun. She hadn't noticed it before.

Fatigue prevented Emma from engaging in conversation. "I'm sorry," she said. "You're the one who's been out in the wilderness for three days, and I'm the one falling asleep." She managed half a smile.

"You should go on up to bed," Dthau-Mahsz suggested. "I will be there shortly." He held her gaze as she nodded. Exhausted, she pushed away from the table, deposited her plate in the sink and headed up to her room. She wasn't aware of when he'd finally joined her.

Emma massaged her temples, trying to ease the throbbing in her head that had woken her. She probably needed to drink more water or something. Sighing, she made her way to the kitchen in the dark, rubbing sleep from her eyes. They had barely been in bed for two hours, and now the pain was too bad for her to even try to get back to sleep.

She looked through her cupboards for some kind of soothing tea, but everything turned her stomach. She hoped this wasn't going to turn into a migraine. When the kettle boiled she poured the steaming water into her cup and froze when she caught sight of the fridge calendar. Leaning in closer she started counting backwards. Her heart beat wildly when she realised she was over two weeks late.

Her hands trembled as she grabbed a blanket from the mudroom. She needed a bit of air. She had never, ever been late before. Part of her felt giddy, and excited at the possibility, but she didn't know how Dthau-Mahsz would feel about her news. He was always gentle around kids, and they seemed to be drawn to him, but they had never discussed having any of their own.

Emma sat outside on the old wooden bench beside the door, tucked her feet under her and wrapped the blanket tightly around her body. She began listing signs and symptoms of pregnancy, checking them off in her mind. She'd have to get a pregnancy test this week to be sure, but there didn't seem to be any doubt left. She pulled the cover tighter around her shoulders and smiled inwardly at the idea of being pregnant.

She heard to front door open and stiffened. Dthau-Mahsz stepped quietly onto the front porch as the first golden rays of daylight appeared over the mountains. She watched as he admired the sunrise, and then looked up at him with a smile, catching him shiver in the cool spring air. "Come sit," she said, opening her blanket to invite him in.

"You look tired today." He examined her closely as he sat down next to her. "Are you sure you are feeling all right?" He brushed a lock of hair from her face. "Why are you up so early?"

She shrugged and leaned her head on his shoulder. He slid an arm around her, pulling her in close, and the link intensified. She sought comfort in it. "I couldn't sleep," she said, letting out a small sigh. "Headache."

"Is there something bothering you?"

She shook her head. "No, it just happens sometimes."

Emma felt him probe through the link. She felt him come to the conclusion that something was off. He took the time to examine the situation more closely, making her smile. "How long have you been feeling this way?" He probed deeper.

"Hey, stop that!" She resisted his scrutiny, pulling back hesitantly before finally opening to him, so he could explore the link. She hadn't known how to tell him, and she honestly had no idea of what his reaction might be, but it wasn't something she wanted to keep from him.

He laughed out loud when he found her secret. "You carry my child," he said through the link and he let his happiness flow freely. He kissed the top of her head.

"You're happy?" she asked, unable to hide the relief in her voice.

"I am more than happy. Thank you so much for this." He lifted her onto his lap and surrounded her with his love.

They laughed and cried together, hugging and kissing. "I love you," he whispered.

"*I know*," she answered back through the link.

She breathed a sigh of relief. "We had never discussed having children," she said, still wrapped in his arms. When he pulled back abruptly, she looked up at him. "What did I say?"

"Am I to understand that here, on Earth, you discuss having children?" He was not able to hide the disbelief in his tone.

"Well, yes. I don't understand your reaction." She leaned heavily on him, feeling fatigued again.

"Your planet has one of the highest rates of abandoned children." Emma could sense his irritation and distaste.

"How do you do it on your planet?" She wasn't sure he'd answer, since the only information she'd been privy to about his home had come through the link. She had never validated what she'd seen, either.

"I told you we choose a mate for life. There is no divorce or separation, and when one of the two dies, there is no replacement." He paused.

She frowned, wondering if he thought that explained everything. "OK, I get the part about being married, but we were talking about having children."

He shifted, and Emma wondered if he was becoming annoyed. "We bond to have children. The responsibility of raising a child is not taken lightly."

"Oh, so you had presumed we would have children." She thought about it a little. "I'll buy a test in town this week so we can be sure."

He hugged her tightly and brought her hand to his mouth for a kiss. "I can assure you that our son is fine."

She laughed. "Oh, and you have already assumed it will be a boy?"

He took her hand and placed it over her abdomen. "His soul is already there, within you. Feel it." The link expanded and Emma's heart filled with wonder. She could feel a spark of energy, of life within.

"But how could that be? He's so small...how could I sense him so clearly?" She marvelled at the spark she unmistakeably felt. A surge of protectiveness ran through her and she brought her free hand to cover the hands already on her abdomen. "That's our baby," she whispered.

Dthau-Mahsz removed his hand and stroked her cheek before dropping his head to kiss her. She felt the excitement and joy the prospect of being a father brought him and tears welled in her eyes. She was truly happy.

* * *

Although she had felt the tiny spark of life within, Emma had picked up a pregnancy test just the same. She didn't have to wait the designated minutes before both lines appeared to confirm that she was going to have a baby. Tossing the box into the garbage, she went to the kitchen phone and called Maggie to share the good news. She could hear Renata screaming in the background and she smiled to herself. She would have loved to tell them about feeling the baby through the link, and knowing it was a boy, or in her case, hoping.

Dthau-Mahsz came in from the barn with Bo at his heels and smiled at her. She quickly hung up the phone and rose to greet him. "Feeling better this morning?" he asked. He'd been letting her sleep in every morning since they'd found out.

She nodded. As a grin spread from ear to ear, she held out the pregnancy test. There were no more doubts in her mind and she was ecstatic.

He raised an eyebrow and he held her gaze. "This is more convincing than what you felt?"

"I needed to see it." She didn't feel the need to justify herself. She was going to be a mom.

"Would you like to go for a walk? The weather is beautiful this morning." He held out a spring jacket. Bo perked up at the word *walk* and began prancing about.

Hand in hand, they strolled in silence, each one lost in thought. "I want you to tell me more about your home," Emma said. She tossed Bo's ball and he scrambled after it.

He stiffened slightly, but kept on walking. "We had discussed that," he said softly.

"I know, but you are a part of my life." She paused and let her hand cover her abdomen. "A part of our lives, and I would like to know more about you." When he didn't answer she felt a pang of sadness that a portion of his life would never be known to her. She sighed. "I'm not asking about the technological wonders of your world, just you..." her voice trailed off. She'd only seen glimpses of his life through the link, but nothing to answer her questions or satisfy her curiosity. Her stomach tightened at the thought of him having to leave if he was found and she pushed it away. One worry at a time...

* * *

Emma rinsed the facecloth under cold water and placed it at the back of her neck. For the third day in a row, she'd struggled against the heat and humidity brought on by the mid-July heat wave. Leaning over the kitchen sink she let her mind go blank as the excess water dripped down, cooling her. A strange sensation in her lower abdomen caught her attention. Could it be? It wasn't the flutter her pregnancy book had described at all. It felt as though someone had dropped a marble deep inside of her. Her eyes grew in wonder as she felt it again.

Bubbling over with joy, she headed outside to find Dthau-Mahsz. He'd been fixing the waterline to the trough so the animals had fresh water, and she'd expected to find him out behind the barn. He scooped her into his arms and held her tight before she'd managed to make it down the porch steps. "I felt your reaction," he said, surrounding her with his happiness. "I am looking forward to being able to feel the baby move as well."

"He's really there, isn't he?" she said more to herself than to him.

Dropping to one knee he cradled her tiny baby bump, leaned in to kiss it and then rested his forehead on her abdomen a moment.

Emma passed her fingers through his golden brown hair, living totally in the joy of the moment.

That night, she lay snuggled close to him as he stroked her abdomen. "Do you think he's all right?" she asked.

He stopped moving and searched her face. "Did you sense that something was off?" She felt his concern as the link expanded and he started to probe and evaluate her condition.

She laughed, touched by his concern. "No, I don't think anything is wrong, but I can't help but worry a bit.

"When is the midwife going to come by?" he asked.

She sighed and caught her lower lip in her teeth, not sure how he'd react. "I haven't called for an appointment. I, I'm still not sure about it."

"Would you feel more comfortable if William was to follow you?"

Since the baby was technically half-alien, she couldn't help but wonder if anything would show up on routine tests and feared what might become of her child. This was her baby, and she couldn't bear to take the risk of him becoming some sort of lab rat or having him taken away. "No, I don't know. I need to think about it some more."

"Nothing will happen to our child," he said. She felt reassurance flow and surround her, but she couldn't shake off the 'what-if'.

"Would you be able to sense if he was in trouble?" She hoped he had yet another special ability.

He kissed her forehead. "I would know if he was in distress, but I am quite certain you would know before me."

She thought back to her rotation in obstetrics and she remembered one mom that had come in saying something was wrong. Without taking her too seriously, they had done a quick exam and determined that nothing was wrong. It was only with her persistence that they discovered the baby was not only small for her gestational age, but the cord had begun to atrophy; a condition that would have been fatal to the baby had the mother not held her ground. This reassured Emma, but there were always exceptions.

"Close your eyes," Dthau-Mahsz whispered. The link expanded and she became acutely aware of Dthau-Mahsz at her side, then he directed her attention to a tiny, yet unmistakable presence within her. The life force that emanated from her belly was distinct, and it throbbed with an energy she couldn't deny. "That is our baby. He is strong and healthy, so try not to worry."

A surge of emotion overtook Emma and the tears started to flow. She sobbed openly as Dthau-Mahsz comforted her. "I'm sorry." She swiped at her tears and rolled over for a tissue.

He pulled her back down and held her tenderly, soothing her until she fell asleep in his arms.

CHAPTER 16: *And Baby Makes Three*

"You want me to get your mounting block?" Two-Feathers teased as Emma struggled to get out of the Jeep. He had come by to drop off some feed for the animals.

"I told you to wait," Dthau-Mahsz said as he reached around her belly and eased her out of the Jeep and onto her feet. He held her elbow and tried to help her up the stairs, but she swatted him away.

Both men followed her inside, carrying the grocery bags. She sat down on a chair with her feet apart and struggled to get her boots off, shooting Dthau-Mahsz a warning look as he approached to help her. With a grunt she freed herself from the last boot, and used the arms on the chair to push herself back up onto her feet. She rubbed her rather large belly and smiled awkwardly at it. "Mommy's not sure she's going to last another three or four weeks."

"Neither am I," Two-Feathers said, giving her a once over.

Emma waddled into the kitchen and made her way to the fridge for some fresh juice.

"You think he's dropped into position as well," Dthau-Mahsz said to the shaman. He brought three glasses out of the cupboard and set a plate of muffins on the table.

Two-Feathers nodded. "I would say no more than another twenty-four to forty-eight hours." He pulled out a chair and sat down at the table.

Dthau-Mahsz followed suit and passed around plates and glasses. "That's what I was feeling as well."

Emma put the pitcher of juice down hard on the table. "Should I lie down on the table so the two of you can give me your professional opinion?"

Two-Feathers nodded to Dthau-Mahsz. "That's another sign." He filled all the juice glasses and reached for a muffin.

"It started this morning. I caught her cleaning out the hall closet." He winked at Emma.

"I'll let Morning Star know, she'll probably show up later on tonight." He took a bite of his muffin and looked at Emma with a grin. "Pumpkin, my favorite."

"OK, that's enough, you two. No one's going to call anyone. I still have a few weeks left and –" Emma started.

"And you're not going to make it," Dthau-Mahsz finished. "Sit." He encouraged her, seemingly oblivious to her foul mood.

She shook her head and downed her glass of juice. "There are too many things to finish in the baby's room."

Dthau-Mahsz turned to face her, his eyebrows coming down in a frown. "He will not need his room for quite a while, so there is no rush."

Two-Feather's looked up. "I thought you had already finished the room?"

"Details and finishing touches are apparently still missing," Dthau-Mahsz said not too loud, then turned and smiled back at Emma. He handed Bo a piece of muffin.

She huffed and waddled out of the kitchen but paused when she heard Two-Feathers on the phone. Emma poked her head back into the kitchen as he spoke to the midwife a few minutes, then laughed softly before he hung up. "She doesn't mind coming up, even if it is a false alarm." He sat back down at the table and picked up his muffin. "But she doesn't think it is, either."

Emma rolled her eyes then made her way upstairs to the baby's room. She remembered how shocked Dthau-Mahsz had been when she said the baby would have his own room. There was still so much she would like to know about his world, to help understand his reactions to hers, but she couldn't force it out of him if he wasn't willing to share. He seemed able to control his side of the link and rarely let slip any information from his previous life. It still upset her, so she pushed the whole thing from her mind and entered the nursery.

They had chosen a blue and white Cape Cod theme, with little sail boats and seashell decorations. The room was fresh and crisp, more beautiful than she'd hoped for. She moved to her grandmother's wooden rocker in the corner of the room and sat down. Taking the stuffed, St. Bernard rescue dog into her arms, she hugged it tight and wondered what it would be like to hold her tiny baby in her arms. The baby shifted and kicked, drawing her hand instinctively to her belly.

She let her head loll back against the top of the chair and tried to imagine what her little man would look like. "Are you going to have Mommy's blue eyes, or Daddy's amethyst ones?" She spoke softly to her belly.

A sound from the doorway drew her gaze, and she smiled as her husband stepped in to join her. He moved close to her and lowered himself to one knee. "There has never been a child with amethyst eyes, born of a parent with amethyst eyes to this day." He passed his hand gingerly across her belly.

"I know I have been a little impatient lately," Emma said with a sigh. "And that I can barely get around or do my own thing because of this big ball, but I'm going to miss it." She smiled when he kissed her belly and leaned his cheek gingerly on it. "I'm going to miss times like this too." She passed her hands through his soft, wavy hair.

He pulled back abruptly and placed both hands on her abdomen. "You are having contractions."

"Just Braxton Hicks," she said, "nothing real yet." She closed her eyes and let him complete his assessment of her contraction. Sometimes she wished he could really feel what she felt. It was a shame to be kept on the other side, looking in, without ever truly knowing how it felt to carry a child.

"You are having contractions," he repeated.

She smiled and sat up to look at him. "Yes, but they are just false con –" she brought her hand abruptly to her abdomen as her breath caught. This one was a little more potent than the others. She let out a breath as it passed. "Don't worry about it, it's normal to have contractions this far along."

He stood and leaned in to kiss her. "I will make sure everything is ready, just in case."

"Is the midwife really coming over?" Her mind began to run in all sorts of directions. She'd need to wash and shave her legs. She should probably change the sheets on the bed too. She looked up to catch a slight frown on Dthau-Mahsz's face. "What's wrong?"

"You do not have to change the sheets. If you want a bath, then I will assist you in and out of the tub, otherwise, just relax." He looked around the room quickly and reached for a book from the shelf. "Read this. The midwife has been called to attend a birth. She said she'd be out to check on you afterwards."

A wave of relief passed through Emma. She was in no rush to see her, no matter how kind and gentle she'd seemed. She'd spent most of the pregnancy fending off William as well. She flipped the small book over in her hand. "Where did this come from?"

"I made it for you, and for the baby. You can tell him about your wait for his arrival, share your thoughts." He watched as she opened the book and started flipping through the pages.

Tears filled her eyes when she found the passage he'd written to her, about how happy he was with her in his life. She laughed and brushed away her tears brought on by his letter to the baby. He wrote about when he'd first found out about the baby, about how elated the news had made him. She drew in a breath through clenched teeth and shifted her position. Closing her eyes, she rubbed her belly and tried to ease the discomfort.

When she let out her breath, she felt his hand cup her cheek. Opening her eyes, she met his gaze and gave a wary smile. "OK, so maybe these are contractions."

He nodded. "Would you like to try and relax in the tub?" He waited as she thought it over.

"Yes, I think that would be a good idea. If they are Braxton Hicks, they should stop." She smiled nervously.

He reached for her hands and helped her to her feet, then drew her into a reassuring embrace. "Do not be nervous. I am right here with you."

She let out a sharp breath. "Would you care to do the actual 'squeezing a human being out of your body' for me?"

He laughed softly and kissed the top of her head. "I love you, and if I could, I would."

She nodded. "I know you would." She pointed towards the door. "Bath time."

* * *

Leaning back in the tub Emma rubbed her belly and shifted uncomfortably as another contraction hit. She focused on her breathing and tried to keep her body relaxed. She needed to get out of the tub and walk around a bit. "Ah!" she cried out. She forced herself to breathe. There were no comfortable positions in the water anymore, and she had to get out of the tub, now.

Dthau-Mahsz appeared at her side and wiped her forehead with a washcloth. She kept her eyes squeezed shut through the contraction, forcing herself to breathe. As soon as it was over she looked up at him. "Get me out of here!" she said abruptly.

Sliding his hands under her arms, he lifted her to her feet and held her steady as she stepped out of the tub. Keeping her stable, he reached for her terrycloth robe and draped it over her.

She shrugged it off. "I can't wear it like that."

He obligingly removed it from her shoulders and allowed her to slip her arms through the sleeves. Still holding on to her, he slowly escorted her back to the bedroom. She sat on the bed in somewhat of a daze as she finally accepted that she was in labor. "I can't do this," she whispered.

"Yes, you can," he said softly, reassuringly. He eased the damp robe off her and helped her into a loose-fitting nightshirt. "Did you want to come back downstairs?"

"No," she said hesitantly. "Yes."

He raised an eyebrow but reached for some warm socks. "Put these on, the floor is cold downstairs."

"Did you make a fire?"

He nodded and helped her up. They made it half-way down the stairs when the next contraction hit. Dthau-Mahsz made a move to pick her up but she stopped him with a glare. "Don't touch me," she snapped.

He moved back a step and waited, arms at his side, ready to intervene.

When the contraction passed, she grabbed for his arm and continued down the steps. "I'm sorry," she said. A fire crackled in the hearth, making the living room warm and cozy. Emma smiled at his thoughtfulness and made her way around to look out the window. She was nervous, not knowing what lay ahead of her. Back at the hospital she'd seen many different outcomes, both good and bad. There was no going back now.

* * *

Emma leaned heavily against Dthau-Mahsz as he held her gently and rocked through the contraction. "You're doing fine," he said. His voice was soft, reassuring.

"I brought you some pieces of fruit," Two-Feathers said as he came in to the living room.

"Any news?" Dthau-Mahsz asked.

"I called back and spoke to one of the assistants. The other woman hasn't delivered yet, but they don't think it'll be too much longer," the shaman answered. "Did you want me to call William? He offered again last week."

"No," Emma answered with a grunt. "He's too far away and I don't want to trouble him."

Two-Feathers paused before turning away. "I'll be in the kitchen if you need anything."

Emma felt Dthau-Mahsz nod. She was starting to feel tired and anxious. "It's getting a little too hard for me to handle," she said against his chest.

He kissed the top of her head. "One contraction at a time." His hands kneaded her lower back in a soothing manner.

"Ah!" She leaned forward and grabbed her lower abdomen. "I have to push!" She looked up at Dthau-Mahsz for guidance as Two-Feathers came rushing back into the living room and laid some towels down at her feet. "What, here?"

"Did you want to go somewhere else?" Dthau-Mahsz asked softly.

"Yes!" She pointed to the guest room but gasped as she found herself unable to take a step. A gush of warm water poured out at her feet and the overwhelming urge to push gripped her again. This time, she couldn't hold back.

* * *

Propped up against the headboard of her bed, Emma reached up to Dthau-Mahsz, wanting her baby back. He sat on the edge of the bed and held their son out to her, watching as the baby latched on to drink. "Thank you," he said to her, running the back of his fingers across her cheek.

She raised her eyes slowly from her baby to meet her husband's gaze. "He's so beautiful." She had never realised the strength of the maternal bond. How protective of her little boy she had already become.

"I know you thought we still had a few weeks to choose a name," he said, "but I think we are going to have to settle on one now." He reached out and uncurled a tiny hand, stroking the delicate fingers.

I never expected him to have so much hair," Emma said, caressing the fine black hair. "He looks like he has a tan." She couldn't stop staring at him, touching him and marveling in the wonder that he was. This was her baby, their baby, and he needed a name.

"Do you want me to get the list we made, or the name book?" he asked.

"No. I think we should name him after his father." She lifted the baby and transferred him to the other breast.

"My name?"

She grinned. "Well, I was thinking we could name him Thomas, and call him Tommy." Since her husband didn't have a last name, this would be a way to give his name to their son.

He wrinkled his brow. "Then why not just call him Tommy?"

"Just a wild guess, but you don't have diminutives or nicknames, do you?"

He shook his head. "We have one name."

And that was supposed to be self-explanatory? "But what if there are two of you with the same name, then how do you know who is who?" She removed the baby from her breast and handed him over to the waiting daddy. His easy handling of the baby warmed her heart.

With his son nestled on his shoulder, he gently rubbed the tiny back until a little burp was heard. "Then the father's name is stated for identification purposes." The baby stretched and yawned as Dthau-Mahsz cradled him in his hands. Emma watched as her husband stared at their son, a look of wonder on his face. He handed the burped baby back to Emma and stood, leaning down to kiss her. "I will install the baby's cradle next to you, and then I think we should all get some sleep."

CHAPTER 17: RESCUED

Time passed quickly for the small family and life brought Emma a sense of bliss she didn't think possible. When she would work part time with William, Dthau-Mahsz watched over Tommy, and she was home when Dthau-Mahsz left on S&R operations. Their home life had become harmonious as they worked together and completed one another.

Tommy would soon be two-and-a-half, and Emma could hardly believe it as she watched the sturdy toddler play with his dump trucks in the sand. It felt strange to have neither animals nor chores for a whole week, but Emma had jumped at the chance to be alone with her two men. At first she hesitated about leaving Bo behind, but Two-Feathers had assured her he'd be fine.

The cabin they were staying in belonged to a park ranger, and he had graciously offered its use as a thank you to Dthau-Mahsz for having rescued him from the edge of a cliff, after a bear attack. The change of pace was nice.

A sense of caution through the link brought Emma's attention to her husband. She watched as Dthau-Mahsz became instantly alert. His eyes darted around the area where they were camping, scanning the trees and river edge in such a way that Emma felt the hair at the back of her neck prickle. "*Inside, quickly!*" he ordered through the link. She took Tommy by the hand and led him up the steps and inside the log cabin, a knot forming in the pit of her stomach. To her surprise, the link dimmed down to nothing, leaving only the faint knowledge that her husband was still there.

Tommy protested being brought inside and away from the trucks he'd been playing with so Emma opened the bottom pantry door, giving the toddler access to the pots and pans. With a squeal of delight he waddled over to explore the contents of the cabinet. Through the kitchen window she saw three men step out of the trees and approach her husband. There was something strange about them, something she couldn't quite put a finger on...until her mind registered the clothes they wore. Her stomach knotted as she recognized the same type of flight suit that Dthau-Mahsz had been wearing when she'd found him.

Stiff and formal, the men showed no signs of familiarity as they spoke to her husband, yet her chest constricted, making breathing difficult as she accepted the fact that they were not from Earth.

She grabbed for a chair and sat down, her legs shaking so bad she could barely stand. He'd once told her that he'd have to go back if ever they found him, and she wasn't sure what that meant for her or their son. The door opened and Dthau-Mahsz entered, his expression unreadable. "We need to talk."

Immediately on her feet she blinked back tears with a nod.

Tommy stopped banging pot lids together and his face lit up when he caught sight of his father. "Daddy!"

"Where'd they go?" Emma asked with a tremor in her voice. She had expected them to come in.

"They have returned to their ship." He pressed his lips together, his face pale.

"Are you leaving?" she whispered.

He let out a sharp breath and gestured for her to sit. Tommy waddled over to his father, holding out his pot covers and Dthau-Mahsz scooped his son up into his arms. "We have things to discuss." He settled himself on the edge of the couch and spoke softly to his son a moment before setting the toddler back onto his feet. Tommy gave his father a toothy grin and made his way back to the cupboard.

"Are you leaving?" she asked again. Her mouth had suddenly gone dry and she could barely breathe through the tightness of her chest.

The link swelled, slowly easing the tension in Emma's body, soothing her and joining the two. She understood that he had no choice but to leave. Dizziness swirled about and she let herself slip, unable to resist its pull.

Images of Dthau-Mahsz's world, life and duty flew past at an alarming speed. She resisted his sense of duty, claiming they came first. That was where his responsibility was supposed to be...

All around her she saw the faces of those who had been saved by Dthau-Mahsz's ship and crew and she felt his pain when people were lost. Anger pushed up from within. "I don't want to understand," she heard herself say.

Then come with me, he said through the link.

A sob wracked her chest and the images faded. She was in his arms, and she had no idea of how she got there. She let herself cry openly, feeling helpless. "I don't want you to go," she blurted out.

"Then come with me."

She stiffened and looked into his eyes, searching them. "You're serious."

"I cannot force you to come. I do not want you to stay behind, but I cannot remain here much longer." His voice was without emotion, but the link betrayed his outer calm. Emma could sense a mixture of emotions just under the surface. He was heartbroken at the thought of leaving his family behind. He was afraid she would not adapt well to his world, and that he would lose his family either way.

"I don't understand why someone else can't do the job, it's just a job." Her tone rose sharply at the end and she started shaking. "You can't replace family!"

They sat there in silence as he held her. The only sound was that of Tommy sifting through the pots and banging the covers together.

"When do you have to leave?" She wasn't sure if she spoke the question out loud or not.

"The scout ship will first complete their evaluation before returning to the Osiris." He hesitated, presumably wrestling with his guarded life.

"Is the Osiris your ship?" Would he answer now? Were they finally going to discuss his other life?

"No, my ship is the Phoenix." He leaned his head against the back of the sofa and let out a slow breath.

"Please talk to me," she said. Her chest tightened at the thought of losing him.

He kissed the top of her head and held her tightly. "In our society, position is determined by a series of evaluations." He paused a moment. "I do not even know how to begin to explain..."

"Show me, the way you showed me pictures through the link. Please." She watched as his expression changed and he finally nodded.

"Close your eyes, and do not be afraid, these are but images." He cradled her as she eased back into the comfort of his arms, of the link. She found herself in a blank room and jumped back in surprise when she saw the scene of an accident form. People cried out for help with her in the midst of it all, barking out orders while she offered assistance. Rapid decisions and physical interventions had her mind swirling. Breathing heavily, everything faded away and the log cabin reappeared.

"What was that?" Fist curled over her chest, she struggled to regain control of her breathing.

He stroked her cheek with the back of his hand. "It was a scene from my initial evaluation. Essentially, there are images at first, and they transform into situations that change according to your response." He passed a hand through his hair. "It measures intelligence, reflexes, physical condition, decision making abilities, creative skills, problem solving and so many other aspects, until the person's place is clearly identified." He took her hand in his and unrolled her fingers. "Relax." He kissed her fingers.

"Wow, we fill out a whole bunch of questions from a guidance counsellor and according to our answers they narrow our field of study." She leaned heavily into him. "How long does the exercise last?"

"The initial evaluation is five hours long." The baby toddled over, smiling and Dthau-Mahsz reached down and pulled Tommy up onto them, tickling him until giggles erupted.

"And then what happens?" She caught her son as he pushed himself off the sofa, steadying him so he landed on his feet.

"Specific training begins so we can prepare for our place."

She waited for him to add more info to his comment. She didn't get it, too many pieces were missing. She sighed. "Do you go off to school after that? Do you have universities or training academies?"

Hesitantly, he shook his head. "No. Specific training is done wherever the student is. The program is individually tailored to meet both the student's specifications and their future role in our society." He let out a breath, betraying the calm of the link.

Emma had a hard time imagining a teacher preparing individual lessons for every student. How could a proper evaluation and control of the student's progress be maintained?

A soft chuckle escaped Dthau-Mahsz and he kissed the side of her head. "You are thinking in terms of your own experience within your system. There is one teacher for every twenty or so students, each one progresses within a group receiving the same instruction until age fifteen. Between fifteen and eighteen, and still in a group setting, a more narrow teaching with personalized elements to prepare the student for specific training is carried out. At eighteen the student begins specific training by being assigned to work in his future domain. A mentor follows each student outside of the training periods so instruction continues." He paused a moment. Gliding his hands along her arms, he took her hands in his.

"Is this a four year program?" She shifted to look at him.

He closed his eyes as a smile spread across his face. She watched as his lids opened and light hit his amethyst eyes, making them glow. "Each person evolves at his own rate, until he or she is ready to assume their place."

"And who pays for all this?" She wondered about student loans or fees to run such an elaborate program.

He stood, lifting her with him before lowering her to the ground. "We do not have or use currency."

She knew by his tone that the discussion was over. And she knew she could not imagine living without him, or raising their son without a father. "What do we do now?" She chewed her lower lip nervously.

"For the next few days, we will stay here at the cabin as planned. When we return home, you will have to make a decision." He moved closer to Tommy and ruffled his son's hair, then dropped down to play with him.

Emma's heart ached. How could she not follow him to the edge of the galaxy? How could she leave her home behind, and what made him think she wouldn't like it? Her emotions tumbled through her, making any coherent thought impossible.

Supper felt strained, each one lost in thought. "I need some air," Emma said.

Dthau-Mahsz nodded. "Let's go for a walk. It will do us all some good." He headed for the closet for the carry rack and strapped it onto his back.

Tommy scrambled over to his father, arms in the air to be picked up. "Up, up." He pointed to the rack.

Emma scooped him up. "Let me put him in his pyjamas, he'll probably fall asleep." She quickly stripped her little man and dressed him in a warm sleeper, ready for their outing. Lifting him up and into the rack she grunted. "He's getting so heavy," she said. If Dthau-Mahsz left, he wouldn't be carrying him in the rack anymore. With a sigh, she pushed the thought out of her mind and grabbed a sweater. "Let's go." At least the fresh air would do her good.

Dthau-Mahsz held out a hand and Emma moved in close as they walked slowly down the hard-packed, earthen path. Emma drew in a breath of fresh mountain air. "I love the smell of the wild blossoms," she said. "There's just something so stimulating, yet somehow soothing about it."

He gave her hand a squeeze and looked over to meet her gaze. "I love how you notice these things, how you take pleasure in them."

She half-expected him to add that he would miss them once he'd left. "Would I be allowed to go with you?"

He stopped walking and frowned at her. "Although our situation is unique, I can assure you that it is what is expected."

"Oh..." her voice trailed off as she thought about living in space. She had no idea what it would be like. Her greatest life changes had been between city living and life in the mountains. She did not have her parents anymore, and there were no other family members to take into consideration. She'd miss Two-Feathers. "Could we come back to visit?"

"I do not think it would be possible, not unless it was duty related."

She had no idea what that meant. "What could I do if I did go with you?" Emma asked meekly.

"You are a nurse, a teacher; you could refresh your training and continue one or the other. Your first duty is to Thomas, which is not a bad thing, since you would have until he entered school to learn." He pointed to a doe that had stepped onto the path and froze at the sound of their voices.

They stood there, watching, while Emma's mind thought about her options. "What if I don't adjust?"

The surge in the link confirmed it as his greatest concern. "Then I will return you here."

"But you won't be able to visit."

"I could not keep such a promise." He started forward as the deer slowly made her way back into the trees.

She let out a breath of frustration. "How can you claim that family is of the utmost importance? The moment they find you, you go running off without any consideration for us." She couldn't hide the anguish in her voice. Her mother had always said that things happen for a reason; she just wished she knew why.

He turned sharply. "I trust that is not what you think of me."

"No, I'm sorry." She laid a hand on his arm and followed, walking in silence. She wasn't one to lash out, but she felt as though her world had been torn apart and nothing would ever be the same, no matter what decisions were made in the end.

She looked up and smiled at the sleeping child on his father's back. Making a quick adjustment to his head she tapped on Dthau-Mahsz's shoulder to let him know she was done. Her heart ached at the thought of losing these moments. This was more than moving to another country, and she had no idea what this country was like. "How did they find you anyway? I mean, they just walked out of the trees."

He stiffened before coming to a halt. "They detected my implant." He made no move to continue on or add to the answer. He just stared at her, waiting for the information to sink in.

She frowned. "Like a tracking device or something?"

He tilted his head in a half nod. "Of sorts."

She felt nauseous. "You have a tracking device implanted somewhere inside your body…" Would she be expected to subject herself or her son to something of the sort?

He reached out to her through the link, offering some comfort, but not forcing himself on her. "I have, in fact, two implants. As do all my people." He turned to face her completely, taking both of her hands in his. "You must wait to learn more about us. Incomplete bits of information cannot form a just image. This is one reason I hesitate to share, especially since you cannot compare it to anything from your experience here."

"Where is this implant?" She couldn't push the thought of it out of her mind.

His eyes searched hers and she wasn't sure he was going to answer. Instead, he reached out and touched the back of her head and slid midway down her neck. "They are here."

She shivered. "Why?" The thought of it unsettled her, talk about control.

He let out a breath, but held her gaze. "The first is the tracking chip. And its sole purpose is so we do not lose one of our own. It is a precautionary measure that has been carried out for hundreds of years."

"Then why not get them a bracelet?"

He smiled understandingly. "A kidnapper could remove it."

"And you have so many kidnappers that this became standard practice?" Did she want to live in such a place?

He shook his head. "No. It came to be so long ago, the practice was maintained since there is no harm to the recipient, and on the few occasions that a child has been lost, it provided rapid retrieval." He cupped her chin. "Just think about all the people that I have helped locate with the search and rescue team. They would have been found within minutes, not hours or days. The same goes for plane crashes, children who wander off or any situation where someone does not come home."

"Well what about soldiers, they'd be like sitting ducks?"

"The frequency is not listed in public information banks. People do not simply have knowledge of one another's location...you are again applying my situation to your world. It would not work the same here."

She didn't know what to think. "You said you had two, what's the other one for?"

"An interface. Children receive it before they start school and use it all through the learning period. Some adults choose to leave it active throughout their lives, while others have it phased out so only the simplest commands are exchanged."

"I don't understand." She moved in closer and he slid his arms around her.

"I know. This is one of the reasons I did not talk about my world." He opened the link and offered her comfort.

Emma drew in a deep breath and accepted the contact. She needed him. They needed him. "But why you...why do you have to go back?"

He kissed the top of her head. "You know why."

Her shoulders slumped and a tear slid down her cheek as she continued to lean into him. She felt defeated. "I want to go home."

He pulled back to look down at her. "You don't want to stay the next three days as planned?"

She shook her head. "And do what, pretend everything is fine? The minute we return home everything will fall apart! I can't." Her body began to tremble and she wasn't sure her legs would carry her back. At that moment she didn't care.

He tightened his hold on her and nodded. "Very well, we will head back tonight."

CHAPTER 18: *Say Goodbye*

They pulled into the driveway in the middle of the night and all was dark except for the porch light. Bo barked frantically from inside the house.

Once out of the Jeep, Emma turned and leaned back against it to look up at the stars. Instead of marveling in the beauty, she felt betrayed. She pulled open the back seat and freed her toddler from the confines of his seat. She wondered if these things were even needed in space.

She pushed past Dthau-Mahsz, who was already heading back to the car for his second load of baby gear, and headed upstairs. Her little man barely stirred as she tucked him snugly under his covers. Tears started to flow and there was nothing she could do to stop them. She turned and slid to the floor, still leaning against the crib. With her face in her hands she sobbed openly now, feeling so helpless in the face of what was yet to come.

Quiet footsteps made their way up the stairs and padded down the hall to her side. Dthau-Mahsz dropped down onto one knee and scooped her up into his arms. She didn't look up at him; she just continued to sob as he made his way back to their bedroom.

She awoke, still in his arms, as the first rays of sunlight spilled into the room. Stiff and sore, she eased out of bed and headed for the shower, hoping the water would help her muscles. Her heart ached, she felt empty, void of all hope and joy.

The warm water streamed across her body, blending with the last of the tears as Dthau-Mahsz stepped into the shower with her and held her close. She turned towards him and kissed him with an uncontrolled passion. She couldn't bear to be without him, even if that meant leaving her world behind.

Sensing her decision, his emotions exploded through the link and he cried with her. "I could not imagine my life without you."

The days leading up to their departure passed in a blur. Two-Feathers had agreed to stay at the house to care for the animals while Emma was gone, and if he had no sign of her by year's end, the house and animals would be his. The paperwork had been drawn up, leaving nothing but the date to add. She had phoned Maggie and Renata, telling them she was going to give life as a military wife a try, and they accepted her story. She'd promised to contact them if possible, but she already knew it would never be.

Emma stood out in the yard, watching Tommy play with Bo and his ball. Tommy would throw the ball and giggle when the dog faithfully brought it back. She was going to miss her dog, her animals and her life in the Rockies. She still had no idea what to expect of a life in space. That had yet to be seen. Curiosity grew at the thought of a new adventure. It intrigued her, but the thought of being confined to a space submarine scared her.

The toddler froze and pointed behind Emma. She turned to look over her shoulder and felt an icy shiver roll down her spine as she saw the two men standing a few feet behind her.

"Mathezar!" Dthau-Mahsz greeted the older of the two men warmly, and Emma was surprised to see the two of them embrace. The younger man stood stiffly off to the side, waiting silently. "Belek," Dthau-Mahsz finally addressed the latter.

Belek nodded curtly, but held his position.

Mathezar wore a two-tone grey jumpsuit. He was not as tall as Dthau-Mahsz, but his stocky build gave him a solid appearance. His hair reminded Emma of the timber wolf, with its black and brown strands mixed together. He was looking over Dthau-Mahsz in a calculated, professional manner. If she had to guess, she'd say he was one of the medical personnel.

The other one, Belek, wore a dark blue jumpsuit similar to the one she'd found Dthau-Mahsz wearing after the crash, but he filled his out with a finely toned body, not unlike a bouncer's. His jet black hair and eyes contrasted his olive complexion nicely, but his stiff mannerism said he wasn't a people person. She guessed he was some kind of security guard.

Tommy waddled over to his father, holding the ball in one hand. Bo danced around hoping to retrieve his ball, but the toddler's attention was on his father. "My son, Thomas," Dthau-Mahsz said proudly to Mathezar.

The older man's face lit up. "My daughter, Jayden, is two."

"So, you did bond with Trenika. I offer my hopes." Dthau-Mahsz held out a hand to Emma, inviting her into their circle. "This is Emma, my wife."

She moved slowly towards the group, not sure how to act. She greeted the men with a nod, and stood to the left of her husband.

"Mathezar is the ship's senior medical officer, as well as a friend from long ago," Dthau-Mahsz explained. Turning to Belek, he pressed his lips together, nipping a grin in the bud. "This is Belek, part of our security detail." The young man obviously took his job seriously.

The doctor dropped down to Tommy's level and Emma saw him stiffen. His eyes shot up to Dthau-Mahsz. "He has amethyst eyes?" The shock in his voice was disquieting.

Emma frowned. "Does it matter?"

Dthau-Mahsz held up a hand and the doctor rose, not saying a word. "No, it is just that they are rare." Emma caught the sharp look he gave the doctor and intended to call him on it later.

"Would you like to come in for some tea?" Emma offered.

The doctor hesitated, but Dthau-Mahsz nodded towards the door. Both men immediately turned and moved towards the entrance, and Emma had to wonder about her husband's role in his world.

Belek stood stiffly by the door; eyes alert. Emma shook her head. What had he expected to be a threat out here? She set the kettle on to boil and pulled out a plate of fresh fruits and the date-nut bread. Out of the corner of her eye she saw that Dthau-Mahsz had settled Tommy in his high chair and was cleaning his hands and face. Reassured that her husband didn't seem embarrassed to perform his fatherly duties in front of his crewmembers, she finished setting the table and relaxed somewhat.

If she was going to go through with her decision, then she'd have to deal with these people on a daily basis. She liked the doctor, and might even enjoy working with him. She poured the tea and settled next to Tommy, discretely listening to the men's conversation. To her dismay, not much of it made sense.

"The Phoenix had been offering support to the Osiris until a new commander could take her," the doctor explained. "However, and still to this day, no other candidates have been identified. The

Nocturne lost an engineering detail during a transfer accident, so they replaced their missing crew with our crewmembers..." his voice trailed off.

Emma felt Dthau-Mahsz react through the link. He wasn't happy about the others pilfering his crew. He was obviously very protective of them, something she could easily imagine, but the intensity of it shocked her.

"Did you come with the Aurora?" Dthau-Mahsz asked.

"No, Commander," Belek answered. Emma was sure his cheeks flushed a little. "The crew was anxious to return to duty, so we decided to leave the Osiris to its functions and headed here as soon as we had received the news." He lifted his eyes to meet the commander's. "Now we can all fulfill our destiny."

Her husband closed his eyes in a slight bow of acknowledgement. What did that mean?

"The Phoenix is in orbit?" Dthau-Mahsz asked for confirmation.

"Yes, Sir." Belek replied.

Lips pressed together, her husband nodded. "Very well. Finish up here and return to the ship. We will prepare our transfer and contact you as soon as we are ready."

Both crewmen stood. Well, then they must be finished, Emma guessed. Either that or they didn't care for tea and cake. Belek pulled a black band from his wrist and handed it to the commander who immediately placed it on his own.

The three men headed outside while Emma tended to Tommy. She was surprised when Dthau-Mahsz came back not a minute later, alone. He sat down beside his family and let out a breath. "Are you ready?" He brushed a lock of her hair from her eyes and took her hands in his.

She shrugged. "I guess I'll have to be." She had no idea what to expect, so how could she be ready? She looked around the room. "What can I bring, or should I bring, for that matter? I haven't been able to make up my mind."

He gave her a half smile. "You do not need to bring anything, except maybe a few mementoes." He held her gaze.

Her brow creased. "Oh, OK then. I guess packing won't take long." She looked around the room. She'd want to bring her recipe book and photo album, the baby's favorite toys and blanket, but aside from that, what was there to bring? She hardly thought bringing her entire library or antique dishes made sense. When she'd returned from the city she hadn't brought anything back with her. It had been her girlfriends who'd dragged her stuff back, after keeping what they'd wanted of it. She wasn't a materialistic kind of person. "You have baby clothes on board? And a bed and high chair?"

He smiled. "Everything you may need, yes." He tilted his head, pondering something. "Though I am not sure you will appreciate our furniture."

"What's that supposed to mean?" What'd they sit on, cardboard boxes? Plastic ones? An image of cube furniture came to mind and Dthau-Mahsz laughed.

"Nothing like that, I assure you." He brought her hand to his lips and kissed her fingers. "All of our seating is individual. They can be pushed together, but there are no couches or settees, as you refer to your grandmother's sofa."

"Could I see it before we go?"

He nodded. "Now?"

Her stomach knotted. "We can go now?"

"If you like." He pulled her to her feet and turned to free the baby from his high chair. Holding the half-asleep toddler against his chest he tapped the black band Belek had given him.

"Commander," a voice filled the room.

"Molecular transport," Dthau-Mahsz said in a tone resembling an order.

Emma didn't have time to say a thing before her kitchen faded away and was replaced by a sterile looking room. Her legs went leaden and Dthau-Mahsz put an arm around her to steady her.

"Welcome home, Commander!" the blonde crewman behind the glass wall exclaimed. They all seemed to have different colored jumpsuits, Emma noted. She wondered if the colors meant anything.

"Sit down, cadet. Do not scare the commander off," the other, older man quipped. A grin spread across the dark features, flashing white teeth. "Good to have you back, Sir."

Dthau-Mahsz nodded. Emma could feel the emotion bubbling up inside of him. He was happy to be back, but she could sense that he was torn as well. At least she knew his time on Earth with her meant something. "We are going to take a quick look around.

We shall be returning to the surface shortly."

"Of course, Sir," the older man said. "Commander, you have been moved to the Senior Staff section," the crewman added nervously.

Dthau-Mahsz frowned.

"Your room wasn't big enough for a family," the cadet blurted out. He cringed when he saw the look the other crewman gave him.

"Thank you," Dthau-Mahsz said. Amusement lit his eyes. "And just where have you put me?"

The door opened and Mathezar entered. He nodded at Emma and the commander. "Allow me." He turned and walked out of the room.

Emma shook her head. OK, she must have been affected by the weird means of transportation, because these people seemed to catch on with little information. She stepped out of the grey, dimly lit room and into a bright, ice-blue colored corridor.

There seemed to be someone standing at every corridor junction, just waiting to greet her husband and welcome them aboard. Though this touched Emma, she wasn't sure how their reaction to her husband made her feel. He seemed to be of great importance here, and she wasn't sure if she could ever fit in. She drew in a breath and forced a smile as they made their way slowly towards their quarters. Not a house…but maybe something like an apartment?

Mathezar pointed to the door in question and it slid open. She wondered if anyone could just walk in at any time. Dthau-Mahsz motioned for her to enter, and he stepped in behind her. The room was dark and devoid of life. It felt as though no one had ever lived here.

She looked around at the dimly lit chamber, not knowing where the light came from. The dining area was obvious with a table and four chairs. Wood? She wasn't sure, at least it didn't look like any form of plastic or metal. Ironically, the other room, the 'living room', was bereft of life. It held six modular chairs, not quite upright, so possibly for relaxing? She moved closer and touched the dark, almost blue-black moulded form. It was rubbery to the touch, but not cold as she'd expected. She sat in it and was surprised at how comfortable it was, even though she would have preferred something in a little more of a sitting position. She let out a yelp and jumped to her feet when the chair shifted below her.

Dthau-Mahsz chuckled and wrapped an arm around her, pulling her closer while Tommy slept soundly on his shoulder. "Think of it as a smart recliner."

She covered her face with a hand and giggled. "Don't let one of those loose on Earth." She sighed and looked around the room from the safety of his arms. Each chair had a small table at its side and there was a large oval table in the middle of the room. That was it. No shelves, plants, pictures, nothing. Her eyes were drawn to the port hole and her breath hitched. Earth appeared slowly from the bottom left side of the oval aperture. "Oh, it's beautiful," she whispered.

Slipping out of his arms she made her way to the window. The view gave her goose bumps as she leaned into the window to stare down.

After a moment Dthau-Mahsz spoke. "You have yet to see the washroom and bedroom."

She looked up and turned to face him. "Lead on," she said.

The bathroom was simply amazing, and the shower was the best. It was encased in a glass-like cylinder that lit up when you stepped inside, and the water streamed from the ring around the top. Except for a metal disk embedded in the wall, there were no taps or faucet. He showed her that temperature was chosen by touch. The disk went from cold to hot as she passed her fingers along the edge.

The bedroom, on the other hand, left her indifferent. A bed, no head board or decorations, a desk and a closet, that was it. She sighed. Prison cell decorum, she mused. He moved the sleeping toddler to the bed and stretched. "He was getting heavy," Dthau-Mahsz said. He pulled Emma down to sit on the edge of the bed and knelt before her. "You can change and decorate as you please. If this is to be our home, I want you to feel comfortable in it."

She nodded and leaned into him. It was sad, scary and the beginning of an adventure all at the same time. Living in space...

He rubbed her back a moment before pulling away. "Shall I ask Mathezar to watch Thomas so we can go collect out things?"

She shot up. "No. I want him with us." She fidgeted, shifting her weight from one leg to the other.

He stood, gave her a reassuring look and opened the link. She immediately relaxed, and drew in a deep breath. How did humanity get along without such an amazing source of contact and reassurance?

"Let us go back to the farm house and collect our things," he whispered.

* * *

Two-Feathers stepped into the mudroom carrying milk and eggs. He smiled when he caught sight of Emma in the kitchen. "Thought you'd left without saying goodbye."

She looked up. Tears threatened to spill. "I could never do that." She moved closer and threw herself into his open arms. She was unable to hold back a sob and began to cry.

He held her until she stopped shaking, and when she pulled back she saw that he, too, had been crying. "I hope you can visit." His voice cracked.

"Me too." She drew in a deep breath. "Take care of the animals."

He dipped his head, eyes filling with tears again. "I have to go now," he said. He never liked 'goodbyes'.

She nodded, not trusting herself to speak. She eased herself into a chair and let herself cry some more, oblivious to her surroundings.

Dthau-Mahsz appeared behind her and placed his hands on her shoulders, gently massaging them. He had been back on the ship to deliver her chosen belongings and now it was time for them to leave. "Two-Feathers was here," she managed to say.

He wrapped his arms around her and squeezed before lifting her to her feet. "Yes, I spoke to him in the barn a few minutes ago." He turned her around and lifted her chin, searching her eyes. "Are you sure about this?"

She nodded and wiped away the tears with the back of her hand. "I want to get back to Tommy. I don't like leaving him with strangers." She had finally accepted to let Mathezar watch over Tommy since dragging the sleeping child back and forth made little sense.

"I know." He tapped his wrist com, and gave the order.

Emma tried to hold onto the image of her home, but it was quickly replaced with her new reality.

"Welcome back, Ma'am," the older crewmember from before

greeted her. The cadet he'd been with last time she'd come onboard had been replaced by a dark-skinned crewmember she hadn't seen before. She marvelled at the electric blue eyes and lack of whites.

"Thank you," she said as she followed her husband to their quarters. She already knew how to get there from the transport room, and though she was anxious to get back to her son, she was also a little curious to see more of the ship.

When she entered her quarters, she found the doctor sitting in the living room, where she'd left him. All was quiet, so Tommy had probably slept through the move. "Go and sit," Dthau-Mahsz said gently. "I will get us something to drink."

"I just want to check on Tommy first," she said. Not waiting for an answer, she entered his room. The tiny form slept soundly in the middle of his bed, like he did back home. His favorite stuffed animals and blankets were strewn all around the crib, and Emma reached down to pull the fleece comforter up to his shoulders. Satisfied, she made her way back to the others.

"How is he?" Dthau-Mahsz asked. He held out a cup.

"Sound asleep." She accepted the warm mug and inhaled the chocolaty aroma. "Should I be drinking chocolate before bed?"

With a look of reassurance her husband gestured for her to sit. "Our chocolate has a soothing effect on the body." He turned to the doctor who was sipping from his own cup. "Did you have any trouble with Thomas while we were gone?"

Emma turned to watch the doctor's reaction, more than to hear his response. "Not at all, he's been asleep since you left. I didn't have to do anything." He looked at Emma, curiosity in his eyes. "Dthau-Mahsz has told me you are a nurse."

Her cheeks warmed. "Yes, but I'm not sure I would be of any use in this world. I know nothing of your ways."

The doctor frowned. "Did you not nurse him back to health when you found him? Healing is healing."

She shrugged. "I suppose. I'm not sure I could learn all your procedures and methods."

"You are being too hard on yourself," Dthau-Mahsz said. "There is no pressure, no deadline. You can take all the time you need to learn."

"Why don't you come by tomorrow?" the doctor asked.

"Standard procedure is to give all new crewmembers a physical. You can watch while I examine the commander."

The commander made a face. "That is just his way to assure he gets to examine me," he said dryly.

Emma giggled. "All right then, I accept."

"Hmm, but what he did not tell you, was that you would be examined next," Dthau-Mahsz added.

"Well, what better way to learn than to experience?" she replied with a shrug. Although she was curious, she couldn't help but feel a little apprehensive. She was much more at ease performing the exam than being examined.

The doctor grinned. "I think I'm going to like you."

CHAPTER 19: STARTING ANEW

The next morning, the strange recliners were the first thing to go, and Emma was delighted by the chocolate brown, leather-like sofa and arm chairs that now occupied the middle of the room. A low, rectangular planter, almost as long as the sofa held most of the plants she'd brought from home. Somehow, Dthau-Mahsz had produced everything she'd asked for; right down to the bookshelves Emma had filled with the meagre mementoes she'd brought along. It actually felt like a living room now. The port window showed nothing but stars, and though the view was remarkable, she missed the crisp, blue rocky-mountain sky. She let out a sigh. She missed her animals and her home too. Shrugging it off, she focused on the task at hand...making this place home.

"Two-Feathers gave this to me," Dthau-Mahsz said as he set a little figurine down on the table. It was a Ktunaxa tribal dancer, dressed in traditional garb.

Emma smiled with a pang of sorrow, but resisted the urge to pick it up. "That was nice of him." She looked around the living room again.

He followed her gaze. "I like the changes you have brought to our quarters," he said. "It feels very warm and inviting."

She turned to face him. "I don't know if you have people over or not, I wasn't sure how they'd react to the changes." She caught her lower lip in her teeth. She moved closer to him, stepping into his embrace, relieved that he hadn't become distant since donning his uniform and role. He seemed to have lost his outdoor-cedar scent, much to her dismay. His distinct, almost spicy-musk scent remained. She closed her eyes and leaned in on him.

He kissed the top of her head. "Mathezar is expecting us in medical bay shortly." He rubbed her back, slowly kneading her tense muscles. "We will be able to have supper, or end-of-day meal, as we call it here, right after."

"End-of-day meal," she repeated, pulling back to step out of his embrace. "I'll get Tommy ready."

He nodded. "Do you want me to help?"

She shook her head. She needed to do something that was the same here as it was back home. Within minutes, she joined her husband, holding Tommy's small hand as she followed slowly. In silence, the group made their way down the endless corridors and Emma looked around, trying to make sense of her surroundings. Every corridor was the same ice-blue color, with a dark blue runner in the middle of the floor. There were no signs or markings on any of the doors, with the exception of a dark rectangular panel at the occasional junction.

Dthau-Mahsz paused beside the panel, and lightly touched it. An image of the corridors appeared as it immediately came to life. "This is where we are," he said, pointing to the three dots on the screen. "Every room is identified on this deck and you can shift views by tapping here." He slid a finger down the smaller cross-section view in the lower right-hand corner. "You can also speak directly to the CPU from anywhere on the ship, and it will answer what you want to know."

Her eyebrows knit into a frown, and she looked up at him. "Who is that?" Maybe it was some sort of communications officer.

A sympathetic smile crossed his face. "It is the Central Processing Unit, a computer that monitors all systems. You can talk to it, or him, and he will answer." He placed a hand on the small of her back and led her down the corridor. "If you can wait for end of day meal, I will show you around the ship after the good doctor is done with us," he offered.

"Yes, I'd like that very much." She wanted to feel at home here as soon as possible, to erase the pang of unease from not knowing or understanding her surroundings. At least Tommy was small enough that he'd never notice the change.

The antiseptic-like smell of the infirmary lingered just outside the doors, causing Emma's stomach to recoil, rather than find comfort in it. Strange, since it had always been a reassuring smell when she'd worked as a nurse. Maybe the fears surrounding her inadequacies were the cause.

To her surprise, the room was not as brightly lit as the corridor, and there was no turmoil or sense of urgency to be felt. Mathezar appeared from his office on the left and greeted the group with a smile. Without saying a word, he led them to the far end of the room and Emma froze when an exam table popped into existence.

"It's a particle curtain, to maintain privacy," Dthau-Mahsz explained. He turned her around so she could see that the entrance was no longer visible. They had curtains and closed exam rooms back at the hospital, but she couldn't deny that this was an amazing concept. OK, her curiosity was definitely piqued, and she was looking forward to seeing what other interesting things they had.

"We are able to move the beds according to our needs, placing them into different groups and configurations," the doctor explained. "This is but one of the five beds in this pod. For now, they are in a star-shaped formation."

Emma passed her hand on the table's glass top, expecting it to be cold and hard. Her eyes widened as the table gave way to her touch and her hand sank slightly into it. Warmth surrounded her hand and she pulled back, realizing that she was being watched.

"Commander," the doctor turned to his first patient. "Would you be so kind as to oblige us?"

The commander's left eyebrow rose as he pressed his lips together. He tugged on his uniform top and turned to sit on the table, before lying back. Emma scooped Tommy up into her arms, so she could move in closer. With a start, she stepped back from the table as a burst of colored light appeared under Dthau-Mahsz's head and began to move slowly downward.

The doctor motioned her forward, and he reached out for Tommy. She watched in disbelief as her son willingly transferred to the stranger's arms.

A semi-transparent, holographic image of her husband appeared over the podium at the foot of the exam table. The image rotated slowly and the doctor pointed to the dark umber shading on the image. "These would be the injuries sustained in the crash." He pointed to the ribs, the forehead and thigh. He traced a line on his forearm. "This one came a little later."

Emma nodded. "That's incredible." She leaned in closer to examine the readout to the left of the image. "You can get all that information from lying on this table?"

The doctor gave a curt nod. "You can call up specific

information if need be."

She frowned. "Such as?"

"Whatever you need." He tapped on the readout and pointed. "Everything from basic vitals to the electrolyte balance, enzymes, hormones, blood-oxygen levels and more can be accessed instantly."

"Now that's a time saver," Emma commented. "Not to mention non-invasive."

Mathezar nodded. He brought the image of the commander's now healed ribs back up. He traced the image with is finger and leaned in closer. "Did you bind the ribs?"

"Yes, why?" She wondered if there was something wrong with the way his ribs had healed.

"Do not question yourself so much," the doctor said in a reassuring tone. "His injuries have healed well. We could regenerate the tissue and replace it, as well as remove the scars from his leg, forehead, and –"

"That won't be necessary," the commander cut him off. He sat up, swung his legs over the edge of the table and hopped down. Tommy smiled and leaned out towards his father who gladly took him from the doctor. "Shall we put you down on the table now?" Dthau-Mahsz asked Tommy.

Tommy shook his head, *no*, then giggled at the face his father made. Dthau-Mahsz smoothly settled the toddler onto the exam table and Tommy went silent as his little body settled into the warmth. The doctor placed a small crystal disk on the toddler's forehead and he went still. "What's that?" Emma asked, a frown forming on her face.

She jumped slightly at her husband's touch on her shoulder. The link flared. "He will not harm our son."

"They create an electromagnetic response in the body that act somewhere between a sedative and an anaesthetic," the doctor explained.

"What do you mean 'somewhere between a sedative and an anesthetic'? Is that really necessary?" She brought a hand to her mouth. "What if he reacts?" The link flared and her breath caught. Calm surrounded her and she was unable to counter.

"There is no danger, and it's not chemically induced," Mathezar reassured her. "He's awake, just calm."

Taking Tommy's small hand into her own, she leaned down to kiss him. He tilted his head towards her and gave her a sleepy smile. *He is fine*, came through the link, but sheer panic threatened to engulf her.

As soon as the beam of light had made its way down the Tommy's body, the holographic image of her son appeared at the foot of the table, and Dthau-Mahsz removed the crystal disk from his son's forehead. Tommy stretched and yawned sleepily, then flipped over onto his belly and pushed himself into a sitting position. Ignoring his parents, he pressed into the warm, soft surface of the exam table, obviously fascinated with it.

Feeling uneasy about her reaction, Emma turned her attention to the test results. Her stomach knotted when she caught sight of the doctor's face. "What's wrong?"

Grey eyes glanced up at her for a second before returning to the results. "There is nothing wrong, but the cerebral cortex shows heightened activity."

Dthau-Mahsz scooped Tommy up. "Which means what, exactly?" His tone was sharp.

The doctor raised a hand. "It means nothing, other than he might be more sensitive to his surroundings, to thoughts and emotions." He focused on the results again, calling up a different sequence. "Has he shown signs of headaches?"

"No," Emma said. "He sleeps well, and isn't jumpy or irritable."

With a nod, the doctor collapsed the holographic image and turned his attention to Emma. "Then we'll leave it at that." He gestured towards the exam table with a sweeping motion. "Your turn, now." He looked from the commander and back to her. "Do you want him to leave?"

She let out a laugh, thinking about the difference between an exam here and one back home. With a wry smile she turned to her husband. "He can stay." She settled onto the table, surprised at how it adjusted to her body. The warmth was so inviting that she immediately relaxed.

Crystal disks in hand, the doctor leaned over her. "Could I place one on you, just so you know what it does?" His eyes searched hers.

Trapping her bottom lip in her teeth she nodded. Might as well, she thought. "Sure, why not."

Without hesitation, Mathezar placed one disk on her forehead. "For an adult, we normally use four disks," he started to explain. She felt calm, and drew in a deep breath. "What you feel now is the result of one disk." He moved the disk to her temple and placed a second one opposite the first. Emma felt detached from her surroundings, the way you do when you first wake up, but haven't yet regained total consciousness. He proceeded to place a disk on the inner side of each of her wrists and she drifted off. She could hear what was going on, but everything had taken on a dreamlike quality.

Emma drew in a deep breath and stretched, feeling calm and well rested. She gave her husband a sheepish smile when she caught him watching her. The corner of his mouth turned up. "If you wish, we could leave you here to get some sleep. You were quite restless last night."

She felt her cheeks heat as she propped herself up on an elbow. "How long have I been asleep?"

Dthau-Mahsz chuckled softly. "Approximately five minutes." He shifted the now sleeping Tommy and grabbed hold of Emma's arm to help her sit up.

"Thanks." She swung her feet over the edge of the table and slid to the floor. "Where did the doctor go?" She turned full circle but couldn't see past the confines of the group of beds.

"In his office, waiting." Dthau-Mahsz nodded over his shoulder. "Come."

No one spoke as they sat around the doctor's desk. The office looked surprisingly like an office, with a desk and chair for the doctor, along with two other chairs facing him. How disappointing. The desktop looked like a rigid version of the exam-table's glass-like surface, and when the doctor leaned his elbows on it, the table-top began to glow.

Emma looked from her husband to the doctor. "Is there something wrong?"

"No," the doctor answered reassuringly. "All of you are fine. Thomas shows heightened receptivity, but if you say he has not shown any ill-effects then it's nothing to worry about."

The commander straightened. "What sort of ill-effects, and what would be the cause?"

Mathezar furrowed his brows and focused on his desk top, bringing an image of Tommy's brain into view. "These areas of the brain are more active than what I normally see in members of our species." He moved things around on his desktop, calling up more info.

"Is that a bad thing?" Emma asked. She wasn't sure what to make of the situation. Her baby had always been easy-going and content.

The doctor tilted his head, looking unsure. "From what I saw of your living environment, he hasn't been subjected to either a lot of people or technology." He paused to read something on the table top. "This will have probably allowed him to adapt to his heightened sensitivity, though he might find the shift into his new environment to be somewhat difficult." He looked up at Emma and Dthau-Mahsz. "Make sure you let me know if there are any changes in his behavior."

Dthau-Mahsz nodded and stood. "We will." He turned to Emma. "Come."

Forcing a smile in the doctor's direction, Emma stood and followed her husband back to their quarters. She shouldn't worry; Tommy had never shown any signs of difficulty or distress. She bit her lower lip and hoped he would not have a hard time in this new setting. Time would tell.

CHAPTER 20: THERE'S A PARK?

"Would you like to take a tour of the ship now?" Dthau-Mahsz broke into her thoughts.

She was looking forward to seeing the rest of her new home, but she didn't think it was fair to have her husband carry Tommy around. "We can wait for him to wake up, or get his stroller."

"We will get his stroller," Dthau-Mahsz said. "We can walk while he sleeps."

Emma tried to take it all in as Dthau-Mahsz took her around the ship, showing her the different sections and departments found in the main saucer. Pausing by one of the darkened wall panels, he called up the diagram of the ship. He pointed to the three smaller saucers that were affixed to the underside of the much larger main disk. "Each one can be deployed separately. This one houses the arboretum." He pointed to the other two. "Geological and Zoological are here, and the latter is for transfers and Zeno-biology."

Emma grabbed his arm, a spark of excitement building. "Could we see the arboretum?" If there was a park of sorts onboard, she might be able to avoid feeling homesick. She could take Tommy for walks, read, relax. This would be perfect. She caught him looking at her oddly. "Is something wrong?"

He pressed his lips together. "I fear you might have the wrong impression."

"Does that mean we can't go?" She searched his face, trying to understand. Nothing came through their link, so she shrugged. Whatever, if he didn't want to go, there wasn't much she could do about it.

He lifted a hand and touched her cheek with the back of his fingers. "I did not say that." He nodded towards the end of the corridor. "This way."

She imagined a beautiful park-like area as they made their way through the halls. She wondered what kind of strange vegetation she might see. There'd probably be exotic fruit growing from the trees. The familiar smell of earth and vegetation greeted Emma when the door open and she dropped her head to hide her smile. Maybe she could have a small garden.

"Welcome back, Commander," a dark haired woman wearing a green and gold jumpsuit greeted him.

"Thank you." Dthau-Mahsz nodded curtly, then reached back to bring Emma forward. "Emma, this is Trenika, Mathezar's wife. She is one of our botanists."

Her dark amber eyes lit. "I have been looking forward to meeting you." She turned back to the commander and took on a more formal attitude. "How may I be of assistance?"

"I was taking Emma on a tour of the ship. She wanted to see the arboretum," he explained.

"Would you like me to accompany you, Commander?" Trenika asked.

"Yes," he answered. "I may have some questions." He gestured for her to lead the way.

The doors from the lab and office area where they were standing opened to a large space. Emma's heart sank. Precision straight rows of vegetation grew off into the distance. A metal grid walkway lay between each of them. The image of a lush park vanished and Emma's hope for a tiny sanctuary disappeared along with it.

She stood, frozen in place, no longer interested in seeing the arboretum. Dthau-Mahsz must have sensed her reaction, since he stopped mid-stride and turned back towards his wife. Emma forced a smile. "I think I'm going to take Tommy back to our room and let him sleep. You can continue your departmental visit." She moved to take a step back, but he caught her wrist.

"We are already here. Surely you can spare a few minutes of your time." He waited for her answer, not bothering to follow the botanist who had moved on ahead. "What is wrong?"

She shrugged. "I had expected this to be more like a park than a lab. I mean, I understand that these plants and trees are used for the colonies that need the different types of vegetation, but in nature trees are all varied." She waved a hand at the setup before her.

"Not like that." Her voice held a hint of disgust.

"Commander, if I may…" Trenika had come back, and had obviously heard what Emma was saying.

The commander turned his attention towards the botanist, still holding onto Emma's wrist.

Trenika's cheeks pinked. "I took some liberties, while we were inactive." She shifted slightly, looking hesitantly over her shoulder. "If you would permit me to show you my personal corner of the arboretum, I believe your wife might find it more to her liking."

Dthau-Mahsz released Emma and waved her ahead of him. To say that she felt awkward was an understatement, and right now, she just wanted to return to her room and stare out the window. Their steps echoed as they walked along the metal grid work that made up the path. Emma didn't understand why they had bothered; she saw nothing wrong with walking on the ground.

Lost in her disappointment, Emma didn't notice when they stepped through another doorway. As soon as the doors closed, the smell of flowers hit, and she raised her head, surprised by the distinct smell of pine and cedar.

"It isn't much," offered Trenika, "but I converted this area into a place that made me feel as though I was planet-side." She drew in a breath. "I need to walk on soil every now and again."

Emma looked around at the tiny haven. The small square room boasted different coniferous and leafy trees in the far left corner. Smaller shrubs had been planted against the back wall, stopping in the right-hand corner. Flowers were dispersed in a precise pattern around a small bench, carved out of a stump. It was barely big enough for two people to sit on, but it was perfect. "It's beautiful," Emma said.

"Is the sole purpose of this area recreational?" The commander eyed the room in a critical fashion.

Trenika stiffened. "No, Sir. I am measuring the soil for mineral variations and monitoring the impact of mixed vegetation on the area so that I may compare it against our controlled growth method." She shifted around, betraying her nervousness. "Vegetation rarely grows in an environment such as we have reproduced. I am worried we are actually weakening the plants."

"Which is why I rotated my crops in the garden every year,"

Emma added softly.

Trenika's head shot up. "You have grown your own vegetables?"

Emma took a step back and shrugged. "Just what we needed."

Dthau-Mahsz laid a hand on her shoulder. "It was quite impressive, and it fed many families." He shifted his gaze back to the botanist. "You wish to make changes to the layout of the arboretum?"

Emma watched as Trenika drew in a steadying breath before she squared her shoulders and faced the commander. "I would like to grow the vegetation in a more natural setting. I believe, though our intentions may be noble, that the plants would benefit from and thrive more in a different layout."

The commander nodded curtly. "How much time before I can expect to see the results of your study."

Trenika's cheeks flushed. "I could present my notes and observations at out next meeting."

Dthau-Mahsz shifted, studying her face. "If your findings indicate a change in configuration would be beneficial, then why wasn't it implemented already?"

"The chief has refused on several occasions," the botanist admitted. "He has ordered me to dismantle this room."

The commander held up a hand. "I want your notes in an hour. I will handle this." His eyes panned the room one last time. "You will make no changes until I have gone over your findings."

Head bowed, Trenika answered. "Yes, Commander. Thank you."

Emma watched the exchange, not sure what to think. OK, so there was no park-like area, but there was a sliver of hope one would be made available, eventually. She followed her husband out of the arboretum, pushing the still sleeping toddler in his stroller. "I think I'd like to go back to our quarters now." She needed to take a step back, no longer interested in a guided tour.

Dthau-Mahsz nodded. "If you are hungry, we could go eat."

She nodded. Not really sure if she was hungry or not, but it was time to return to their quarters.

Emma lifted Tommy from the stroller and set the now awake toddler down onto the living room floor. She wondered how Bo was doing without them. She missed her dog. Tommy's scream of delight had her spinning around to face her son. She watched in awe as he played with a metal sphere. The ball would open, emitting light and shapes and then snap shut without warning, eliciting a round of giggles from Tommy.

"What would you like to eat?" her husband asked. He was slowly introducing his food to his family.

Emma shrugged. "You choose." Her attention remained on her son and his game. "What is that thing?"

Dthau-Mahsz looked up from the tablet he was holding. "A child's toy." He tapped a few more times on the tablet and deposited it on the table before making his way to his wife's side. "It develops creative and cognitive abilities."

"So do crayons," Emma replied flatly. "Could it be dangerous?"

A look of patient amusement crossed Dthau-Mahsz' face and he tilted his head slightly. "Would you like to try?"

She shook her head and settled onto the couch, not wanting to disturb Tommy. She watched as Dthau-Mahsz settled, cross-legged on the floor in front of his son, and picked up the orb. The globe opened like a flower and a multitude of glowing, colored blocks appeared, floating about. One by one, the blocks piled themselves up. Tommy watched, fascinated. Without warning, the blocks tumbled away and the toddler burst into a fit of giggles.

Emma stared on in amazement as her little man leaned his head slightly down, eyes glued to the floating blocks until they stacked themselves back up. A look of excitement and a toothy grin lit Tommy's face and Dthau-Mahsz beamed with approval. The blocks flew every which way and the toddler giggled with glee. "Did he do that or did you?" she asked her husband.

"I did the initial stacking, he did the rest." He reached out and touched Tommy's hand, attracting the toddler's attention. Holding the orb, the colored blocks fused together and formed a teddy bear that disappeared when Tommy reached out to touch it. As soon as Tommy pulled his hand back, the bear appeared again. Uncertain, the toddler stared at the orb and another animal appeared.

Dthau-Mahsz closed the orb, stood and handed it back to his son. Immediately, the ball burst to life, displaying various shapes and colors.

The door chimed and the commander made his way to escort his crewmembers in with the platters of food. Emma realised that

Dthau-Mahsz must have sensed their arrival and she stood to help set out the meal. She tried to identify the smells but nothing was familiar. The food was still covered so she couldn't see it either.

Tommy, toy abandoned, had been drawn to the table by the aroma and he struggled to climb up on his chair. Dthau-Mahsz gave Emma a kiss on the temple. "You should probably wash his hands. I will serve the meal," he said.

Emma nodded, but rather than take the toddler away from the table, she went to get a wash cloth. She wasn't in the mood for a toddler tantrum.

"I ordered finger-foods for Thomas," Dthau-Mahsz explained. "Our meal is a combination of root vegetables with a grain that resembles your Kasha." His eyes searched hers. "If you do not like it we can order something else from the replicator." He pointed to the small alcove in the wall.

Emma frowned. "I thought that was where we sent the dirty dishes." She spooned a mouthful of the risotto looking dish into her mouth, intrigued by the flavor. It wasn't half-bad and she didn't have to cook it, so far be it for her to complain. She glanced over at Tommy who was busy shoving pieces into his mouth. She offered him a spoon of her dish but he shook his head.

"Do you like it?" Dthau-Mahsz asked.

"Yes," she answered honestly. "It doesn't taste like anything I've ever had before, but it's not bad."

"Good." He watched her for a moment before putting his fork down. "Tomorrow I have to meet with my department heads. We will not be on active duty for another week or so, not until they return my engineering detail." He reached out and stroked her hand. "That will give us a little more time together, to help you settle in." He gave her a hopeful smile.

Her mind ran through her options...and came up blank. There was only so much decorating she could do. There was no park, no outdoors, and no animals for her to tend to. She missed her chores and routine. Maybe she could learn a little more about his world. It had been something she'd asked him about time and time again.

"Should I get a basin to bathe Thomas?" he asked her, changing the subject and pulling her from her thoughts. "He has never been in the shower before."

"Give the shower a try." She didn't think her toddler would

mind. "If it doesn't work then we'll figure something out." A spark of hope filtered in. "Do you have a pool onboard?" Why wouldn't they?

"A pool, as in a large basin of water?" He wrinkled his brow and passed a hand over his mouth. "We have basins containing fish and other marine life in the zoological department."

Emma's stomach knotted. She couldn't imagine what conditions the poor animals lived in after seeing the arboretum. "I meant for recreational purposes, to swim," she explained.

"No. We do not." He let out a sharp breath. "Would you like to try endurance training after my meeting tomorrow?"

She shot a look in Tommy's direction. "We can't just leave him here, and I don't think he could participate in the activity from what you've described of it." She didn't understand. Maybe he wanted a babysitter or something....

"He can come along. There is a level for him to develop motor-skills, flexibility and coordination." He watched her.

"Oh, well then I guess it will be all right." She'd have to wait and see for herself what was involved. She swallowed, trying another venue. "Do you have any recreational activities, choir, band, sports?" She shook her head as she remembered he'd once told her that his people didn't play sports.

A smile tugged at his lips, giving him the look of a patient parent. He shook his head 'no' in response to her question. "We can settle in the living room or go for a walk and I will show you the training room. Thomas might like to play there."

Plates in hand, she rose and deposited the dinnerware in the replicator as he had shown her. She paused. "You said this thing gives food too?"

Rising to his feet in his typical, seamless fashion, he sent the soiled plates on their way and touched the corner of the black frame. Two cups of cocoa appeared and he held one out to her. "My interface allows me to communicate directly with the computers on board." He pointed to the panel that appeared on the right hand side of the replicator. "You can use touch." He pointed to food then drink. Touching 'drink', another list of options appeared. "Just keep at it until you narrow down your selection. Or you may speak directly to it." He gestured for her to give it a try. *For Thomas* he instructed through the link.

She touched the corner of the frame and the panel lit up. Clearing her throat, she said, "Hot chocolate in a child's sippy cup, please." With a half-hearted smile she looked at her husband. "Does it know what a sippy cup is?"

He laughed softly. "We shall soon find out." He pointed to the replicator. It looked like someone had removed the door to a micro-wave and mounted it flush into the wall. "It would appear as though it does." He withdrew the cup and handed it to her.

The chocolaty aroma filled Emma's senses and she inhaled deeply before taking a sip from her own mug. The effect was soothing and she closed her eyes to appreciate it. "I think I would prefer staying in tonight."

He nodded, making his way to where Tommy played on the floor with his orb. Emma waited a moment before she moved to settle onto the couch. She had managed to create a cozy room, but she missed her fireplace. Normally they'd head out to tend to the animals after supper, but that was no longer possible. She missed her dog. She would have liked to bring him along, but after seeing the arboretum, he wouldn't have had a place to run either. She forced the thought aside, placed the drinks on the end table and joined her men on the floor. She wanted a closer look at that ball.

Dthau-Mahsz looked up at her. "Would you like to give it a try?"

"I wouldn't know what to do." She'd rather watch for now.

"Come," he insisted.

Hesitantly, she moved in beside the boys. Dthau-Mahsz scooped up the ball and offered Tommy his sippy cup in exchange. Holding the orb out to Emma he lifted her palm and gently deposited it in her hand. "Tell it to open," he said.

"Open," she repeated dutifully.

He chuckled. "With your mind."

She shot him a glance. *Open*, she said in her mind, but nothing happened.

"See it in your mind," he prompted.

Through clenched teeth, she saw the orb open, and to her amazement, it complied. A smile spread across her face as she let out a breath, mesmerized by the glowing shapes. "I did it."

Tommy, having finished with his cup toddled over and plopped down before the orb. The blocks fused and shifted, forming a rudimentary dog. Both parents watched as the dog defined itself, until the unmistakable 3-D image of Bo floated above the open orb. "Bo," Tommy called out. The orb snapped shut, taking the dog with it.

"That was very good," Dthau-Mahsz praised his son. Emma, on the other hand, felt a pang of sorrow. He may be small, but he obviously remembered what had been left behind.

"Maybe we should give the shower a try. If it doesn't work, it won't be too late to find an alternative solution." She needed to do something before she let her emotions take over.

"Perhaps we could take a walk before we put him down," her husband offered.

"If all goes well, then sure." She scooped up her son and nibbled on his belly. Tommy giggled as he tried to wiggle free.

Dthau-Mahsz returned their cups to the replicator and made his way to the shower along with his family. "Should I get in alone and show him first, or do we all go in together?"

Her head shot up. "All of us?"

He shrugged. "It is big enough." He winked at her. "Where's your sense of adventure?"

To Emma's surprise Tommy loved the shower. He would close his eyes and turn his face up into the gentle stream, giggling and sputtering in the water. Getting him out of the shower was where he began to protest, but Dthau-Mahsz masterfully succeeded in distracting him and getting him into his pyjamas.

In the end, they decided to call it a night. Emma was drained and a little harried. She had hoped for a good night's sleep, but her restlessness followed her into her dreams. Tangled in her covers, she awoke with a start, heart beating rapidly. A feeling of dread squeezed her chest with its cold fingers. Frustrated, she tossed the blankets aside and padded into the living room.

She chose a seat that allowed her a view of the stars. She'd be lying if she said it wasn't beautiful, but to never plant a garden, play in the snow or watch a sunrise from her front porch again...could she do it? Cooking wasn't even possible here. She grabbed a throw pillow and hugged it to her. Maybe once she had a purpose in this society, she would feel better about the change in her life. She adored her husband and couldn't imagine living without him, so making an effort to adapt wasn't even an option.

Her heart felt heavy, and her chest tightened as she swallowed back a tear. It would somehow work out. She had to believe that.

Warmth, laced with a feeling of calm flowed through her, and she abandoned herself to its comfort. Eyes closed, she let Dthau-Mahsz scoop her into his arms and hold her. "It was a long first day for you." He kissed the top of her head and shifted her into a comfortable position. "We could bring Thomas to play group for two hours tomorrow. If he adapts well, then you could look into your training as a nurse," he offered. "You had so many occupations at home, you will need something to keep yourself busy."

Emma let out a slow breath. "I'm not comfortable leaving him with strangers."

Gently, he brushed the hair from her face. "He will be with a small group of children only a few doors down from medical bay. You and I will only be a few seconds away at any given time."

She nodded, feeling herself drifting off to sleep. "I'll go see it. He might enjoy having someone to play with."

CHAPTER 21: DAY TWO

A gentle caress on her cheek brought a smile to her face. Emma stretched and yawned, feeling refreshed. "Good morning," Dthau-Mahsz said. He sat on the edge of their bed, wearing his uniform. "My meeting is in a few minutes. I will return as soon as I am done." He trailed the back of his fingers across her cheek. "Breakfast is on the table. I imagine Thomas will be awake shortly."

"Why didn't you wake me?" Emma threw the blankets aside and moved to get out of bed, but Dthau-Mahsz held her gently by the shoulders. "It is still early. You needed to rest. Go take a shower and wake up slowly. The CPU will inform you if Thomas rouses before you are done, so there is no need to worry. " He leaned in to kiss her and was gone before she could protest.

Emma stood and looked around the bedroom, unsure of what to do. She decided to hurry and shower before her little man awoke. Making the bed could wait.

She had time to dress before her son began to stir. He hadn't shown signs of distress since their arrival, though sleeping in so long was unusual. "Mama!" a little voice called out.

Emma smiled and made her way to Tommy's room. "Good morning." She lifted him from his bed and brought him to the bathroom before getting him dressed. Breakfast was still on the table and Emma sighed. It must be cold by now.

Tommy climbed into his chair as Emma lifted the covers, surprised to find everything warm and appetizing. That's when it dawned on her, the comment Dthau-Mahsz had made about plates keeping the food warm. Nice.

Breakfast was tasty and mother and son ate heartily. The door chimed and Emma looked over at Tommy. "Do you think we should answer it?" she whispered in his direction. His answer came in the form of a brisk nod. She pushed away from the table and stepped around to the door. Nothing happened. "Can you open the door?" Emma asked the CPU.

The door slid open and Trenika stood, holding a dark haired little girl in her arms. "I hope I am not intruding," she said. "I was going to bring Jayden to the play center and thought you might like to come along. Mathezar mentioned you would likely be spending some time upgrading your nursing knowledge..." her voice trailed off. "Am I being too bold?"

Emma laughed in spite of herself. "No. Do you want to come in? I'm afraid we're not quite ready to go anywhere, and I don't think I am expected today." She stepped aside as Trenika entered and stood by the door. Emma gestured towards the living room area. "Please, make yourself at home. We were almost finished eating, I just have to tidy up and we'll be ready in a few minutes." She decided it would be nice to check out this play center and the idea of spending a bit more time in her field would be welcome.

Trenika moved closer to Emma's plants while Emma sent the dirty dishes on their way. "What a wonderful idea!" she exclaimed. "I should have thought of this."

"You don't have house plants?" Emma asked. She couldn't get her head around the concept, but then she recalled the arboretum. It was almost as if they were afraid of the vegetation.

Trenika shook her head. "No." She leaned in closer to the pothos on the book shelf. "Isn't this one toxic?"

Emma nodded. "If you eat it." She wiped Tommy's hands and face, set him on the floor and cleared off his place setting. There really wasn't anything else to do. "I guess we're ready." She made her way over to her guest and watched as the toddlers greeted one another.

"Did you really grow your own food?" Trenika asked as she scooped Jayden into her arms.

Emma held out her hand and led Tommy towards the door. "Yes. Don't you grow your own food back home?" What the heck did these people eat?

"There are those who specialize in the growth of food for the masses, but here onboard, most food is synthesized." She gave Emma a weary smile. "Once a week, we are invited to partake in end-of-day meal in the formal dining room, where real food is served."

Tommy walked alongside his mother as the group made their way down the corridor. "Does everyone dine at the same time?" Emma was wondering if this was a big event.

"No. We each have our assigned days." She put her daughter down as the girl wiggled fiercely to free herself. "She looks forward to her play time," Trenika explained.

To Emma's surprised Jayden took Tommy by the hand and led him through the door, not waiting for her mother. Emma stepped in behind Trenika and watched the group of children as they settled around a woman. Jayden, still holding tight to Tommy's hand, sat with the other children.

"Trenika." A slightly plump woman with white hair and brilliant green eyes stepped closer.

"This is Emma, the commander's wife." Trenika introduced her. "Ilya oversees the children," she explained. "Thomas has joined the group this morning."

Emma hesitated. "Well, I would like to see how he fits in before I just leave him here."

Both women turned to face her. "He appears to have settled in just fine," Ilya said.

"But what if there is a problem," Emma asked.

Trenika rested a gentle hand on Emma's arm. "You will be in medical bay, three doors down, and the CPU can instantly locate you should need be."

Emma looked over at her son, seemingly engrossed in whatever activity was going on. Music appeared to come from the orb at the center of the children, and the group swayed and laughed in time to its rhythm. "If you're sure..." She forced a smile and looked at Trenika for support.

The botanist laced an arm through Emma's and led her towards the door. "Mathezar is waiting, and I am expected in the arboretum." She gave Emma's arm an involuntary squeeze. "The commander has approved the reorganization of a quarter of the arboretum." Her eyes lit with enthusiasm. "We will organize the vegetation to resemble a more natural state, and we might even be able to walk on the soil!"

Emma felt her mood lift. "Will you be able to grow vegetables?"

Trenika paused. "I don't know." A look of mischief crossed her face. "One victory at a time. But wouldn't it be wonderful?" She gave a carefree laugh. "A few days ago I thought I would have to dismantle my study plot." She gave Emma's arm another squeeze. "Thank you."

"Oh, I don't know that I had anything to do with it." Emma felt suddenly awkward.

"But you did! The commander referred to the wonderful garden you grew during his time on your planet." She brought her hand to her heart. "I would have loved to see it."

"Is this medical bay?" Emma shifted her attention to the door. She paused, hesitantly. "I don't think I was supposed to show up today."

With a wave of her hand she brushed Emma's concern away. "Would you like me to come in?"

"Not unless you want to see your husband," Emma said.

Trenika laughed. "I will see him soon enough. If you are certain, I'll be on my way."

With a nod of conviction Emma squared her shoulders. "Thank you for stopping by this morning." She turned and entered medical bay. To her surprise there was more activity then on the day she had come in. Was that only yesterday?

"Emma," Mathezar called out to her. "Could you give us a hand?" He took her by the elbow and guided her behind a particle curtain. "We have had an outbreak of sorts amongst our survey team. The details were unclear."

"What can I do?" She looked around at the empty bed pods.

The doctor reached out and attached a small chip to the underside of her collar. "This will allow you to see through the particle curtain. It also acts as a bio-shield." He pointed to the head of the exam table. Each one is the same and the phy-disks are here." He pointed to a small slot near the underside of the head of the table and removed the four crystal disks he'd placed on her during her exam. "Escort each patient to a bed and place the disks on them before you do anything else."

She swallowed. "OK."

He gave her arm a quick pat. "Thank you. Our security detail will be bringing them in any minute now." He pointed to a setting on the podium at the center of the five beds. "Activate the quarantine field immediately after getting the disks in place. We want to get them settled and keep them as calm as possible." Without waiting to see if Emma had any questions, the doctor left the bed pod area.

People started appearing at the far left corner of medical bay before she had the chance to react. They must have been transported directly here from wherever they were. Moving quickly, she met a guard and led her first patient to an exam table. Still holding the four disks, she swiftly placed them on his temples and wrists. She expected him to almost fall asleep, but she could see he was still agitated, though he didn't seem able to move.

"Get the quarantine fields up!" Someone called out to the room.

Emma moved to the podium at the foot of the exam table and activated the field. She looked over towards her patient and saw the colored beam making its way slowly down the length of her patient.

"Over here!" a guard called out. He was struggling to support a man. Emma grabbed another set of disks and moved in quickly to lend a hand. With two of the disks in place they were able to escort the subdued crewman to the waiting table. He rolled to his side and began to wretch. Emma moved in closer in an attempt to place the other disks on the man's wrists but the security guard yanked her back.

"What are you doing?" she asked, flustered. "I have to settle him."

Her eyes widened as a rather large, pink mass oozed from his mouth and landed with a splat on the floor. It was moving! Emma stood back in horror and watched as the guard moved quickly. An alarm sounded and a silvery dome appeared over the object, or creature. Emma suppressed a shudder and moved to her patient's side to place the other disks on his wrists and lie him back down as the guard activated the quarantine field.

Mathezar moved to the podium and looked over the hologram from the first patient. Three masses, identical to the one on the floor, moved about the abdominal area, and Emma couldn't help but stare. Shaking it off, she moved to escort yet another crewmember to a bed.

By the time the twelve-man team had been settled and purged of the parasites, Emma felt invigorated. Maybe she could fit in and work here after all. The technology was amazing and the way they could help their patients here seemed almost magical. She drew in a deep breath as she sensed the approach of her husband.

"Report," Dthau-Mahsz ordered the doctor.

The doctor passed a hand over his mouth. "The situation is under control. All parasites have been eliminated, and only one member of the medical team became contaminated." He waved them towards his office. "All members will be under quarantine for the duration."

"Why was Emma involved in this task?" The commander's tone was sharp.

She laid a hand on his arm. "I didn't mind helping." She had something to look forward to, some way to contribute.

Hard eyes held her gaze. "This parasite, had it infected you, would have forced you to be quarantined from your son for twenty-one days." He paused a moment and his expression softened. "It is important that you familiarize yourself with the dangers before you volunteer your services."

Emma dropped her gaze.

"I had activated a bio-shield around her," Mathezar offered.

Dthau-Mahsz shifted. "You should not have let her in medical bay today."

"What's done is done," Emma said.

"If you are ready," the doctor spoke up. "I will prepare a series of evaluations that you can take at your leisure. Once they are done, I will be able to set a study program and then we can decide on the times you will come in to work."

Dthau-Mahsz shot his friend a look but said nothing. "Back to the report on our crewmembers' condition, Doctor."

Mathezar nodded. "The report states that the planet's inhabitants became fearful of our team, believing them to be demons of sorts." He waved his hand in the air. "The inhabitants even blamed them for the seismic activity. They began throwing the parasites at them, and, well, our team was not prepared to deal with that."

The commander raised a hand to his jaw. "I will have the Osiris handle it until our crew is complete and back on its feet." He stood and motioned for Emma to follow. "It is time for Thomas to have lunch."

Mathezar stood and locked gazes with Emma. "Thank you for your help today."

With a nod Emma moved to join her husband. She was pleased to have been able to help, and now she had something to look forward to.

Dthau-Mahsz and Emma stepped into the play center to find their son in Ilya's arms. He was red faced, and had obviously been crying. Tommy launched himself into his father's arms and tucked his head tightly against the commander's chest. "Explain," the commander barked out.

Ilya remained unflustered. "He started rubbing his ears and whimpering. We were going to call for you, but you came in." She spun to catch a child as he scooted by. "I have told you not to run, Emran." She leaned closer to the child to whisper in his ear. When the child nodded, she set him down and turned back to the commander. "His discomfort began only minutes ago, we would have had him seen in medical bay had you not come in."

The commander nodded. He placed a hand around the back of Tommy's head and Emma watched as her son settled somewhat. "I will have Mathezar take a look at him." He turned, laced an arm around Emma's shoulders and led the family away.

Now, what? Emma thought. She wondered if this is what the doctor was referring to about Tommy's heightened sensitivity. Was it being around so many kids at once? Could it be the technology?

Mathezar was waiting as they entered medical bay. "Ilya informed me of the situation."

Emma frowned. That was fast. "Is this what you were worried about?" she asked.

The doctor led them to an isolated area and motioned for Dthau-Mahsz to put the toddler down. Even with the crystal disk in place, Tommy withered on the exam table. Mathezar frowned and placed a second disk on the boy, sliding the first to the left temple.

Emma brushed the damp hair from Tommy's forehead, watching as his breathing slowed. He appeared to have fallen sleep.

Dthau-Mahsz moved closer to the doctor, watching as the holographic image appeared. The doctor's eyes went wide. He tapped away at the panel on the podium and removed a small, flimsy patch from a slot in the podium. Moving in next to the toddler, the doctor gently turned him onto his side and brought Tommy's head to his chest, exposing his neck. Emma watched as he applied the thin orange patch to the base of Tommy's skull. The patch began to glow softly.

No one said a word as the doctor returned to the holographic display. His eyes lit and he let out a breath. "It's working."

"What's working?" Emma asked softly.

"Mathezar pointed to the holographic readout. "I am able to create a barrier of sorts, so that he is not affected by his surroundings. Our society uses thought to communicate, much more than yours did, and our technology is adapted to receive our thoughts, this is what he is sensitive to."

Will he always need this barrier?" Dthau-Mahsz asked before Emma could.

She shifted her gaze back to the doctor, waiting for his answer. Tommy seemed to be asleep now. Her heart ached. How many other hidden dangers lay in wait here?

"I am sure he will adjust and that he will not need it for long. From what I saw of his living environment; he was quite isolated from any source of electromagnetic energy. City living would have been more intense for him, but he would have developed a tolerance for it." The doctor called up more information before moving back to Tommy's small form. He removed the crystal disks and moved aside, gesturing for Dthau-Mahsz to pick him up. "You should let him sleep in his bed, but he will most likely be ravenous when he awakes."

Gingerly, the commander moved in and scooped up his son, cradling him to his chest. Emma could feel the concern he felt for their child.

"Thank you," Emma said to the doctor.

Mathezar nodded. "If there is anything, don't hesitate to call on me. I will stop by later on this evening to check on him."

Dthau-Mahsz nodded. "Come," he said to Emma.

Something was up. She could feel it through the link.

Once inside their quarters, Dthau-Mahsz settled Tommy in his bed and came back to join Emma in the dining area. She was going through the list of foods, feeling frustrated. "I don't recognize any of these."

He moved in closer and dropped a kiss on the side of her head. "Is there something in particular you feel like eating?"

She shrugged. "Vegetable stew would be good."

He nodded. "Let me see what is being offered in the dining hall. Maybe there is something you would find pleasing." He went to collect his digipad, the tablet he consulted frequently and searched through this evening's menu.

"How is that right?" She waved angrily at the replicator. "Your crew have to eat from this thing most days, and yet you can eat fresh whenever you feel like it?"

He lowered the digipad and frowned. "Most of them have eaten from it all their lives. *I* insist they eat real food at least one day a week, believing it to be healthier than amassed atoms and molecules." He tapped something into the pad and deposited it onto the shelf along the wall. He reached out for her and guided her to the couch.

She resisted, at first, then allowed him to lead the way. She felt helpless, frustrated that she couldn't protect her son from the dangers she wasn't even aware of. She'd give anything to be able to take Ruby for a ride up the ridge, out behind the house, right now. She needed to clear her head. She needed to understand this place.

He sat down on the sofa and pulled her close, letting her lean against him. "You need time to adjust. You cannot simply jump in and expect to know everything, and no one expects you to, either. Do not be so hard on yourself."

She sighed. "You didn't have any trouble fitting in," she said, bitterness in her tone. She thought about how he seemed to figure everything out, and once he'd learned something, he could do it as though he'd done so all his life. "I don't even know what to protect my son from over here, at least on the farm it was clear."

The door chime sounded and they both rose from the couch. Rather than follow her husband to the door, Emma went to check in on Tommy. Moving silently to his bedside, she reached out to stroke the soft cheek. He sighed deeply at the touch and turned onto his side. Gently, Emma rubbed his back, wanting to see if he'd stir. "Did you want to come eat? Are you hungry?"

Scrubbing at his eyes with his tiny fists, he nodded and stretched. Holding his arms out to Emma, she scooped him up and held him tight before making her way to the bathroom to wash up.

* * *

After their meal, the three of them sat on the living room floor, playing with Tommy and the homemade modeling dough Emma had brought from Earth. She didn't want him to play with his orb, afraid to cause him discomfort. She was busy making farm animals for him as he and his father played with them, making the sounds of each one.

When the door chime sounded, Emma looked over at Dthau-Mahsz nervously. He offered her a reassuring smile as he stood. "It is Mathezar."

Oh, yeah. He had said he'd stop by, she remembered. She stood to greet him.

"How is he?" he asked before the door had closed behind him.

Dthau-Mahsz waved him towards the living room. "He is fine. No sign of distress."

Emma watched as the doctor approached her son. He reached out to touch a bright yellow horse. "What is this?" The look on his face was priceless.

Emma took a blue blob of dough and placed it in the doctor's hand. "You make things with it." She watched as he squeezed and even smelled the dough.

"I trust you did not come solely to play with Thomas' modeling dough?" Dthau-Mahsz retorted. Emma wasn't sure if his tone was one of annoyance or amusement.

The doctor handed the dough to Tommy and sat on the couch. The lines around his eyes more pronounced than Emma had seen yet. She sat across from him, waiting for her husband to join them.

Dthau-Mahsz stood, arms crossed tightly across his chest, waiting. A look of warning in his eyes, the same look he's shot his friend when he'd noted the color of Tommy's eyes. "What's going on?"

CHAPTER 22: THE TRACKING CHIP

The doctor avoided the commander's scrutiny, turned to face Emma, and began. "I am not sure how much you have learned about us through Dthau-Mahsz, or since your arrival, but in our society we use cognitive abilities more than you do. We also have a learning chip to facilitate the interface between man and technology." He paused, watching her reaction and Emma was sure he caught her shudder.

"So I've heard, and the thought of it turns my stomach." Her insides twisted. "You're not thinking of putting one of those things in my son, are you?" Her tone rose slightly and she had to struggle to control her breathing.

Mathezar raised a hand. "I wouldn't advise the interface until he has adapted to his surroundings, it would be too much for him." He took a moment to observe the toddler at play. "The filter seems to have solved the problem for now."

Dthau-Mahsz moved to Emma's side, shooting another look in the doctor's direction. Emma could feel the tension through the link. She wasn't used to that feeling. She was normally the high strung one. He took her hand in his. "I believe the good doctor is referring to the tracking chip, not the learning interface." His eyes searched hers.

"Why would you want to do that to our son?" she whispered. Her chest constricted. She wanted to scoop up her son and leave this crazy place. Dthau-Mahsz tightened his grip on her reassuringly.

"Do you know why he crashed on your planet?" The doctor asked.

Emma heard her husband's breath catch. "He never spoke of his world while we were together," she said honestly. "What does that have to do with anything?"

The commander raked a hand through his hair. "I have told you how our place is selected in our society. If someone becomes a pilot, he is the best there can be. He is not careless, he does not make mistakes, and he does not crash."

Emma frowned. "If there is a mechanical failure, then he can be the best pilot from your world, he's going to crash."

He gave her that patient smile again. "Not if the engineer is the best that can be."

She shook her head. "It all seems rather presumptuous."

The doctor raised his hand to cut them off. "We are getting off topic."

OK, he's cranky, Emma thought. "No, we've never talked about the crash. I found him, end of story." Or beginning, she mused.

Mathezar looked at the commander. "What has he told you about his eyes?"

"I'm sorry," she said. "I don't know what you're trying to get at." She shot a glance at her tense husband. "All I know is that his eyes are rare, even amongst his people." She was starting to get annoyed. Why didn't he just come out and say it? Then it dawned on her. "You were attacked?" She looked from the doctor to her husband. "But what did that have to do with your eyes?" A sickening feeling gripped her. "Did someone want you for your eyes?" It sounded too incredible to believe. Images of Rhino horns and bile from living bears flashed in her mind, the harvesting of parts of living creatures. "We're not talking about an animal here..."

The doctor leaned forward. "No, we are not. We are talking about your son."

A burst of anger crossed through the link and Dthau-Mahsz stood. "Thank you for stopping by."

To Emma's surprise, the doctor stood, head slightly bowed, and left their quarters without another word. She brought her gaze to meet her husband's and waited for the explanation to the doctor's insinuations.

Dthau-Mahsz moved to sit across from Emma. He kept a tight lid on the link and Emma didn't know what to expect. "I ask that you allow me to tell you everything, without interruption. I will answer your questions afterwards."

She nodded, mouth going dry. She didn't want to know why he

simply didn't *show* her as he'd done in the past. Her unease grew at the lack of contact through the link, but she sat and waited, hoping it wasn't as bad as it seemed.

"The night you found me, I had been fleeing the Binari. They have come to believe that amethyst eyes hold some kind of magical power, and have taken to hunting the few who possess them." His tone was low, level, and sent chills down her spine.

Questions began popping into her mind, screams of protest bubbled up, but she nodded for him to continue.

He looked over at his son. "There is a legend that states that those born with amethyst eyes will have a special gift, but the child with amethyst eyes, born of amethyst eyes, will have the greatest gift of all." He brought his gaze back to her, locking with hers.

Her child was in danger.

"Mathezar believes we should put the tracking chip in place immediately. This would alert us if anyone ever tried to leave with him." He paused a moment, opening the link slightly. "Had he been born here, he would have had it already."

Emma sighed, feeling almost dizzy. This was surreal. "Did something happen to make you think it was dangerous for him?" She didn't know if he was done, but she'd heard enough.

"No one knows of his existence beyond my crew." He drew in a breath. "I have made it clear to those who have met him that they were not to speak of his eyes."

She swallowed. "Do you think he is in danger?"

"The danger is there. We cannot pretend that it is not. It would be careless of us not to take precautions." He leaned down to pick up his son, who had lumped together all of his animals. "The unexpected attack on our crew today has made the good doctor overly cautious. Though I must admit, he is right to want to take precautions."

Tommy offered the colorful mass to his father.

"Thank you. Would you like to go take your shower?"

Tommy smiled a toothy grin. "With Daddy," he said.

"Yes, with Daddy." He looked over at Emma and smiled. "What about Mommy?"

The toddler nodded enthusiastically. "And Mommy."

Apparently their discussion was over. Emma would have to think about what she'd heard. She understood that there was a real danger, but for now, the fear of the implant was greater. She wondered if they expected her to get one too. She shuddered and followed her men into the bathroom.

The discussion of a tracking chip had been put aside for now, though it was never far from either of their thoughts. As long as one or the other could be within walking distance of Tommy, Dthau-Mahsz had agreed to give Emma time to accept the inevitable.

She had been spending up to four hours a day in medical bay, as her learning and training progressed. In her down time, she'd take Tommy to the arboretum and help with the planting and reorganizing of the new plot. He enjoyed playing in the dirt, much to the dismay of the chief botanist. Dthau-Mahsz had managed to restore his crew and the family had settled into a routine of sorts. Things were working out and she was happy, though she still had her moments of homesickness.

"I will be planet-side for the afternoon," Dthau-Mahsz explained over breakfast. "The survey team wanted to see if a continental transfer would be preferable to a planetary evacuation."

Emma frowned. "Isn't it better to try and keep these people on their own planet?" She pushed some cut fruit pieces into Tommy's plate. He really liked the blue fruit, with its own particular flavor.

"Unfortunately, the difference in continents is as varied as going from a northern climate to the desert on your planet." He ruffled Tommy's hair.

Spooning another bite of porridge into her mouth Emma thought about the people below. "Are they going from cold to hot or hot to cold?"

"Hot to cold, why?" He wiped Tommy's face and set him on the floor.

She took the last spoon of porridge and pushed her bowl back. "They are going from a hot, dry climate to a cold climate, but with seasons?"

"Yes." He stood and cleared the plates from the table. With a mug in each hand, he sat back down and offered Emma a cup of cocoa.

"I'm sure they'll adapt, but I hope for their sake that it's the summer months so they have some time to adjust." She preferred seasons and couldn't imagine life in a desert climate. She lowered her cup, bringing her attention back to her husband. "You're uncomfortable about something." She could sense it through the link.

He brought his amethyst eyes to meet hers. "This will be the first time I leave you alone with Thomas." The link remained in check, letting Emma know there was more involved than he was letting on.

"This is where I had been attacked, where I fled from, years ago." He held her gaze.

Emma swallowed the dry lump forming in her throat. "Do you think the same thing will happen again?" Her voice was barely a whisper.

He shook his head. "No, but it makes me uneasy to leave you behind."

She reached out through the link. "We can stay here this afternoon. I want to dust and sort through Tommy's clothes and toys."

Dthau-Mahsz nodded. "We can go to the ship's stores now, and he will be issued clothing for his size."

"Sure, why not." She rose to get Tommy. "I could go this afternoon if you would rather do something else before you had to leave."

"I would prefer if you remained in our quarters." His tone was a little sharp.

"We will." She trusted him, and if he felt they should stay in, she'd respect that, but he'd have to give her an explanation when he got back.

The link opened slightly. *Thank you.*

* * *

The afternoon passed in a blur, and Emma relaxed in their clean quarters, reading some of the materiel Mathezar had selected for her while Tommy napped. She was covering various case studies when she came across an incident where someone had been abducted by the Binari. The name hit a chord. They were the ones Dthau-Mahsz had mentioned, the ones that had been after him.

The abducted man had been found hanging by his feet, arms bound behind his back, while he slowly emptied himself of his blood through puncture wounds to the neck and groin.

She sat up, leaning forward as she read the case study. Her heart rate kicked up a notch as she read that a film of sorts had been sprayed across his eyes, drying them out. She imagined her husband, her son, taken by these horrible beings.

She read on. The patient had been found, so close to death that he had to be put into stasis. At the time it was not known if he could be saved, and if so, whether his eyes could be restored.

At the end of the paragraph there was a photo of a Binari. Emma gagged. The bald, grey-skinned creature was right out of a nightmare.

The digipad fell to the floor and Emma hurried to check in on her son. Moving closer to the bed she looked down at her precious bundle, sleeping soundly in a jumpsuit that mimicked those his father wore. At the time, she hadn't been able to resist, but now she wasn't sure she wanted him to be associated with his father's world or this particular danger.

Her insides began to shake, and an irrational urge to scoop him up and run grew within her, but where would she go? She felt like a sitting duck out here in the middle of space, trapped in the ship. This danger didn't exist back home. No one had given more than a second thought about his eyes, because the color is both startling and unusual. There was no need for a tracking chip, or being confined to quarters while her husband was away. Why didn't he tell her about this before they came here?

She was finally beginning to feel at home, finally carving out a place in Dthau-Mahsz's world, and now a fear gripped her so tight she didn't know what to think. How could she remain here with such an ominous danger to her son, not to mention her husband? She struggled to control her breathing as her mind raced.

Could she even protect her son from these creatures? They had gone after her husband, they knew he existed, surely they'd try again. Someone forced their way into Tommy's room and a scream burst from Emma's throat. Grabbing for her son, she scooped the startled child and tried to make a break for the door. Strong arms clamped down around her and she fought to break free, screaming frantically. She failed to register the security uniform, worn by the one who held her. The urge to escape overpowered her senses. She needed to save her son.

Dthau-Mahsz came into their quarters at a run, and locked his arms around his family. "What happened?" He moved them towards the wall, keeping a hold on them.

"All clear, Commander," one of the guards spoke.

"Are you sure?" Dthau-Mahsz asked.

"Yes, Sir," Belek replied. "Should we stand outside the door?"

"Stay until you have verified that no one has come on board. If there are any passengers, remain until the last has left." Dthau-Mahsz escorted a shaking Emma and a crying Tommy to the couch. Passing a hand over his son to make sure he was all right, he turned his attention to Emma. "What happened?"

A flood of reassurance surrounded the family, and they huddled in it for a moment, until Tommy made a move to wiggle free. "No!" Emma tried to grab him but Dthau-Mahsz held her, hushed her.

"He is safe."

Slowly, the panic cleared as she rested in her husband's arms. She could feel that he had been frantic because of her reaction to what she had read. "I'm sorry," she said.

"What happened?" he asked again.

"I don't know. I was reading the information Mathezar gave me and there was a case study with those beasts and the eyes, and I got so scared..." She drew in a shaky breath.

Dthau-Mahsz stiffened. "Mathezar to my quarters," he called out.

Emma pushed up from his chest. "Oh, no. Don't take it out on him." She was still having trouble breathing.

He cupped her chin and looked into her eyes, searching. "He had no right to cause you such distress."

The door chimed and Emma stiffened. Dthau-Mahsz removed his arm from around her, stood in his typically fluid fashion, and went to greet their visitor.

The doctor entered, grim-faced and took a seat across from Emma, without saying a word. She felt bad for him.

Dthau-Mahsz sat stiffly beside her, and she could feel him straining to remain calm. "Explain." He tossed the digipad over to the doctor.

Mathezar lowered his eyes. "I had hoped to incite Emma to have the tracking chip implanted in your son, for his protection." He lifted his eyes to meet Emma's. "You need one too. It is more prudent under the circumstances."

The commander rose, outrage pulsing through the link. "That is not your call! I will not betray my wife's trust and impose such a thing."

The doctor sputtered. "You would risk your son's life because of an irrational fear of our ways?"

"You would do well to mind your business and let me tend to mine," Dthau-Mahsz exclaimed.

Emma blinked back tears. It was getting hard to breathe again. She couldn't do this anymore. She needed to go home where things were safe for her son, where she didn't doubt her ability to protect him.

Dthau-Mahsz whirled to face her. "Is that your final decision?"

"I don't know," she whispered.

Her husband shot a glance in the doctor's direction. "If I had felt my child's life in danger, then I would have done everything to convince my wife of the necessity of the chip." He drew in a breath through clenched teeth. "No child has ever been targeted, and I have taken precautions onboard to insure the safety of my family."

"Are you willing to take the chance, knowing of the prophecy? Knowing that he is unlike any other?" The doctor was unable to hide his frustration.

"That decision rests with myself and my wife." He narrowed his gaze. "Do you doubt my ability to oversee my family's well-being?"

The doctor shook his head. "No." He looked at Emma. "I did not wish to cause you such distress, but I had hoped you'd reconsider the chip."

Dthau-Mahsz let out a sharp breath. "We will discuss your indiscretion at a later time. Confine yourself to quarters until further notice." He dismissed Mathezar with a glare.

As soon as the door closed behind the doctor, Dthau-Mahsz turned to Emma. He stared at her in silence, a long while, gingerly opening the link to get a sense of her deepest feelings.

"Was the case study you?" She asked, averting his gaze.

"No." He reached out and touched her cheek, coaxing her to look at him.

"Did he survive?" She wasn't sure she wanted to know the truth.

"No." He shifted, taking both of her hands in his. "He had lost too much blood."

"Did he have a tracking chip?"

She saw the muscles of his jaw tense. "Yes."

She leaned into him. So even with the chip there was no guarantee her son would be safe. "What does the prophecy say? What is so important about it?"

He kissed the top of her head. "No more than what I have told you. It claims that the child with amethyst eyes, born of amethyst eyes, will have the greatest gift of all."

"What is your gift?" She let him hold her, seeking comfort in his arms. She turned her attention to Tommy who was busy with his orb.

"The ability to sense others," he answered softly.

Of course. He'd used it often with the S&R team. "What do we do now?" She couldn't shake the uneasy feeling in the pit of her stomach. "How will I know he will be safe? Or you?" She let him into her biggest fears, into her broken confidence. She had already lost both parents in a freak accident, and as an ER nurse, she was all too aware of how fragile life could be.

"Today's incident has shown us that I cannot perform my duties properly under these conditions, and that my fear for your safety is greater than I care to admit." He asked, though she knew he could sense her decision. "There is no way for me to keep you safe unless I keep you under surveillance while I am away."

"I think we should go back to Earth. At least until he is older." She said in a voice so low it was barely audible. "No one will come looking for him there, and the chip won't give him away."

Dthau-Mahsz remained silent as he went over their options.

"You can't focus on your job if you have to run back every time I panic about something, and the one time you don't take it seriously, might be the time we need you most." Her heart felt as though it would break at the thought of not having him at her side. What else could she do? "I couldn't stay here if something happened to you…"

"I should have considered the dangers before I brought you both here." The sheer intensity of his sadness at the possibility of being separated from his family was almost enough to make Emma change her mind. "No. You are right to want to return home."

Part of her felt a burst of joy at the prospect of returning home, and another crumbled at the thought of life without her husband. "What if he wants to be part of your world?"

Dthau-Mahsz sighed heavily. "When he becomes an adult, I will return. I will allow him to spend some time with me so he can choose for himself." He tightened his hold around her and they fell into silence.

So that was it. A life altering decision made in the blink of an eye. She only hoped he would find a way to visit from time to time.

*E*PILOGUE: *H*OME, TO *B*EGIN *A*GAIN

Emma stood in the kitchen of the old farm house with her arms wrapped around herself. It felt strange to be back after two months away. Dthau-Mahsz was chatting with Tommy, and she watched as he affixed a small stone pendant around the toddler's neck. He gave the boy a kiss and set him down on the floor before turning to Emma. He held out a pendant to her, and stepped forward to tie it around her neck as well. "If ever there is an emergency, join the two halves together, and I will come to you."

She looked at the crystal flecks in the stone, then lifted her eyes to meet his. She would miss looking into those beautiful, loving eyes. She would miss everything about him.

Two-Feathers stepped into the kitchen with Bo and a basket of eggs. He looked from Emma to Dthau-Mahsz and nodded. Dthau-Mahsz had somehow told him they were coming home. The shaman bent down and scooped Tommy into his arms, bringing him to the cookie jar.

Dthau-Mahsz led Emma towards the living room, and gently guided her to the settee. He sat close and took her hands in his. "Close your eyes."

She nodded, closing her eyes in total trust. She gasped as the link flared to an intensity never before experienced. He showed her how to seek out their memories, how to relive them, not just remember them.

When she opened her eyes, she saw that his glistened with unshed tears. She leaned into him for one last kiss. "I will always love you," she whispered.

"And I, you." He brought her hands to his lips. "Sometimes, in the depths of your sleep, you may find me there, waiting for you." He stood and drew her into his embrace. "Tell Thomas about me. Tell him I love him."

Emma nodded, tears streaming silently down her cheeks.

"Say goodbye to Two-Feathers for me." He took a step back and tapped the wrist com. His eyes held hers as his form faded into silence.

I love you, came through the link and Emma smiled to herself. She drew in a steadying breath and went to find her son in the kitchen. Her husband was there, alive in her heart, and as present as ever.

About the Author

Over the years I have worked as a nurse, a school teacher, a martial arts instructor, baseball, figure-skating and gymnastics coach as well as an artist, selling my paintings in an art gallery. I have been part of an orchestra, flown planes and gone on wilderness hikes. I am an officer in the Canadian Forces, and though I have taught on different military bases, for now I work primarily with cadets. Writing full time is my next goal.

Connect with Debbie

WEBSITE: http://welcometomywritingworld.weebly.com/
BLOG: http://amethysteyesauthor.blogspot.ca/
TWITTER: https://twitter.com/amethysteyes01

BOOKS BY DEBBIE BROWN

Amethyst Eyes

Amethyst Eyes: The Legend Comes to Life

Rebirth

Emma... to Begin Again

DEBBIE BROWN

www.ingramcontent.com/pod-product-compliance
Lightning Source LLC
Chambersburg PA
CBHW061228170626
46809CB00007B/2562